GRACE MOUNTAIN

Grace Mountain

A Novel

The redemption of a family betrayed

Inspired by a true story

Bobby C. Scarlett

To Misti,

Best Wishes !

Bobby Scarlett

West Creek Publishing

Grace Mountain
By Bobby C. Scarlett

ISBN 978-0-9894677-0-4

Copyright notice

Library of Congress Cataloging-in-Publication Data

Printed in the United States of America

Cover and book design: Janet Elliott

Front and back cover photography: Bobby Scarlett

Author photograph: Gloria E Foy

To Brandon, Riley, Colton, Dakota and Addison Grace
You each captured my heart the very first time I saw you
And you still make your Paw Paw smile.
Always know that you are loved.

Acknowledgments:

A special thanks to Carol Grigg and Carolyn Jones for the much-needed help and encouragement during the formative parts of this endeavor.

I am especially grateful to my Aunt Marie, Great Aunt Alma, and Great Uncle Will, who still keep our legacy alive.

Thank you to Luis, for the encouragement to write daily.

And a sincere thanks to Ted Anibal, the editor of this book, whose skill, dedication, and empathy is greatly appreciated. We have become friends.

In Memoriam

In memory of my Great Aunt Ora (February 4, 1920 – September 24, 2010). She was the backbone of the family. She never saw the finished book, but our times spent remembering and discussing the early days I will cherish forever.

Most of all, this book is dedicated to the enduring memory of my beloved Grandma Grace. A part of my heart left with her. She was adored, and now truly missed by all.

Grace Mountain

When my eldest grandson, Brandon, was just a small boy and started taking forest walks with me, I began referring to the small mountain behind my grandmother's house as Grace Mountain.

Although not its official name, "Grace Mountain" seems most appropriate for my family, as we have been walking its trails for more than a century.

I am gratified that Brandon still calls it Grace Mountain to this day.

There is a balm in Gilead, To make the wounded whole;
There is a balm in Gilead, To heal the sin-sick soul.
Sometimes I feel discouraged,
And think my work's in vain,
But then the Holy Spirit
Revives my hope again.

From the traditional African American Spiritual
There is a Balm in Gilead (circa 1854)

Contents

Preface

Extraordinary events lie hidden within the lives of many families that may never be revealed. Some are amazing in their accounts, and some are just too unpleasant to divulge. This is one such story of an exceptional woman who endured and managed to rise above countless hardships, while sustaining her faith and kind spirit. She was a gentle and caring lady as I observed throughout the years I lived with her in a small, wood-framed house in the Cid community, south of Thomasville, North Carolina. Although deceived and betrayed by the very ones she loved, she never spoke of her past oppressions, nor did I ever hear a harsh word spoken against any who were hurtful to her.

I feel honor in my endeavor to convey the incredible and eventful life of Grace Scarlett — my grandmother, called Grandma Grace. I tell this story along with the help of those who recall many of her experiences first hand.

Prologue

1976
A Secret Revealed

The news of their father's sudden death in another town had unexpectedly arrived through a third party. Although he had been hospitalized for the past seven days, his three children had no way of knowing he was ill, since that third party was the only other person in his town who knew these children existed.

His three children were now making preparations to begin the hour-and-a-half journey. On this day, their travels would lead to an unusual and somewhat suspenseful meeting that would culminate in the funeral of a man they never really knew. Nearly forty years earlier, this same man abandoned his three children and their mother, leaving them to fend for themselves while he disappeared from their lives.

Now that he had died, they realized that the secrets and deceit their father had asked them to keep from his present family would, since finding him, soon be revealed. A tinge of sadness accompanied their apprehension as they traveled north to their destination in Danville, Virginia.

Their minds were preoccupied with questions: How would they confront this situation? How would they be accepted, and how would they feel about the people they were about to meet? Each queried the other on their thoughts, and with each mile they became more anxious — almost as anxious as the day that first led to his discovery.

How do three siblings just show up and disclose that they are family to two sisters who never knew they existed, they wondered, especially at a time of grieving the loss of a man they presumed was their father only. Adding to their grief was the shock and disappointment of discovering he had also kept secrets from them for their entire lives.

The events that led up to this day had begun many decades earlier, setting into motion a chain of events that none of them could have ever imagined.

Grace and Clinard

Marie

Clyde

Chapter 1
Seeking Independence
1923

It was getting late when Grace stepped to the kitchen window holding her baby sister, Ora, as she pulled back the cream-colored linen curtain and faced the field where her family worked. With her other little sister, Ruth, under foot, she strained to see if any of them were on the way back. It was time to be finishing up and returning for the day. Her sister, Maggie, just two years younger, was in the kitchen preparing the evening meal for the Grubb family's hungry brood. The mouthwatering aroma of homemade biscuits wafted through each room.

To Maggie, cooking came naturally, so she took on the responsibility of preparing most of the meals.

Sister Tura was fourteen and acquiring many of Maggie's culinary skills as she helped.

"Ain't they on the way in yet?" Maggie asked.

"I don't see 'em," Grace answered. "They must've had more to do today."

"Supper's ready and I wish they'd come on while it's hot."

"Well, it can't be much longer," Grace assured. "Girls, let's go in the sittin' room and play some games."

"Yeah, Grace!" they exclaimed.

Grace could always keep the girls occupied when they became restless and she realized Ruth and Ora were getting hungry, so she led them into the next room until the others arrived.

Grace was now twenty and the oldest daughter still living at home. There was a pure and humble innocence about Grace, simple and modest in appearance and dress, as there was no money for extravagances that she was not even aware were lacking. High cheekbones complimented her deep-set green eyes, with smooth, fair skin like her mother's, and she featured a softer, more feminine version of her father's prominent square jaw. Her thick, wavy, shoulder-length brown hair was combed back and to one side.

Grace had endured an anxiety condition since childhood, and had been physically sick more than most. For that reason, she was not asked to work in the field with the rest of the family. Her youngest sister, Ora, was now three and had also been very sick at birth, so their mother entrusted her to Grace's care, intent on the arrangement being beneficial to both girls. Grace felt contentment as she rocked Ora through the day and hummed or sang favorite songs and hymns.

It was for Grace's best friend, Ora Gallimore, that she was allowed to name her little sister when she was born. A few years earlier, her older brother, Bud, had been dating Miss Gallimore at the time of her sudden death, and all presumed he would have eventually asked her to be his wife. Grace had developed a special bond with her and loved her as a sister. Months later, she had urged her mother, Dora, to let her name the baby, and realizing the heartbreak and loss Grace still felt, Dora lovingly relented.

It was now planting time, but Grace stayed in the house to care for little Ora, as well as Ruth, while the others went to work in the field.

Being inside day after day allowed time for Grace to often reminisce about certain events. Occasionally her older sister, Emma, and the memories she had of her came to mind.

Emma was the first child born to Walter and Dora, and was six years old when Grace was born. Their brother, Bud, was almost four at the time.

Shortly after Grace's birth, Dora developed a condition commonly known then as milk leg. Finding that she was unable to care for the three young children she now had, Dora and Walter asked each of their parents if they could help with them until Dora's health was better. Dora's mother, Sarah, agreed to keep Grace and Bud until she could get well, but Walter's mother, Jane, adamantly agreed to take only Emma. When Dora recovered and was ready for the children to return home, Jane was not willing to give Emma back.

Many years earlier, Jane's own little girl had died, also named Emma. Jane lost three other children as well, all at very young ages, so this grandchild filled a painful emotional void. Walter and Dora were extremely troubled with the situation, but felt they should not dispute her refusal at the time, considering Dora's recent illness.

Although Walter and Dora eventually brought Emma back home, she suddenly disappeared one day and was discovered back with her grandmother, Jane.

From that point on, Emma remained with her grandparents until she married and moved to the Farmer community, a few miles away in Randolph County. She returned home only for visits and, unfortunately, had been instructed by her grandmother to call her father and mother "Walter" and "Dora," as others called them.

Today, as was usual, all of the available family, along with Grace's younger brother, Jess, were helping Walter finish up in the field and around the farm. He had George, the white horse, pulling the plow, and Bob, the old trusted mule, standing by to assist with other tasks.

With Walter and Jess the only two men in the household now and such a large farm to care for, everyone had to work a little harder. Jess had to help his father with more of the chores since his only brother, Bud, had married two years earlier. Bud moved into a house within sight of the old homestead, but he and his wife, who was also named Grace, had chores of their own now. And with a four-month-old baby, their home life was even more demanding. Even so, Bud helped his parents whenever he could.

Walter, Dora, and their children in all appearances were happy and comfortable in the two-story, roughhewn farmhouse they built in the heart of rural Cid community. They taught all the girls the household and farm tasks as soon as they became old enough to work, each taking turns equally at milking the cows and churning butter. They took freshly churned butter to the spring, wrap and pack it in a crock, and place it in the cool water running through the spring house, which served as one of their only sources of refrigeration. One of the girls would go to the spring each morning to get butter for breakfast, sometimes as early as four o'clock. Grace attempted the trip a few times when she was younger, but became too scared and nervous and ran back to the house exclaiming she had seen a bear down there.

Eleven-year-old Bessie and nine-year-old Cletie were now taking on more of the responsibilities and helping out in the field. Youngest siblings Ruth and Ora attempted to help, but often ended up playing games or playing house.

Grace peered out the window once again and saw everyone coming up from the field and through the yard.

"They on the way, Maggie, and they a-lookin' tired and hungry!"

The work in the field was done for the day and their appetites grew by the minute.

"Jess, you think you can get ol' Bob back in his stall?" Walter asked, as they neared the barn. "You know how stubborn he is."

"Yeah, he tried to kick me yesterday, but I'll get 'em in there one way or another," Jess replied.

"Put him and George up and head toward the house. We'll feed up after we eat," said Walter.

As the tired family neared the house, they caught the delectable smells of supper and suddenly their steps didn't seem quite as weary.

They all paused at the well covering for a moment of shade and a thirst-quenching break from the hot evening sun.

Grace watched from the side door as Dora drew a bucket of water.

Dora was petite, with deep-set eyes accentuated by high cheek bones and a fair, smooth complexion. She possessed a calm and patient disposition, keeping her long hair in a bun at the crown of her head, and was often seen donning an apron.

After cranking the rope around the wooden drum until the bucket was raised, she slid the cover back across the well top and let it rest there.

"Hand me the dipper there on the nail," Dora said, as she took and dipped it in the bucket of cold, deep-drawn water and passed it around for a few quick sips.

"Boy, am I glad this day's done!" Tura said.

"Me, too," echoed Bessie and Cletie, as they took turns washing their hands in the old agate pan.

"Why don't Ruth get to help?" Cletie asked. "She's old enough to."

"Oh, she'll be helpin' soon," Dora said. "She's a-growin' up fast."

"Here, girls," Dora offered, as she handed them a cloth hanging from the post to dry their hands. As they finished, they entered the back door one by one to sit and catch their breath for a moment before the call for supper.

Maggie soon stepped out exclaiming in her customary wit, "It's ready and you better get in here and eat, cause it sure ain't a-gonna eat itself."

They all filed into the dining room, found their usual places, and were quickly seated on the wooden benches along side the handmade table. Sometimes they talked a little too loudly, but no one dared to start eating before thanks were given. Once the "Amen" resounded, the lively buzz resumed among the eight siblings present. It was sometimes known to be a happy and jovial clamor, but sometimes it rose to a swell of discord until Walter intervened. They passed the serving bowls around as the delectable smells became heaping portions on every plate.

As they finished the evening meal, they all chuckled when little Ruth rubbed her tummy and announced, "Ooo, I'm tight as a tick!"

"Daddy, I'm gonna check the rabbit gums if you want me to feed and water up the animals while I'm there," Jess offered.

"Okay, but you need to watch for pilot snakes now," Walter warned. "It's about time for 'em to be a-comin' out."

Pilot snakes were to be avoided at all costs because they were more dangerous than common copperheads. However, the black

5

snakes, often found stealing eggs, were of no harm except to the eggs or baby chicks. And, maybe to his sisters' nerves.

An egg was always left in the nest to keep the hen coming back to lay another. But when it kept disappearing, Walter had an idea and decided to place an old glass doorknob decoy in the hen nest. He hoped it would fool the chickens and discourage the snakes from eating the family's next breakfast.

"Look, everybody!" Jess yelled, as he walked back from the barn with a large, black snake he carried on a long stick. The snake had an obvious knot inside and some of the girls shrieked at the sight of it.

"He thought the doorknob was an egg and swallowed it," Jess said, with a laugh.

The rest of the family thought it was quite an odd sight. The girls had always feared snakes of any kind, and watched curiously from a safe distance.

"Well, that'll sure be his last meal," stated Walter.

The girls returned to the kitchen as Walter and Dora convened to the early summer evening coolness of the front porch to relax. They wondered who might stop for a visit as their children played nearby.

It seemed family or neighbors were always stopping by to visit and chat, and the front porch, lined with straight-back caned chairs and rockers, was a favorite social spot.

Meanwhile, Grace washed dishes while the younger girls helped clean up the kitchen.

Oddly, Grace enjoyed washing dishes, even in childhood. She never considered it to be a chore and, apparently for her, was good therapy. When she was done, she could excuse herself and let the girls finish up. They certainly didn't complain and were happy with just drying and putting the dishes away. Besides, Grace was not fond of all the drama the girls could create when they were in the same room for too long. This was usually one of the last chores of the day, so after finishing, they were off pursuing their own interests.

Grace slipped out of the house through the side door and

sat on the steps alone, sensing a feeling of repose in the calming breeze. Time alone was a rarity with such a large family, but on her more confident days, Grace entertained thoughts of independence and making some kind of life for herself. She loved her family very much and felt a responsibility for the seven younger siblings, even though they frequently helped look after her as well.

She thought back to just a year earlier when her mother gave birth to a stillborn baby. Grace worried terribly about her mother and felt compelled to take any burden off of her that she could. Even when her mother had regained her strength, Grace continued to be concerned.

In the distance she could hear the faint whistle of a train as she sat in quiet reflection. The sound stirred feelings of restlessness. Just then the lonesome cry of a whippoorwill echoed her feelings. Grace contemplated that she was twenty years old and still living at home, and wondered what the future held for her. She wondered how it would be to somehow gain enough independence to venture out of her safe haven, as sheltered as her life had always been. Even though the thought of taking that first step terrified her, she knew it was a choice she would someday have to make.

As she sat daydreaming with her face cupped in her hands and elbows on her knees, she pondered getting the courage to just step out and do it. She had heard family and friends talk about the cotton mill in Thomasville. It was less than fifteen miles north of where she lived and much larger than the town of Denton a few miles south, where they often shopped. But even if she found work, how would she get there? She had neither driver's license nor means of transportation, and she didn't know of anyone who made the daily trip there and back.

Rays from the setting sun began to shimmer through the newly budded trees, and dusk was inevitable. Realizing she had sat there longer than intended, she was about to get up and join the family, unaware that anyone had walked up.

The worn and squeaky screen door opened suddenly, accompanied by a brash voice.

"What are you doin' out here?"

"Oh, Maggie! You scared me half to death!" Grace scolded.

"Well, I was just wonderin' where you got to."

Grace composed herself for a moment and then began.

"I just been thinkin' what it'd be like to get a job in town. It'd be nice to earn my own money and I'd be able to help mama and daddy out a little and I could buy a few things I need."

Maggie just stood in the doorway as if trying to perceive this sudden idea.

"I'd hate to leave Ora," Grace continued. "But I know Tura and Bessie would help mama with her. If I don't try, I ain't never gonna have nothin' of my own."

"Well, I'd like to get a job, too," Maggie announced. Maggie was known for offering her honest opinion. "But I don't see that happenin'. I can just imagine what mama and daddy would say about that with all there is to be done around here. I don't think they'd ever agree to it."

"I can't stay home forever," Grace asserted. "I'm gettin' older, you know."

Grace sat in thought for a moment and then said, "Don't you think they could manage without me here for a while? Mama is a lot better now."

"Well, if you're intent on doin' it, I don't reckon it would hurt to ask," Maggie replied.

"You wanna go with me to talk to 'em?" invited Grace.

"I'll go with you, but I wouldn't expect too much if I were you."

Grace hesitantly proceeded toward the front door with Maggie closely following out onto the porch where Walter and Dora sat conversing about the day's events and how scandalous the world seemed to be getting.

"Why, do you remember that girl at the last wheat thrashin'?" Walter asked. "She set right down on that boy's lap, just a-makin' over him. Can't imagine a girl doin' such a thing!"

"I guess that was a little ill mannered. I'm sure her folks

raised her better," Dora replied.

"Well, you'll hear tell of her a-gettin' that boy in trouble before long," declared Walter.

Grace and Maggie thought it only a funny event at the time, and at this point they just wanted to find a place to break into the conversation.

"Daddy…" Grace anxiously started. "I've been thinkin' lately. How would you and mama feel about me gettin' a job? I thought you might know somebody around here who works in town. I could save up some money and help you and mama out," she cautiously continued. "Ora's a lot better now and…"

"Grace…" Walter interrupted. "You ain't got no business a-goin' off to work. You ain't able to hold down a job all day long. You know how your nerves are. An' besides, we need you here to help out right now. We're just beginnin' to get the fields planted and we can't get it done without everybody's help. Your mama has to work in the field herself. I just don't want you a-goin' off like that."

"But Daddy, a lot of girls younger'n me go to work in town."

"I think you best forget about it for now," Walter repeated.

She realized further argument was futile, and resigned with a disappointed "Okay," and retreated inside the house.

Grace walked back through the front room with Maggie still in tow. Maggie had no chance to give her any verbal support whatsoever.

"Well, I told you how that'd go," Maggie reminded her, as Grace glanced back, giving her the 'Don't you say another word' look.

Back on the porch, Walter sat silently for a moment as if he knew what was coming before Dora even spoke.

"Walter, you know she's old enough to do as she pleases if she took a notion."

He paused for a moment and said, "I reckon so. But how'd we ever make do with all the summer crops?"

"We could manage somehow if we had to, but I doubt she could find a way to get to work before summer's end, anyway,"

Dora reassured. "Why don't you talk to her and agree to help her find a ride to town this fall if she'll help us through the summer? It might give her somethin' to look forward to, if that's even what she still wants to do by then. The field work'll all be done by that time and it wouldn't be as much a burden on us."

Walter agreed, and was content in the clever idea as if it were his own.

Grace, meanwhile, escaped to the solitude of her upstairs bedroom that she shared with the other girls, changing and slipping into bed early, hoping to collect her feelings before the other six girls would come up and intrude upon her thoughts. She lay there in the quiet room with only the resonance of chirping crickets outside. She was disconcerted but resigned to the idea of living at home indefinitely. Still, she wondered and dreamed of possible places and adventures not yet experienced, until she finally drifted off to dreams of distant realms.

Chapter 2
The Arrangement

A faint sound awakened Grace early the next morning just as twilight roused the first chorus of songbirds that seemed to echo clear across the meadow. She lay there in the silent room listening to their jubilant announcements of a new day, having no recollection of anyone else entering the room the night before.

She envied the cheerfulness of all the carefree birds outside her room.

I guess it's just as well I stay here. Maybe daddy's right, she thought.

Gradually, the first beams of morning light pierced the small window. Still fresh in her mind were the thoughts of the day before, as though she hadn't slept at all. It was Saturday morning and she could hear her mother downstairs in the kitchen. She knew there was a lot of work to do that day so she got up and readied herself to go help prepare breakfast. She walked down the narrow, creaky, wooden steps as lightly as she could, trying to step on the familiar, less noisy places, so as not to disturb the younger ones still sleeping, and then through the kitchen door.

"Good mornin', Mama."

"Mornin', Grace. You up earlier than usual."

"I fell asleep early last night. Just thought I'd get up and help you with breakfast."

"Wanna start up the fire for breakfast?" Dora asked.

Grace stepped to the woodbox and got enough kindling and paper to get the cookstove started. The fire was starting slowly, so she stood by watching until it finally caught up enough to add a couple of larger pieces.

"Grace, I think your daddy wants to talk to you today," Dora said, in a composed tone.

"If it's about me wantin' to get a job, I already give up on the idea of goin' to work, Mama, so he needn't to worry about it now," Grace replied.

"Well, he just wants to talk to you, honey."

"Okay. But he really needn't worry about it. I know he needs me here, so I'm not gonna mention it anymore."

Grace put more wood in the stove and slid the lid over the firebox. Dora was getting the biscuits started as Walter walked in with ham slices retrieved from the smokehouse.

"Grace, are you the early bird after the worm?" he joked.

"I guess I am. I just decided to get up and help mama."

"Maggie went to the spring this mornin', but I think she's back and in the front room. Go get her so she can help with breakfast," Walter advised, as he pulled the heavy iron skillet off the wall and set it on the stove.

Grace exited without hesitation, as she wasn't sure what more her daddy had to say. She suspected he would just reiterate the conversation they had the day before and really wanted to avoid discussing it further.

Grace returned to the kitchen with Maggie following and they began helping their mother. Later, Dora said, "One of you go get the rest of the girls for breakfast."

"I'll go get 'em, Mama," Grace offered.

As they returned, they all sat down to eat and discussed the chores that needed to be done that day.

Dora said, "Girls, as soon as we get done in here, we need to get those apples ready for dryin'."

"And, Jess, we need to repair some of those fences on the lower end," Walter added.

As they finished, one by one they got up from their seats. Walter and Jess headed down to the pasture and Grace made her way to the sink to start the dishes, relieved that no one had mentioned the previous day's discussion.

The women began to prepared pots of food in preparation for dinner as well as the next day's Sunday meal that would cook while they did other chores around the house.

When they finished inside, Dora said, "Grace, have the girls help take the chairs, pans, and buckets out under the oak tree. I'm gonna see if there's any more on the ground. When your daddy gets back, he'll get the ones out of the grain bin that's already been picked."

When Walter and Jess returned at noon, the family gathered back around the table for dinner. As soon as they were finished, they went back outside to work.

Walter brought the buckets of apples and set them down by the chairs. He then brought the old sheets of tin out of storage that they used for drying apples, then he and Jess went back to fence mending.

Dora scrubbed down the tin with the help of Grace, Maggie, and Tura, and then proceeded to the straight-back chairs under the big oak to peel and slice what would become a small mountain of apples.

Seconds later, Dora rose from her chair and said, "Ya'll didn't bring my good knife and this one's not very sharp. I'm goin' inside to get it. Keep peelin' and I'll be right back."

Dora disappeared through the side door while the girls continued to peel apples. Just then, Tura let out a squeal and threw her apple along with her knife.

"What'n the world's wrong with you?" Maggie snapped.

"A fetched worm crawled up my finger!"

"A little ol' worm ain't a-gonna hurt you. You fetch that knife and get back to work."

Cutting her eyes toward Maggie with a slight tilt of her head, Tura inquired, "Why do you have to be so bossy, Maggie?"

"I'm gonna be more than bossy, young girl, if you don't get busy!"

"Tura," Grace consoled, "get your knife and I'll see if I can't find you an apple with no worm."

Tura cautiously picked up her knife with two fingers to inspect it as Grace leaned over to hand her a wormless apple and whispered, "Yes sir, that Maggie sure is bossy," as they both giggled and smiled.

"What's so funny?" Maggie snapped.

"I said, 'Bessy, that Macintosh sure is glossy,'" Grace casually answered, as Tura snickered again.

Throughout the early afternoon as they peeled and sliced pans full, the girls and their mother talked and touched on most every subject that interested them until the soaking apples were ready to be spread out in the sun to dry.

The day was swiftly slipping by, so they all returned to finish their other tasks in the house.

When most of the cooking was finished, Maggie said, "Bessie, help me carry the food out to the well." They covered the bowls and placed them in the bucket and lowered it down the well to keep the food cool until the next day.

Grace helped Dora put three or four inches of water in the washtub and set it outside in the sun to warm for bathing the children later in the day.

It was late afternoon when Grace stepped out back to retrieve the remainder of the wash from the clothesline. She was about to go back in the house just as Walter came up through the backyard from the barn.

"Grace, come here and set down for a minute. I got somethin' I wanna talk to you about."

They both sat down on straight-back chairs in the patchy grass next to a worn area that encircled the well house. Feeling slightly apprehensive, Grace clutched the garments she held and shifted her gaze to the distant hills beyond Silver Valley as Walter began.

"After you asked about gettin' a job in town yesterday, I talked to your mama and if that's what you wanna do, I'll help you find a ride later this fall if you'll just help us out here through the summer."

"Really?" she replied, as her disquieted look quickly faded, unable to mask an obvious glimmer of excitement.

"I don't mean to put extra burden on the family, Daddy, but I will be here to help out in the evenin's," Grace quickly assured.

"Well, your sisters are old enough to take over and help out a little more. You've looked after Ora real good, and she'll be fine now." Grace stood up shifting the clothes to one arm, leaned over and embraced her dad with the other.

"Thank you, Daddy," she exclaimed, beaming as she hurried to the back door.

Maggie walked through the kitchen doorway as Grace entered.

"What're you smilin' about?"

"Daddy just said he'd find me a ride to town if I get a job this fall. He asked me to just help out here the rest of the summer."

"Well, glory be!"

"I can't believe it either," Grace added, as she proceeded to the kitchen where Dora smiled, already aware of the news Grace was about to share with her.

Throughout the evening, she reveled in the reality of finally going to work, elated and even carefree. The concept of town life kept entering her mind as she prepared the younger ones for their Saturday baths in water that was getting a little soapier with each one.

The older ones eventually move the tubs to the little room on the side porch to take their own baths.

That night when she went to bed, Grace had a new awareness of even the little things — the room hinting of talcum powder, slightly masking old but familiar and comforting smells of line-dried linen, cedar furniture, and the fragrance of flower blossoms one of the young ones left on the dresser earlier that day.

Chapter 3
Sunday Wayfarers

Grace awoke early the next morning with renewed excitement. She got out of bed and woke the other girls to come down for breakfast and then to get ready for church. After everyone finished eating and got dressed, they walked the short distance to their wood-framed place of worship, just in sight of their home, sitting up on a small hill where the dirt road passes by.

Several neighbors and family friends had already gathered early and were chatting around the front steps as Grace and her family arrived at Walter's Grove Baptist Church. Others were moving wagons that their families rode in on and others were tying up horses for the duration of the service.

Walter felt particularly honored to have donated the land for the church. Out of respect, the members named the church after him. Walter greeted the group and bid them a good morning as he marched his children, in stair-stepped fashion, up the steps and in the front door. Grace noticed a couple of the younger men looking her way, so she nodded hello and gave a cordial smile. A couple of the young men in particular seemed to show an interest in her. They had attended church together for quite some time and had become casual friends over the years. In fact, Grace had gone on outings and events with each of them. The young men seemed quite awed by her and always possessed a very courteous manner, but her feelings so far had not been mutual. Even so, her heart was stirring with excitement and she wanted to share her upcoming venture with anyone willing to listen.

Grace was still holding Ora and whispered, "Ora, you gonna have to be quiet during the service now."

"Alright, Grace. I will."

They all filed in one by one, down the aisle and into their familiar family pew where they reverently waited for the service to begin. The floor creaked as members entered and found their respective places among the echoing chatter in the wood-slatted room that featured a stately pot-bellied stove at the front.

Other members walked over to their pew to greet them before the service started.

Soon everyone was seated as a refreshing breeze drifted through the open church windows. The song leader stood and instructed everyone to take out the old songbooks and turn to "Amazing Grace."

It was Grace's favorite song, not because of her own name, but because of her profound convictions. On this day, she sang each word with unbridled zeal. The singing concluded and the congregation sat intently as Preacher Hough began to deliver his message.

The little ones occasionally squirmed until they got the stern look from Walter or Dora.

The message was "The Worldly Evils that Await to Deceive Even the Very Elect." Grace absorbed every word and determined in her mind that those worldly evils would not be her fate no matter what she faced in her future quest. After the conclusion of the last invitational song and the final amen, the congregation stood in dismissal. Some of the members lingered, engaging in fellowship for a little while.

"Brother Hough, y'all still comin' over for dinner?" Walter asked, as they departed.

"Be there shortly," he answered.

The Grubb clan proceeded down the bank and followed the deep-rutted drive to the dusty road that led back to their home just a stone's throw away. The exhilarating warmth of the noonday sun gave the kids an irresistible urge to skip and stray ahead of the group. "Girls, you stay close while the wagons are leavin'," Walter ordered. "You got plenty of room to run at home."

As the family walked, the only thing that briefly took Grace's mind from her upcoming endeavor was the sweet smell of blossoms wafting from the trees and bushes that grew wild alongside the road. She paused only a moment from her brisk walk to break off a few clusters of blooms for savoring on the way home.

"Daddy, do you know anybody around here who works in Thomasville?" Grace asked.

"Well, yeah, as a matter of fact, I do. Luke Thomas works in town. If I'd a thought, we could've asked him before we left church. When I see him next time I'll ask if he minds givin' you a ride to work this fall. I see him comin' through here on his way in the mornin's. You could offer to help out with the cost of gas. I'm sure he wouldn't mind. I think he's a little sweet on you, anyway."

"Oh, Daddy, I don't think so."

Grace was thinking that God always seems to have a way of working things out and wished they could just go back and ask him right then, but she knew that wouldn't be possible while they had the family all headed toward home.

After a few quick preparations, company arrived and the dinner hour passed rather quickly with abundant and lively conversation. Afterward, everyone sat back and relaxed. To Grace, the fact that it was Sunday made her heart feel lighter, for Sundays always seemed more serene than any other day. She felt secure while the family conversed, laughed, and chattered, as all were either in or around the house most of the day. It was such a beautiful day that Grace decided to gather up a quilt along with Ora and sit on the green patch of grass under the large, old, oak tree while she watched her play. Grace simply admired the clear, blue sky with white, boisterous clouds floating by.

Soon, the company left and everyone settled in for the evening to savor the time left before bedtime. However, with so many girls in one place, there was no discounting occasional disagreements and dramatic outbursts, until Walter finally demanded peace and quiet.

Chapter 4
Harvest Gathering

"The days just have a way of slippin' by," Dora exclaimed.

"It don't seem that way to me, Mama," Grace said.

"Well, you're still young, honey. The older you get, the faster it goes. Summer's almost over," added Dora.

The crops were tended and harvest time was near. The summer's heat was gradually waning and the air was getting crisper and cooler, hinting of subtle autumn smells with leaves turning shades of golden browns, reds, and oranges. Grace had never been away from home before and was becoming more anxious as fall neared, realizing what was about to happen would change her life more than anything she had ever done.

Wheat-threshing time was fast approaching, and this was the year for everyone to meet at the Grubb farm for the much-anticipated event. Preparations were under way for what would be an impressive gathering of hard work, good food, fellowship and fun.

"Everbody'll be here Thursday. We need to get finished up," Walter kept reminding, as he and Dora made final provisions for the occasion.

When Thursday morning arrived, the kids ran to find their dad and squealed with excitement.

"Daddy! They comin' in with the big machines!"

The neighbors were invited and came early from all around the countryside. They brought their large machinery for gathering and threshing the crops. The corn harvest was always large and farmers needed help with the shucking.

The lady folks had been cooking throughout the morning while the men worked in the field and, around lunch time, they arrived with pots of food.

"Grace, you and the girls help the women with puttin' the

food out," Dora instructed.

They placed all the food outside on a long, makeshift table that Walter had made from rough lumber.

"Mama, just look at all the food they brought," Bessie exclaimed. "It looks like a spread at the church homecomin'. There's chicken pie and green beans and corn and pinto beans and collard greens and cornbread."

"Well, Bessie, did you miss all those biscuits over there?" Dora asked, and chuckled.

"Oh, yeah. And look at all those pies and cakes. Mmmm," she uttered.

The ladies sent word for the men to come in from the fields and eat. They rode in with wagons full of corn for the corn husking and heaped it into a mountain-high pile for everyone to take part in later that day.

When the food was served, the men ate heartily as the women kept refilling their glasses with southern sweet tea from gallon jars.

"I'm tempted to just lounge back and take a nap now," said one of the farmer friends when he finished eating. They all agreed in jest, but knew their day's work was far from done.

"Well, boys, time to get back to the fields."

The threshing resumed and lasted until late evening. When the men came out of the fields, the ladies had supper ready and waiting once again.

After they finished eating they built a bonfire. Everyone was eager to start the corn shucking and the games they always enjoyed after the long day. Sometimes they would have a contest to see who could shuck the most ears of corn. The gathering was more about fun than work.

The crowd all gathered around the mountain of corn as someone said, "Now remember boys, whoever finds a red ear of corn gets to pick a girl to kiss. But you have to catch her!"

It wasn't long until one young lad found such an ear and announced, "I choose Grace."

"Oh, no!" Grace exclaimed, as she bolted to the house when

he walked her way. Everyone laughed, but Grace didn't find it as comical as they did.

Grace eventually returned to the group when she heard someone announced, "Let's start the games. We'll play Tap In first, and then Drop Hanky."

"Grace, you know when you drop a hanky, a boy gets to kiss you," said one of Grace's friends.

"Well, I don't plan to drop a hanky for anybody today!" she declared.

It was nearing dusk as the games and joke telling were finished, so they brought the desserts back out to signal the end of the event.

"Much obliged to you all for helpin' today and bringin' the good food," Walter and Dora said, while the neighbors gathered up their belongings.

"Walter, we'll be back tomorrow to finish up what we didn't get done today," a neighboring farmer assured. Full up and bone tired, the neighbors made their way out the dirt driveway and back toward their respective homes.

The men returned on Friday and spent a few early hours in the field before going on their way again.

Realizing the kids would soon be cooped up in the house when winter arrived, Walter always allowed them one pleasure before taking the grain to the mill.

"Okay, kids, the grain bin's full. You can climb in and play awhile."

Chapter 5
Finding a Ride

Early on Saturday morning, Walter loaded up a portion of the grain to take to the Rush and Cole Mill in Denton for grinding.

"Grace, you gonna ride with me to the mill today?"

Grace readied herself to go along as she most always did.

"Walter, I think we'll all ride along today," Dora replied.

Dora gathered up a few quilts to wrap the kids in and let them ride on the back of Walter's old, faded-black T-model truck.

Life on the farm was routine, and although Denton was a small town with only a few hundred people, after growing up in country seclusion, it was exciting for them to see the sights.

To the children the mill looked massive, and they all seemed spellbound watching the grain being turned into flour. It was very dusty from all the grinding, but they loved the smell of grain that permeated the air.

When they were finished at the mill, Walter took them over to Workman's General Store for lunch. Even though it was no comparison to the meals they served up back home, they looked forward to the special treat of cheese crackers and the soda pop that Walter always bought for them.

They noticed all the buildings that lined the dirt street, and all the people walking to their favorite stores. A few horses were tied to posts on the side streets. They could see the Denton Hardware Company and the bank down the street on the corner. The water tank with a sturdy wooden crisscross structure supporting it was a prominent feature down a ways and across the street. They observed one store in particular, right beside the general store, where ladies frequented. Walter's girls had always wanted to venture inside to get a glimpse, but never got the courage. Two local women sold hats there and the girls assumed there wouldn't be enough money to buy the kind of hats they saw customers walking out with.

As they all sat on the store's wooden bench and around the porch's worn edge, Walter caught sight of Luke and figured it would be a good opportunity to inquire about Grace's transportation to work.

"I see somebody down the street I need to talk to for a minute. You all stay here 'til I get back." Walter headed down the wooden sidewalk to the next block.

"Hey, Luke. How you been?"

"Doin' good, Walter."

"You still workin' in Thomasville, I reckon?" Walter inquired.

"Yeah, I'm still there, for now, anyway."

"Luke, Grace wants to get a job at the Amazon. I promised her I'd try to find her a ride this fall and was wonderin' if you'd mind lettin' her ride with you. We pretty much got all the harvest in and I don't think she's gonna let me forget about it."

Luke's eyebrows raised as Walter's request captured his full attention, for he had thought of asking her out sometime but had not found the right opportunity.

"She'd be willin' to help pay for gas," Walter affirmed. "Of course, I gotta get her up there somehow to apply for a job first."

"Well, Walter, I'll be glad for her to ride with me anytime she needs. In fact, she can go up with me to apply if she wants. Only thing, she'll have to hang around there all day 'til I get off work."

"Well, I thank you and I'll talk to her and let you know at church tomorrow. Be a-seein' you soon."

"Sure thing, Walter. You all take care now."

Walter walked back as everyone was finishing their snacks.

"Watn't that Luke?" Dora asked, getting Grace's attention.

"Daddy, did you ask him about givin' me a ride to work?"

"Yeah, and he said he'd take you to apply for the job, too, if you want him to. We'll have to let him know tomorrow when to pick you up."

"When can I go?" Grace asked excitedly, trying to repress her eagerness.

"Whenever you want to," he said.

She was thrilled and quite chatty all the way home.

As soon as they got there, Grace went upstairs and again checked her selection of clothing she chose months before to make sure she had made the right choice. She laid the modest, homemade cotton print dress out on the bed to give it one last inspection, and then hung it back in the wardrobe.

That evening after supper, Jess was eager to inspect the rabbit gums he and his dad built and set throughout the woods behind the garden and beyond the creek.

"You better check good before tryin' to get 'em out. You don't wanna be a-bringin' back no skunk smell," Walter warned, jokingly.

"Needn't to worry. If one gets in there, that's where he'll stay," affirmed Jess.

Always hoping for a rabbit, he just never knew what he would find, so he was cautious. Fortunately, he hadn't encountered a skunk yet, although he had heard the tales of what that could be like.

'Possums must love the apples used for bait, too, because that seemed to be the primary catch. But, today's catch was a full-grown rabbit, and Jess took pleasure in presenting it held high to the family as he returned.

"Just put him in the box out at the tool shed," Walter instructed. "We'll fatten him up for a couple of days and then he'll be ready for your mama to make one of her good ol' rabbit stews."

The next day, after Sunday service, Grace kept a watchful eye for Luke until he walked up where she and her family were talking to friends.

Luke always possessed a friendly smile and had become quite stout from all the heavy work he was accustomed to. A few strands of blond curly hair fell from under his hat onto his forehead.

"Grace, hear you needin' a ride to work," he said. "I talked to your daddy yesterday in Denton and wanted to let you know you're welcome to ride with me anytime."

"Daddy, you think I should go tomorrow to apply?" Grace

asked, as she turned toward Walter.

"Luke's offerin' you a way there and you should go if that's what you want."

She faced Luke squarely and said, "Okay, you can pick me up in the mornin'. What time should I be ready?"

"I'll be by around six o'clock," Luke said. "That'll get us there a few minutes early."

"Okay, Luke. I'll be ready!"

"You all have a good afternoon."

"You, too, Luke. And thanks for your help," Walter replied.

"Well, Grace, looks like you set for a way to work."

"Yeah, and I'm beginnin' to get nervous about goin'. I don't know what to expect," Grace stated.

"Just do the best you can and everything'll be fine," assured Dora.

That night, Grace escaped to her upstairs bedroom early, pulling her dress back out of the wardrobe, hanging it on a hook near the door, and placing her hose and other items across the cedar chest.

She slipped under the quilt and snuggled in, predetermined to fall asleep quickly, but that didn't happen. Her mind was reeling with anxiety, nervously wondering what she would experience the next day. After exhausting efforts, she would drift off and wake up time and again with the feeling she had only slept for a few minutes. When she awoke early the next morning, she thought she had overslept. She jumped out of bed to find no one else awake, but decided to stay up. She proceeded to get dressed and attempted to relax a bit while the house was quiet.

It wasn't long before the others got up and were getting ready for a day of work while Grace had breakfast. Soon, Luke pulled up the driveway to pick her up.

Dora handed Grace a brown bag with a ham biscuit and left-over vegetables she had prepared from the day before. Then Dora and Walter wished Grace well as she slipped on her sweater and headed out the door.

"Hey, Luke," Grace greeted, as she entered the car.

"Mornin', Grace. How are you today?"

"Doin' good, thank you. Hope you are."

"There's a little chill in the air. I guess we better get used to it cause cold weather's on the way, but, I like this time of the year the best," Luke replied.

Detecting Grace's anxiousness, he tried keeping the conversation going to occupy Grace's mind during the drive. Soon they arrived at her destination and Luke let her out in front of the office door at the Amazon Cotton Mill.

"There's a store down the street there where you might want to go to pass some time when you get through with the interview, if you don't have anything else to do. I'll be back here to pick you up around fifteen 'til four," Luke said.

Grace entered the office, feeling slightly awkward and nervous as she walked up to the desk. She said hello and informed the receptionist that she was there to apply for a job. The receptionist smiled and handed her an application.

"Fill this out and bring it back to me when you finish," she instructed.

Grace filled it out as best she understood and took it back to the receptionist.

As she looked it over, she asked, "Grace, do you have any experience in this type of work?"

"No, ma'am," Grace replied grimly.

"Well, that's no problem. We'll need another spinner soon. You would need some training, but after that you should be able to handle it just fine. When can you start?"

"I can start whenever you want me to."

"That's great. My name is Eva, and if you have time, I'd like to take you through the mill to show you what you'll be doing."

"I've got plenty of time. My ride won't be back to get me 'til this evenin'."

"Good. Let's go see what you think about it. You never know, you might just master this job before leaving here today," Eva said cheerfully, as Grace returned her smile.

Eva, who had long, thick, brown hair, displayed a big, welcoming smile, and looked to be only a few years older than Grace. Her warm and friendly personality made Grace more comfortable as she followed her into the plant where she encountered rows of machines humming at full speed. Some of the machines were so loud she could barely hear anyone speak, and others had an almost soothing effect. But, it was apparent to Grace that very hard work was involved.

As they moved from one department to another, Grace felt a bit self-conscious. It seemed all eyes were following her as she passed by their departments to the spinning room.

Eva introduced Grace to Claire, a slim and modestly but neatly dressed lady with a most pleasing appearance. Claire was operating machines like those Grace would be trained on, and Eva asked Claire to be a mentor to Grace until she came back for her. Grace set her lunch bag down on a table near their work area and stood watching the lady work, wondering if she would ever become as fast and efficient as she was. Claire was years older than Grace, but they quickly became friends as Claire patiently showed her how the job was done.

When Eva returned thirty minutes later, Grace was catching on reasonably fast for a beginner.

"Grace, would you rather come back tomorrow, or keep practicing for a while longer?" Eva asked.

"I'll stay for a while if you don't mind."

"Alright, but if you need anything, just come back to the office."

"Thank you, I will."

She wanted to learn all she could while she had the opportunity, and she began to settle in. Time had passed quickly as a horn sounded.

Grace looked all around the plant as workers began to leave their machines. When Claire saw her puzzled look, she explained, "That's the dinner horn, honey. Get your lunch and we'll go outside and eat."

They both got some water to drink and proceeded out a side door to picnic tables under the trees.

It was a sunny day with a cool breeze as they sat down and took out their lunches while other workers joined them. Claire began to introduce Grace to the others as they all asked about where she was from and about her family. Many of the city residents seemed fascinated as she answered questions about her home life in the country. When she wasn't answering questions, she sat quietly and observed the group talking and laughing until the horn sounded again, and they all got up and returned to their workplaces a bit more rested.

Back at the spinning machine, Claire gave Grace a little more responsibility to see how she could handle it, and she only had to assist her a couple of times to keep things running smoothly. Grace's excitement now turned to intrigue as she concentrated completely on her task. She couldn't believe how fast the day had gone when the final horn signaled the end of the shift.

"You done good, Grace," Claire said. "You think you gonna like workin' here?"

"Oh, yes ma'am. I'll see you tomorrow, Claire."

Grace stepped back into the office to assure Eva that she would be back the next morning.

"Well Grace, what do you think about it?" Eva inquired.

"Claire said I did pretty good to have never done it before."

"I'm sure you did. You have a good evening and we'll see you tomorrow."

"Thank you," Grace replied, as she proceeded out the front door to wait for Luke.

Grace stood outside the front door of the cotton mill assessing all the tasks she had accomplished throughout the day, and was eager to get home and tell the family.

She hadn't been there very long when she saw Luke's car as he turned down the street and pulled up for her.

As she climbed in, Luke smiled and asked how her day went. She enlightened him with every detail as they drove home. When they arrived, they agreed to share the ride the next day as she got out of the car and thanked him. Luke waved and drove away as Grace walked toward the house.

Grace had barely closed the door before questions started flying through the room. "Did you get a job?" one asked. "How much money you makin?" asked another. "You makin' things out of cotton?" "Are you gonna buy me somethin' now?"

"Girls, girls, let Grace get settled before you ask so many questions," Dora pleaded.

"Oh, it's alright Mama," Grace chuckled, and proceeded to tell them about the nice lady she had met named Claire and of all the day's events all over again.

Chapter 6
The Festival

Grace met her ride the next morning as she did for days to come. Luke had wanted to invite Grace to the Everybody's Day Festival, but hesitated, feeling she might think he was too forward. The event was to take place the following Saturday, so he knew he'd better do it soon or she might not be able to go.

The following morning on their drive to work, Luke took his chance. "Grace, I was wonderin' if you might like to go to Everybody's Day this Saturday."

"I don't know. I've never been to one before. What is it?"

"Your guess is as good as mine," he quipped. "It'll be a first for me, too. I hear there's a parade."

"Well I'm sure they can do without me at home for a day. I think they're gettin' used to not havin' me around — maybe a little too much!" she jokingly mused.

"I'm sure they miss not havin' you at home like before," Luke said, in an assuring manner.

"Yes, I guess so."

On Saturday, Grace began getting ready early amid many questions and queries from the girls, but she didn't dare tell them where she was going. Realizing it would be difficult to get away if they knew, she just told them she had asked Luke to take her someplace.

It had looked like rain earlier, but the sky was clearing up as the sun began to burn off the early morning fog, promising to be a beautiful day.

Luke finally pulled up the drive near the side door, and little eyes peered out the windows when they heard the sound of the engine. Even though it was a trifle cool outside, Cletie and Ruth conveniently strolled slowly out the door holding hands and around the house, shyly craning just to get a better view of Luke.

They were always asleep when he picked Grace up in the mornings and had seen him at church time after time, but now he was on their turf and occupying Grace's time that was supposed to belong to them. Grace told them bye and waved as she and Luke backed out and drove off.

"They're curious little things, ain't they?" Luke said, as they both chuckled.

As Luke and Grace neared town, there was a multitude of other vehicles already parked and others looking for spots. Luke parked on the next street over from Main, getting as close as he could so Grace wouldn't have to walk any further than necessary. As they walked up the hill toward the tracks, they could already see makeshift tables with homemade wares and crowds of people as they approached.

"I don't think I ever seen so many people in one place," declared Grace.

"Have you seen the big chair they built in the square last year? It's really somethin' to see."

"No, I don't ever remember comin' to Thomasville but one time, and it was a long time ago. I don't remember a lot about it."

"There it is," Luke informed, as they walked across the tracks.

"My goodness, how'd they build that thing so big?"

"They say it took three men workin' ten hours a day for a whole week," Luke explained.

"What'd they make it out of?" Grace asked, curiously.

"I was told Thomasville Chair Company built it out of enough wood to make a hundred chairs. And, that the brown seat is covered all in Swiss steer hide, whatever that is."

"It looks so real. I wonder how tall it is?"

"I think the chair itself is over thirteen feet high. And with the base it's settin' on, it looks to be every bit of twenty-five feet high," Luke continued. "They say it's the biggest chair ever built."

"I don't doubt that," Grace replied. "Can we walk closer and look at it? I ain't never seen anything like that before."

As they got closer, a crowd had already gathered to admire the city's new icon. Grace, as everyone else, appeared dwarfed and stood there in awe of its size.

"I wish the girls could see this," Grace stated, as she gazed in amazement.

"Maybe we can bring them to see it one day," offered Luke.

"All of them girls?" Grace exclaimed. "You have no idea what you'd be gettin' into!"

"Maybe not," said Luke, as he laughed.

They proceeded down the dusty street, past venders with food and merchandise of all kinds, noticing in particular a man pushing a cart with small bags full of a pink and blue cottony substance hanging all over it.

"What's the stuff that man's got in those bags?" Grace asked.

"I'm not sure. I'll ask him when we get closer."

As they strolled by, Luke inquired, "Mister, what is that you got there?"

"It's called Fairy Floss, son. Would you like a bag?"

"What do ya do with it?"

"Why, you eat it," the man replied.

"How much?"

"Just a nickel, my good man."

"Think I'll try one, then."

Luke dug deep into his pocket and brought out five cents to pay the man, was handed a bag, and the vender rolled his cart on down the street.

"Grace, you wanna try some first?"

"I think I'll let you test it out before I try it. It looks like a big, colored cotton ball to me," Grace replied, warily.

Luke opened the bag, pulled off some of the soft cottony stuff, and stuck it in his mouth.

"Hmmm. Well, it was good while it lasted," he said, and chuckled. "It just sorta melts as soon as you put it in your mouth. Here, try some."

Grace pinched a small amount and cautiously tried it.

"Mmmm. This is good," she exclaimed. "And ain't it funny how it just sorta disappears so fast?"

They both took turns reaching into the bag during their stroll until they had divided the last piece.

Hearing a brass band coming from somewhere down the street took Grace's mind away from watching the first few parade cars in the procession. The beat of the drums and the live music gave her an unexplained feeling. She couldn't determine if it made her nervous, sad, or just excited. As the band passed, floats followed towed by tractors, late-model cars and trucks represented people of importance, adorned with ribbons and flowers made of paper. Grace especially liked one float in particular. It was draped with fabric and carried queens dressed in finer attire than she had even seen. The regal ladies smiled and waved to everyone on the street and Grace was amazed at the spectacle. The parade finally ended with a finale by the band, and Grace was still smiling as she and Luke crossed the street and made their way back to the car.

"Did you enjoy the parade, Grace?" Luke asked.

"I sure did! It was the most fun I've ever had!" she proclaimed. "Thank you for bringin' me. And thanks for that cotton stuff, too."

"You're welcome," Luke answered, then added, "Did you see that old moonshine mountain man in that jalopy?" as they both laughed.

For the entire trip home they recapped each of their Everybody's Day experiences with amazement and laughter.

When Luke pulled up the driveway, they said goodbye and Grace got out of the car. She walked to the door through swirling leaves carried on a light September breeze.

Her family greeted her as she began to tell them all about her tour of Main Street and the big chair. The girls earnestly begged her to take them to see it and were finally content when she assured them that she'd take them all someday.

"Grace, dinner is still on the table," Dora informed. "We just finished. You need to go on in and eat so they can finish cleanin' up the kitchen."

"Okay, Mama."

They all followed her to the table as Ora and Ruth crawled

up close on their knees, and the others leaned in to hear more of her amusing adventure and asked a myriad of questions about the event and parade.

Chapter 7
We're Having Turkey This Year

Grace was anticipating Thanksgiving Day the following Thursday. It was less than a week away and would be the first break from work since she had started in September. She decided to get a turkey for the family dinner this year since she had been able to save most of her pay. She had also been able buy her dad a new straw hat and a few shaving items he didn't usually buy for himself, plus new dress goods for her mom and sisters.

Normally, they just had chicken or ham on this holiday. When Grace announced her intention to buy a turkey, Walter replied, "You needn't spend money for a turkey. Chicken'l be just as good."

But Grace insisted that she was getting a turkey regardless, and so he finally obliged.

Grace recruited Walter to find a bird before Thursday and bring it home. After inquiring around the countryside, he found a neighboring farmer with a flock of turkeys. He picked one out and asked the farmer to hold it for a couple of days until he could get back with a cage.

On Wednesday, Walter and Jess placed a large, wire cage on the truck bed and drove off to pick up their future dinner.

When they returned, everyone ran out to see the unusual, big bird. And he was not a happy bird after being uprooted from his domain and jostled about on the truck. He gobbled, ruffled his feathers, and his neck changed colors as they all watched.

"Look how red his neck is gettin'!" Cletie exclaimed. "Wait a minute, now it's turnin' white!"

They all laughed at the odd actions of the turkey.

"Where's Grace?" Walter asked.

"She's in the house and won't come out," the others said.

"Grace!" Walter belted. "Come on out here and see this turkey you bought!"

"I don't wanna see it, Daddy."

"Why not?"

"If I'm gonna eat it tomorrow, I sure don't wanna make friends with it."

"Well, suit yourself," replied Walter, as the girls laughed.

Early Thursday morning, Walter was out with the ax and Dora and Maggie were boiling water in the black cast-iron pot out back.

"Boy, the feathers on this bird are sure tougher to pluck than a chicken's!" Maggie snorted. "Sure hope the meat ain't this tough."

After a little persistence, the turkey was clean and ready for the oven. They cooked it all morning, then around noon, it was prominently displayed on the table, surrounded by bowls filled to their rims with traditional country holiday fare.

Since Grace provided the main course, Dora and the girls prepared all the extra trimmings. As the family shared the meal, there was a thankful spirit sensed more by everyone that day than at anytime in the past, and Grace felt humbled and grateful that she was now able to contribute to the well being of her beloved family.

The following week, everyone was back on their usual schedules. As they entered into the first week of December, the days had gotten noticeably shorter and colder. Grace was thinking about what gifts she could buy for the family as she realized time was running short. Christmas was getting ever closer and she wondered what her budget would allow, for she was now spending more on needs for the family. She already had a few things in mind, but she didn't know how she would get uptown. She felt she was imposing on Luke if she asked him to go out of his way just for her. Maybe she could look in Denton on a Saturday when they went there with daddy, she thought, but it would be hard to shop if the whole family was there.

As they drove to work, Grace finally asked, "Luke, will you be goin' back into town anytime soon?"

"I can go back anytime. It's just up the street a ways. You need somethin'?"

"I'd like to check on a few presents for the family. I don't have Christmas presents for anybody yet, and it's just a couple weeks away. I did get a few ideas from the store windows when we went to Everybody's Day."

"We could ride uptown one evenin' after work and you could look around a bit," Luke offered.

"Oh, I wouldn't want to keep you from gettin' home, Luke."

"I think we could do that and still get home at a decent time. We could actually go tomorrow evenin' if you want to. Just let your folks know you'll be home a little late."

"Are you sure?"

"Sure I'm sure," he said, lightheartedly. "It'll be fun."

Chapter 8
The Doll

The next evening, Luke picked Grace up after work and they headed toward town. She had already determined that Ora would have her first doll this Christmas.

"Ready to go shoppin'?" Luke asked.

"Sure," she answered, cheerfully.

After a short drive, Luke said, "We can park close to the square this time. Won't be near as many people here today as last time. Where you wanna start?"

"How about that five and dime down there?" Grace suggested.

They walked across the street and stepped up on the sidewalk. Grace marveled as she passed store windows, pausing occasionally to admire the bright and sparkly Christmas decorations and colored electric lights she had heard about.

Amid a display of toys in one of the store windows, Grace saw a doll. They stepped inside and watched as the sales clerk picked it up and handed it to Grace to examine. It had what looked like real hair and eyelashes. It wore a lavender dress with lace round the neck, sleeves and hem, and little button-up shoes.

Merchandise there appeared to be of a slightly higher quality, so when the clerk informed them of the price, Luke realized from Grace's expression that it was too expensive for her budget.

He intervened for her and said, "We'll get back with you. We're just lookin' now."

"Boy, I'd have to spin a lot of cotton for that," she said, and they both laughed as they walked away.

"The five and dime will probably be your best bet," Luke suggested. "I believe you'll find a better deal down there."

As they neared the door of the department store, they immediately caught the buttery aroma and sounds of corn popping.

Grace could hardly wait to get inside. This was the first time she had been anywhere to experience something like this, and she felt she was at some grand event.

There was so much to look at as they scaled each aisle that had been well stocked for the holiday. She finally spotted dolls in a section of the toy department and picked up the first one she came to. She looked at the price and quietly said, "Let's see what else they got." She picked the next one and then put it back, again with a look of disappointment.

"They're a little expensive," Grace said.

"No need to worry, we can check somewhere else," assured Luke.

"I feel bad havin' you come all the way up here, but I think I'm gonna have to wait. These ain't as expensive as the one down the street, but I'll still need a little more money."

"Would you like some popcorn, Grace?"

"It smells awfully good, but I probably should save what I got for presents," she replied.

"Don't worry, it's on me."

Luke walked over to the popcorn stand, made his purchase and proudly delivered it to Grace.

"Thank you," she said, coyly accepting it as she sampled the first few kernels. She marveled, and said, "This is much better'n what we pop at home."

"Yeah, it's those fancy corn poppers with all that butter they have here."

As they made their way to the front door, Grace happened to glance toward the left window display. Under a Christmas tree, she noticed a small doll she hadn't seen in the toy department. It looked to be just the right size for a little girl like Ora.

"Hey, look. There's one," Grace exclaimed.

"You want me to ask the clerk to go get it?" Luke offered.

"If you don't mind."

The clerk stepped over to the display, lifted the doll and brought it for Grace to inspect. It was smaller than the fancy doll at the other store, and it had a smooth head instead of real hair, with painted eyes and a simple print dress. It had no shoes, but she knew Ora would think this one was just perfect.

Grace turned the tag over to look at the price, and Luke knew by Grace's smile that she had found what she came for.

After a thoughtful and thorough inspection, she told the lady she would take it.

"I'll wrap it in paper and put it in a bag. It'll only take a minute."

Grace looked around while waiting for the clerk and discovered a few other items she thought would be perfect gifts for some of the others. She took them to the counter and was met shortly with her initial purchase.

"I'm afraid I've found more," Grace offered, apologetically.

"That's fine, dear. Just take your time." the saleslady replied.

After the transaction, Grace picked up her bags and accompanied Luke back to the car, especially pleased with her purchases. They both knew that one evening would not be sufficient to shop for the whole family, so the next evening, they were on their way back uptown. They spent a couple of hours searching as Grace chose the perfect gift for each one.

"Thank you for bringin' me to town again, Luke. I really appreciate it."

"Think nothin' of it."

"Well, I ain't thought about where I'm gonna hide these things to keep the girls from findin' 'em. I surely can't take 'em in with me when I get home."

"You can leave 'em in the car 'til you decide what you wanna do," Luke offered.

"Maybe that'd be best," she agreed.

A friendship progressed between the two as Grace felt more self-assured, and soon she began to open up and talk more during their trips back and forth to work. Being away from family with no one to distract her thoughts was an experience completely different than she was used to. As a result, she sensed more freedom than ever before. She laughed at Luke's funny quips and they discussed future endeavors they each would like to accomplish someday.

"See you in the mornin'. I'll take good care of your gifts," said Luke.

"Oh, I'm not worried. See you tomorrow!"

As this was her first opportunity to ever buy gifts for anyone, she felt especially eager to tell Ora about the doll, but knew she couldn't as she imagined the surprise it would bring when presenting it to her on Christmas morning.

Since Grace started riding with Luke, he had reluctantly accepted gas money from her at times, but she was insistent on paying. However, as she tried to pay him on Friday before the holiday work break, he was very adamant that she keep the money as a gift from him.

"Thank you, Luke. That's real nice of you. Do you have to work on Monday?"

"I'm afraid so. We only get one day," Luke answered. "How 'bout you?"

"The mill decided to let everybody have Monday off since Christmas is on Tuesday," Grace explained.

"Well, think of me while I'm slavin' away Monday," he said with a chuckle.

"I imagine we'll all be pretty busy around here on Monday, too," Grace added. "By the way, do you mind droppin' the gifts off at Bud's? I asked him if I could leave 'em there and he said it was alright. I can walk over there and wrap 'em over the weekend."

"I'll take 'em right now," assured Luke.

Grace had secretly bought a handkerchief with Luke's initial on it, but she hadn't had an opportunity to wrap it. She decided to give it to him in the brown paper from the store.

"Here's a little somethin' for you."

"Thank you, Grace. You didn't need to do that," Luke replied, as he reached the end of the driveway. "Merry Christmas, Grace."

"Merry Christmas, Luke. And thank you for everything. I'd a never got all this done without your help."

"Glad to help," he said.

"Bye, now."

"Bye, Grace. See you Wednesday," Luke said, as she stepped out of the car.

He backed the car up to turn around and paused for a moment to glance her way, watching her as she opened the side door and closed it behind her.

Chapter 9
A Family Christmas

Grace had a lot to do in the four days before Christmas. On Saturday, they all were busy with chores most of the day. They wanted the house especially neat and clean for the holiday. Ora was only three, but she realized the approaching season held something special as Grace told her the stories of Christmas when she had time.

They looked forward to the Sunday morning Christmas play as they bundled up for the brisk, cold walk to church. As the service started, there was a nativity reenactment with scripture readings telling the events of the Christ child. The characters wore sheets of material draped around them, made to simulate the attire of that day. They used a baby doll wrapped in old cloth and laid in a crude, homemade feeding trough from someone's barn. With flickering candles in the windows, everyone seemed to radiate the peaceful spirit of the season. When the service ended, the ladies hugged each other and their families wished one another a joyous holiday before departing.

After the noon meal, Grace said, "Mama, I need to slip out and go to Bud's for a while to take care of somethin'."

When she got there she discovered that gift wrapping took some time since she hadn't had much experience in that capacity, but was proud of her humble efforts when she finally finished her project using brown paper and twine.

Monday morning, everyone was up early with the whole family eagerly volunteering to help with cooking and making the house look festive for Tuesday's big day. An abundance of running cedar grew on the bank above the spring that would make ideal trimmings for the mantle, if someone could be recruited to gather it.

"Jess, would you mind goin' up the hill and pull some of the cedar and bring it back?" Dora asked.

"Be back in a jiffy."

Trying to remember the words as best they could, the older sisters led the others in singing carols while adorning the fireplace with the green runners and extra red berries that Jess found and brought back as a bonus.

When nightfall came and everyone had dressed for bed, they gathered in the warmth and security of the living room, lit by a single oil lamp. Flames from the fireplace created dancing silhouettes on the walls as Walter entered with apples and oranges he had kept hidden away for this special night.

"I'll be right back," said Grace, as she slipped out of the room. Her little sister's eyes lit up with delight when she returned with a small bag and began to pull out colorful sticks of striped candy she had purchased in town. Even the older ones were eager to get one of the sweet treats.

"Roll your orange hard between your hands a few times to soften it and then we'll cut a small hole," Walter explained. "Then, stick the candy Grace got you in the orange and use it like a straw."

They squeezed them, then Walter helped cut the holes as an orange fragrance permeated the room.

"Mmmm, this is the best Christmas treat I've ever had," they all kept saying, savoring the treat as well as the time they enjoyed with family during their private celebration in the cozy farmhouse room.

Later that night, as all the children slipped into bed, Walter placed heated bricks warmed at the fireplace and wrapped them in pieces of cloth at the foot of the children's beds to warm their feet. As they all snuggled peacefully and warmly under mounds of quilts, hearts were content. All was calm, and all was well.

Christmas morning arrived, and with the exception of Ruth and Ora, everyone was up extra early making preparations for the much-anticipated family dinner.

Although the Thanksgiving turkey dinner would be hard to

match, they were content to have ham and farm-grown chicken, green beans picked and corn pulled, and potatoes that were carefully turned out of the dirt rows and stored away back in the summer. There were hot buttermilk biscuits, tops glistening with a fresh, buttery glaze. Apple and pumpkin pies had been baked and covered with cotton cloths in the pie safe. Bud and his wife arrived to join the family dinner with a basket of their own to share.

Grace had managed to keep the meager family gifts a secret, and when dinner was finished, Bud herded Grace off to a corner and asked her when she wanted to get her presents.

"I shoulda thought to let you bring 'em with you. Can I ride back with you when you go home?"

"Sure. We'll go right now if you want."

Once there, Grace exclaimed, "Bud, how am I gonna get these back to the house? I don't have a bag big enough for all of these."

"I can drive you back home," Bud offered.

"Oh, they're not heavy. I just need somethin' I can carry 'em all in," she said.

He stepped out on the porch and brought in a box to load up her gifts. She took one out and handed it to Bud.

"This one is for all of you."

"Now, why'd you go do that?" he scolded gently.

"It's not much. I just wanted to get everybody a little somethin' since I'm workin' now," she beamed.

Bud's wife stepped over to the cupboard for a moment, returning with a bag of freshly baked cookies.

"I just made these and they're for you," she said with a smile.

"Thank you both. Love you," Grace said.

"Love you, too," they both returned.

"Grace, you sure I can't take you back?" Bud implored.

"No, I'll be fine. Merry Christmas to you both."

"Merry Christmas!" they exclaimed.

There was a lilt in her step as Grace eagerly made the short way back home with her treasures. The younger ones were all a-buzz as she walked in with the box, and the others displayed expressions of curiosity and even a bit of wonderment. She handed out each gift in turn, deliberately making little Ora anxiously wait for hers. She finally handed the last one to her. As she tore open the paper and saw the doll, she squealed with excitement, hugging it tightly.

"Oh, Grace! It's what I always wanted!"

The kids normally would have gotten a reprimand from Walter for so much noise and chatter, but he made an exception on this day and just sat back and reveled in the occasion.

Chapter 10
A Snowy Winter

A year of remarkable changes had passed, and as Grace embarked on the beginning of a new one, she wondered what course 1924 would take. She was proud of the independence she had managed to acquire in such a short time, and she was amazed at all she had learned and accomplished. The experiences of home life through the years were not taken for granted, though. She knew they were important. She just never fathomed such a difference between her previous sheltered life and the new one she now embraced.

Although it had not come to mind that much in the past, Grace began to think more about marriage since being away from home, and at times wondered if there was someone special out there for her and if they would ever meet. Her modesty and timid nature prevented her from revealing her thoughts to anyone.

Her sisters could keep a strong conversation going at home and reveal most every fact they knew.

But Grace could keep a secret, as her own family learned when they would come to her confiding personal matters.

Grace had enjoyed all the festive Christmas and New Year celebrations, but now she was ready to get back to work.

Most everyone at work appeared to be jovial and refreshed following the holidays as they talked of their family dinners, church pageants, and other events that took place. Then, gradually over time, they settled back into their normal daily routines.

Grace and Claire still had conversations during lunch, learning more about each other and their personal lives.

"It's always good to hear of families that attend church together," Claire said.

"Mama and daddy raised all of us in church," Grace said. "I love goin' to church and especially the singin'. Amazin' Grace has always been my favorite song."

"I think I might have to claim that one, too," Claire added.

Grace had found a trusted friend in Claire, and felt with her she could confide most anything.

Bidding one another goodbye at the end of the day, they each left the building and found it had gotten quite cold and windy outside.

The sky that had been a beautiful clear blue earlier, had now become heavy and gray with clouds and Grace was surprised to see how quickly it had changed.

"Boy, it looks like snow!" Luke announced when he arrived.

Grace shivered as she entered the car and pulled her coat tighter.

"I hope not. It's only one more day 'til the weekend. Will you still go to work if it does?" she asked.

"It depends on how much it snows. If it's not much on the road, I could make it alright. I guess we'll see tomorrow."

They headed home with Grace hoping the bad weather would hold off.

"Oh, dear," Grace mumbled, as they got about halfway home.

Luke chuckled and asked, "You see it, too?"

"Yes, I thought I saw little snow flakes back up the road but I was hopin' it was my imagination."

"Well, I did, too. I just didn't say nothin', knowin' you'd be disappointed," Luke admitted.

"Oh, well, I guess if it comes, it comes, and I believe they're gettin' bigger. Yep, they are gettin' bigger," Grace moaned.

The wind and snow seemed to be picking up as Luke turned on Cid Road.

By the time they reached the driveway, everything was beginning to get white. He pulled up to the side door as close as he could to let Grace out.

"Remember, if there's not much on the road, I'll be by in the mornin', but if it snows a lot, I won't be goin'."

"Okay, I'll see you if you make it."

The wind was getting blustery now with snow swirling off the edges of the roof, hitting her in the face, while blowing her hair in every direction as she reached for the door. She had to hold tight to keep the wind from pulling the door knob out of her hand and slamming it against the wall.

"Oooo… hurry and close that door, child! That air is a fright," Dora exclaimed, as Grace bounded in.

"It looks like a blizzard, Mama."

"I know. The girls are peerin' out every window in the house. Your daddy and Jess are still feedin' up. I knew somethin' was comin'. I've heard the roar comin' across the mountain all day."

"I was hopin' it wouldn't amount to much so we wouldn't miss work tomorrow," Grace added. "But from the looks of it now, we might be in for a big one tonight."

She occasionally peeped out the door, checking the progression until time for bed, finding the snow a little deeper each time. As darkness fell, the wind continued to howl and the snow could be heard pelting the windows as the wind blew it sideways.

She decided to check one more time.

"Grace, openin' that door all night ain't gonna make the snow stop, you know," Jess quipped.

So Grace then resigned herself to the fact that she would be snowed in the next day and went to bed.

She awoke the next morning with daylight revealing a deep, brilliant snow with heavy-laden tree branches that glistened when the sun peeked through the breaking clouds. It had transformed the landscape into a new, sparkling world. It was so beautiful and peaceful as she stood gazing out the window in awe.

She always remembered being so excited as a child when it snowed. Reflecting on the past with a lighthearted smile, she reasoned maybe it's God's way of getting people to slow down. I would've rather gone to work today, but I'm just gonna enjoy the day, she decided to herself.

Walter and Jess had set out early to clear a path through the deep snow to the barn. The animals had to be fed and the cows milked. Over in the afternoon Dora said, "One of you young'uns take this pan and step outside and get some snow. I got a bowl of sweetened milk ready to make snow cream."

Once they were back with the pan heaped up, it didn't take long for Dora to mix it and dish out the delicious cold treat.

The sun's warmth gradually started to melt the snow the next day, and Grace was soon able to return to the mill.

But it seemed it snowed almost every week, preventing them from traveling their route to Thomasville time and again.

Grace was heard saying more than once, "I'll be so glad when spring gets here!" And some of the siblings would chime in, "Yes, and we will, too, Grace!"

She thought how much easier it would be if she had a room at a boarding house near the mill, but was uncertain if her pay would be sufficient.

"Mama, what do you think about me gettin' a room close to the mill before next winter comes? Several girls stay at boardin' houses close by so they can get to work even in bad weather."

"Well, you would certainly be better able to get to work. It's whatever you want to do, Grace, as long as you find a good place to stay. I know you had rather be workin' than sittin' here waitin' for the snow to leave. Spring is just around the corner, so you got plenty of time. Just ask around."

Spring finally did arrived with summer soon on its heels, and Grace was happy that she wouldn't have to miss any more work. She now, however, was thinking of a solution for the following winter.

When she talked to Claire the next day during break, she asked her opinion.

"If you want to move closer to work, I know a nice lady named Nellie out on Fisher Ferry Street that occasionally takes in boarders," Claire informed.

"I wonder what they charge," said Grace, with a tinge of apprehension. "I don't know if I make enough right now to afford it."

"You could do some part-time work to help pay for the expense. There's a big demand for house cleaning in this area, especially the folks up closer to town. I could probably arrange a couple jobs for you right off with people I know."

"Really, you'd do that?

"I sure would."

"Claire, you're so nice."

"Let me check with them and I'll let you know as soon as I find out."

Claire was as good as her word. A few days later, she relayed good news to Grace.

"I talked to Nellie and she has a room available. I also found a couple of ladies looking for someone to clean. I told them you were a real hard worker," she added.

"I wat'n plannin' to move here 'til later in the fall. You think I should get a room now? "

"Oh, yes. Honey, if you wait 'til fall, there won't be any rooms left. That's when everybody tries to get closer to the factories, just as you are."

"Oh, I hadn't thought of that. I mentioned to my mama about movin' later in the year, but I really think my folks would understand if I explained it that way. Let me talk to 'em tonight and I'll let you know tomorrow. I appreciate you checkin' for me."

"It was no trouble, sweetie."

Later that evening Grace spoke with her mother and explained the situation just as Claire had to her, and then asked her to let her daddy know of her intentions. As Grace awaited her ride the next morning, Walter and Dora gave their approval for her to move.

Grace was hesitant with her news to Luke, but about halfway to work, she gingerly spoke.

"Luke, I hate to tell you this, but I might be movin' to one of the boardin' houses uptown."

"Really? Your folks don't mind?"

"I'm sure they'd rather I'd stay home, but I need to get a room now so they won't get gone before the end of the year. You've really helped me out a lot with errands and takin' me to work and back home. I really appreciate that," she replied.

Luke had become comfortable with Grace's presence during their trips each day, and he was now feeling sad at the thought of the long ride without her.

"Well, I'll miss your company," Luke said. "But I guess I can't blame you. It's a long drive and I know how you feel about bein' stranded at home when it snows. I sometimes wish I could move closer, but I got too many roots down home. The family still needs what help I can give with the animals and I help in the fields on the weekends. But I'm glad you're able to make a change," he assured.

Chapter 11
The Move

Grace could hardly wait to tell Claire, and from the broad smile on her face as she walked in, Claire pretty much knew without asking. She gave Grace directions to Nellie's boarding house just a couple streets over, and she decided to walk there during her lunch break.

She found the house, and unlike the plain wood siding at home, this one was whitewashed with a well-groomed yard. Flowers of all colors were freshly planted, with more blooming in pots around the entrance. And there were her favorites, marigolds, growing in beds against the house.

Grace had always loved flowers and often wished she had a garden of her own. She smiled to herself as she walked up the front steps. She heard movement in the house and knocked on the screen door. After a moment, a short lady, a little on the fleshy side, came to the door. She was wearing a brown floral cotton dress with a stained apron tied around her waist, appearing to have just stepped out of the garden.

"Hello there," Nellie greeted.

"Hey. Are you Nellie?"

"Well, honey, that's who they tell me I am," she said, followed by a hearty laugh and revealing a witty personality that Grace was not quite sure about.

"I'm Grace Grubb. Claire spoke to you about a room for me."

"Yes, child, come on in and excuse my appearance. I'm a plain mess. I've been plantin' and settin' out my flowers all mornin'."

Grace stepped in and glanced around to see a very neat sitting room furnished with an attractive, rounded-arm sofa and two chairs placed invitingly around a large, oval rug of a burgundy, green, and brown braid. The end tables had crocheted doilies that anchored the items resting on top, and there was a large, upright radio against one wall. Hanging above it was a loudly ticking wooden-case clock with a swinging pendulum.

"You like flowers?" Nellie asked.

"Oh, yes, ma'am. I tried to grow some at home one time but didn't do too good. I especially love marigolds, though."

"Well, missy, if you stay around here long, you'll have a green thumb."

"A green thumb? I never heard of that. Is that somethin' bad?"

"Mercy me! No, child," Nellie replied, as she laughed. "That's a good thing. Means you know how to grow things and not kill 'em."

"Oh," Grace said, a trifle embarrassed.

"So, you lookin' for a room. Well, let me show you what I got. This is the parlor if you have company. You're welcome to use the radio if you can find a station. There's only one girl stayin' here for now, and she rents one of the rooms upstairs. There's an empty room up there and one down here. My bedroom is at the end of the hall down here on the left, and the extra room is the one on the right there."

Nellie opened the door and Grace stepped in to inspect it. She looked all around and said politely, "It looks real nice."

"Let's go upstairs and look at the other one," Nellie suggested.

The stairway was much wider than the steep, narrow stairs at home. As they walked upstairs, Nellie asked, "Where you from, honey?"

"I'm from the Cid community, right below Silver Valley."

"Cid... Cid. I think I've heard of that. Silver Valley is just a fer piece down south of here, I believe."

"Yes, ma'am. My daddy and mama farm with the help of most of the kids."

"Hard work makes good young'uns," declared Nellie.

"Here's the other room," Nellie said, as she opened the door. "You might like this one better since there's somebody else up here close to your age. Just walk in and look around."

Grace obliged and looked around, noticing an iron bed with

a rug beside it on the wooden floor and a dresser with a hinged mirror.

"I think I'd like this room if you don't mind," Grace said.

She felt this one would feel more like home since her room at home was upstairs as well. And with another young lady in the next room, she was hopeful they might have some common interests.

Nellie told her what she charged per week, and added, "…which is less than most others ask. The supper meal is included. All I ask is for the ones eatin' to help out with the dishes, and breakfast is available if you like. The town got electricity a while back and it sure is nice," explained Nellie. "I was able to buy one of those new wringer washin' machines and I don't have to use that scrub board anymore. It's on the back porch for anybody that wants to use it. Just don't get your fingers caught in the rollers. Do y'all have a wringer washer at home yet?"

"No ma'am. We don't have electricity yet. I've seen one, but we wash our clothes out back on a wash board and in a black pot over the fire," Grace replied.

"Well, we might have you actin' like a city girl before you know it," said Nellie, sporting another big laugh as Grace thought how southern Nellie sounded, even more so than her own family.

"When you want'n to move in, hon?"

"I'll be back tomorrow if that's alright," Grace replied.

"See you then, dear."

She hurried back to the mill to avoid being late, and informed Claire of her decision. Having her own room with privacy was an exciting thought that kept her mind engaged the rest of the afternoon.

Now, all that was left to do was to go home and start packing her belongings. She was wondering how her family would react when she walked out the door, knowing she wouldn't be coming home that evening. She would be the first girl to leave home under normal circumstances. Reflecting on that, reality began to creep in, and Grace felt a little apprehensive of the change and a degree of sadness at the thought of being away from her family. It was a bittersweet decision, but this is what she had been looking forward to all summer and now knew she had to move forward with her life.

After conveying the news to her mom and dad at home that evening and then to the rest of the kids, Grace began to gather her clothes.

Ora entered the bedroom with a saddened face as Grace was bagging her things.

"Are you never comin' back?"

"Yes, I'll be back. In fact, you can come spend the night with me sometime."

"I can?"

With that, Ora was satisfied. She smiled and gave her a big hug as she ran off to play.

Grace didn't have much more than her homemade dresses and a few personal things, so it didn't take long to pack. She thought of leaving her coat until fall but remembered how the nights could still get chilly and decided to take it with her.

Alone in the bedroom, she felt a little guilty leaving home just as the family was starting to plant again, but her ambition outweighed the guilt. She finished up and went downstairs to join the family.

She explained to the younger girls before bedtime that she wouldn't be home that next evening but would be returning home for a visit soon.

The next morning, Grace took one last look around the bedroom and spotted one of the rare photos taken of her mom, dad, and some of the kids. It was a small photo in a plain metal frame, and she tucked it in her bag before leaving the room.

Downstairs, she hugged and kissed her mom and dad as they cautioned her to be careful in her new surroundings, and reiterated the differences she might not be used to.

She was eager to get to the room and start setting up her living quarters.

After work, she grabbed her belongings at the sound of the

last horn and rushed off to Nellie's.

She had saved enough money to cover the first few weeks' rent until she could start cleaning the houses Claire had arranged for her.

When she arrived, Nellie welcomed her in and invited her to return to supper in about an hour, which would give her time to get everything situated in her room. As she started up the steps, Nellie mentioned that Anna, who lived upstairs, would be home to meet her soon.

Her pride and delight radiated as she placed her personals in the dresser drawer, hung up her dresses, and leaned the rigid family photo against the bottom of the mirror. She was so excited that she envisioned sliding down the banister on her return to the kitchen. What a funny sight that would be, she mused to herself.

She heard someone coming up the steps and was soon greeted by a young lady about her age with strawberry blonde hair and big, green eyes, introducing herself as Anna. She wore a store-bought dress, Grace was almost sure, having a design more intricate than she had ever seen homemade.

"I'm Grace. Nice to meet you."

"Nice to meet you, too. I'm glad to have someone else here. Nellie's a lot of company, but it's been sort of quiet up here at night. If there's anything you need, let me know."

"Thank you," Grace graciously obliged. "If you don't mind, could I go down for supper with you when you go?"

"Sure, I'll be ready in just a minute."

Anna went to her own room and Grace continued putting her things away. It wasn't long before Anna was back at Grace's doorway inviting her downstairs.

After the meal, the three remained at the table, chatting and getting to know each other. Nellie and Anna were glad to have Grace there as much as she was to be there. Even though she had never been away from home, Grace felt like an adult for the first time in her life, and her heart was happy and she felt content.

Chapter 12
A Second Glance

Grace spent the next few days getting acquainted with Anna and Nellie. With Anna working close by, there was time for the two to get out in the evenings after work and walk the neighborhood, at least until Grace's house cleaning jobs were to start at the end of the week.

As they walked down the street, they noticed three young men in the distance coming in their direction. Anna whispered to Grace that they should smile at them if they were handsome. The boy on the right was slightly heavy with light brown curly hair while the one on the left was a skinny, freckled redhead with ears that stuck out. The middle boy, they thought, was quite nice looking. As they got close enough, Anna said hello. After passing, Grace curiously glanced back at the fellow in the middle just as he did the same. She abruptly turned back around, embarrassed to have been caught looking, but flattered that such a handsome guy could have been noticing her. He definitely made an impression on her. He had dark, wavy hair, piercing eyes, and a captivating smile with a mysterious presence that oddly intrigued her.

"You know them?" Grace asked.

"I've seen them from time to time. They probably live somewhere nearby."

Grace wanted to mention the one looking back at her, but didn't feel she knew Anna well enough to confide her personal thoughts without fear of embarrassment.

"We probably should get back," Anna suggested. "It's getting a bit late."

"This has been nice," Grace said, wondering if maybe they would meet the young men on the way back.

They arrived back at the house, but the boys were nowhere to be seen. She wondered who he was throughout the evening, still flattered by the attention.

Grace was now getting into a new routine very different than the one she had at home. She would love to go back and visit family and tell them all about her new experiences, but knew that wouldn't be possible this weekend with all her extra work coming up.

The next evening, Grace heard a car pull up in front of the house and she peered out the window. She realized it was Luke and stepped out on the porch as he got out of the car.

"Hey, Luke. How you been?"

"I'm on my way home and thought I'd stop by to see how you're likin' it here."

"I'm really likin' it up here. Come on up and sit for a while."

"I don't have long. I got some feedin' up and more chores to do now that summer's here."

As they sat down on the swing, he asked, "How's your house cleanin' jobs workin' out?"

"I start this weekend with two. I'm gettin' settled in this week and gettin' to know everbody. They're all real nice and make me feel welcome here."

"I'm glad you're happy with the arrangement."

They both talked and laughed for a little longer before Luke announced that he had to go.

"I saw your folks at church Sunday and they wanted me to ask when you're plannin' to come back home for a visit."

"It'll be hard to get back on a weekend since I'm cleanin'. I guess I could ride down the road with you on a weekday sometime and come back the next mornin', if you don't mind."

"Whenever you want, I'll be glad to pick you up," Luke offered.

"If it's not out of your way, I could go down in about two weeks."

"I'll tell 'em when I see 'em again. Well, you take care of yourself, Grace, and I'll see you then."

The first two houses to be cleaned were fairly close by and

Grace was glad she didn't have to walk very far. She had ample experience in housekeeping back home and gave a little extra care as she cleaned, hoping to please and impress her patrons. When she finished, they bragged and complimented her on a wonderful job. She walked home, sensing satisfaction and thankfulness.

"Grace, would you like to go to church with me tomorrow?" Nellie asked. "Anna goes home to her folks nearly every weekend, and you'll just be by yourself here."

"Yeah, I'll go with you," she answered.

Grace wouldn't be able to get to her church back home, and had not found an opportunity to look for one in the city.

She told Nellie all about her church in the country and all the friends she had there.

The next morning, she found the service at Nellie's church a trifle different than at Walter's Grove. It was quieter and a little more orderly, but regardless, Grace felt inspired by the sermon.

They returned home to have lunch, spending most of the afternoon on the porch rockers talking about family and past events.

The warm day brought memories to Grace's mind — of trips to town with her daddy and she could almost taste the soda pops they had enjoyed there.

The local store wasn't open on Sunday, so she would have to wait.

Monday evening, she decided to go as soon as they finished eating and doing the dishes.

"Nellie, I think I might walk over to the store. Do you need anything?"

"Thank you, hon, but I can't think of anything at the moment," she replied.

Anna would be late coming home that day, so Grace set out on her own. The store was only a block away.

When she arrived, she walked up the wooden steps to the entrance and passed two older men chatting on a bench and spitting tobacco juice over the edge of the porch. She opened the creaky screen door, spotted the drink box in the corner, and headed that way.

There were a couple of other people about the store and a customer standing in the next aisle. She casually glanced that way as she walked by, their eyes locking for an instant.

"Oh, my…it's him," she thought, as she blushed and quickly turned away.

It was the handsome boy that glanced back at her as she and Anna were out walking the week before. Too shy to look back, she could tell out of the corner of her eye that he was looking her way. As she made her way to the counter to pay for her drink, he appeared and said hello, with a smile. Grace shyly returned the gesture, desiring to talk more, but the confidence just wasn't there yet.

She paid for her purchase and exited the store. Every fiber of her being wanted to turn around and go back. But her legs kept moving forward against her will.

All the way back she questioned and chastised herself. Why didn't I just take the time to talk to him? What if I never run into him again? I could have at least found out his name, she scolded.

Back up in her room, she wondered over and over who he was and just hoped their paths would cross again. After all, this was the second time seeing him since moving here. She then decided the next time she would stay long enough to see if he was interested enough to initiate a conversation or if he was just being cordial. He does seem like he's interested, she thought to herself.

Anna was working later than Grace in the evenings for the next week, so Grace repeated her venture to the store alone to try catching sight of him once again. But he had not shown up, and Grace knew she couldn't afford to keep buying a soft drink every day. Although Nellie hadn't mentioned it, she was going to wonder what was up with her walking to the store every evening. Grace was beginning to wonder if maybe she was mistaken in her assumption.

Returning home from a big housecleaning job on Friday evening, she trudged up the stairway to her room for a few relaxing moments. As she sat down on the side of her bed, she heard

Anna's footsteps until they reached her partially open door and then stopped.

She peeped in and said, "Hey, Grace. That you?"

"Yeah, come on in. Pull out a chair and sit down."

"You do your cleaning today?" Anna asked.

"I sure did, and I'm not used to these long hours. I'm thankful to have the extra work, though."

"Just wondering if you might want to go down and sit in the porch swing for a while. Would you?"

"Sure. Let me get these shoes off and I'll be right down."

Sliding her shoes under the bed, she headed down barefoot to join Anna.

"Grace, did you have a boyfriend back home?"

"No. But I did go out a couple times. I usually stayed so busy at home there wasn't much time for that. I took care of my little sister a lot. I miss her, and the rest of them, too."

"Do you regret moving up here?"

"Oh, no. I dreamed of doin' this for a long time. It's just a bit different here than out in the country. A couple of boys at my church was friends, but there's not nearly as many boys there as it is here. Nobody lives real close, and we can't see any of the neighbor's houses, except for my brother's. How about you? You have a man friend somewhere?"

"I have a boyfriend over where I lived with my folks. He doesn't have a car yet but does catch a ride here once in a while."

"Anna, you remember those boys we met last week while walkin'?

"The ones we saw down Fisher Ferry Street?"

"Yeah. That one walkin' in the middle, I saw him at the store Monday evenin'."

"Oh, he was the good-looking one. Did he speak to you?" Anna asked, with raised eyebrows.

"He just smiled and said hello."

"Did you talk to him?"

"I wanted to, but I was too nervous," she admitted. "That day we met 'em, I glanced back to find him lookin' back at me, but I didn't mention it."

"Grace, I believe he might fancy you!"

"Oh, I don't know. You think so?"

"Yes, I do. You need to talk to him the next time you see him."

"How old do you think he is? He looks pretty young."

"I suppose about our age, eighteen or so," Anna answered.

Grace was quiet for an instant, with a smug look.

"What's that look?" Anna asked.

"Well, I'm already twenty-one."

"Really? You don't look that old, Grace. It doesn't matter though. And, he could actually be older."

"He might not be back around, anyway," Grace rationalized. "I ain't seen anything of him since then."

"He'll be back around eventually. I've seen those boys several times. Did you like the looks of him?"

"Well," Grace hesitated, "he was nice lookin'. I just get so embarrassed for some reason."

"Could it be that you're a bit struck on him?" Anna asked, giving Grace a sly look of jest. "We'll just have to keep our eye out for him when we go walkin' again."

The innocent tease prompted a shy response for a moment, but Grace sensed she had gotten to know Anna well enough now to confide in her.

Grace couldn't relay such matters to Maggie back home. She would sometimes appeared slightly envious when attention fell on one of the others, which probably came from her not venturing very far from home. It was just normal sister rivalry, but never on Grace's part, as it had never entered her heart to be jealous of anyone.

"Maybe we can go out walkin' some next week," Grace mentioned.

"Okay, maybe Monday," suggested Anna.

When Anna arrived home Monday evening, she found Grace and said, "Hi, Grace. Have a good day?"

"Yeah. A lot of new work came in today. I'm a little tired."

"I thought about going walking after supper, but if you're too tired…"

"Oh, I'm not that tired," Grace assured her, as they both laughed.

At the dinner table that evening, Anna blurted, "Nellie, Grace found her a boyfriend."

"Really?" Nellie asked, as Anna giggled.

"Anna. You didn't need to tell that," Grace scolded, with a slight grin. "I hardly even know that boy, Nellie. We only spoke twice."

"Where did you meet him, Grace?"

"We saw him and two other boys walkin' down Fisher Ferry Street a couple weeks ago."

"What's his name?"

"We don't know," Anna and Grace both answered.

"We only said hello," Anna replied. "Grace saw him again at the store later, but scampered out like a scared rabbit, without talking to him. We're going walking after supper to see if we run into them again."

"Well, girls, I always say if it's meant to be, it'll happen when and if the time is right," Nellie said. "And when you do think you've met the right one, make sure you get to know 'em well before makin' a commitment. It's easier to get into than to get out of. I was just bless to get a good one, God rest his soul."

They finished the dishes and dashed out the door like two giggling school girls, with dress tails swaying in rhythm as they sauntered down the front walk and up the street.

"Have you ever wondered what life would be like after you're married someday, Grace?"

"I've not really thought about it that much. How about you?"

"I think I'd like enough money for a big house full of nice furniture. After growing up as an only child, I want a house full of children, too. How many children do you want?" Anna continued.

"About two or three would be enough for me. I don't think I'd want to have as many as my mama did, although I admire how well she looked after all of us. I just want to teach my children

71

the right way. I don't really mind how big a house it is, but I'd like to have one that's painted white like Nellie's with lots of flowers growin' around it."

As the evening slipped by, they had not seen the young men anywhere and didn't figure they would, so they headed back toward Nellie's house.

They chatted with Nellie for a while after they returned, and then made their way on up to their rooms.

"Have a good night, Grace. See you tomorrow."

"Good night, Anna."

Chapter 13
They Finally Meet

It was hot and sultry when Grace got home on Tuesday evening, so she gathered up her laundry and marched toward the cooler spot on the back porch where the washer sat.

She met Anna in the hallway and asked, "Got anything that needs washin' while I'm at it?"

"I'll gather up a few things and come out to help you," she said.

After they finished the wash cycle, they repeated Nellie's warning of the rollers to each other a couple times as they continued. And then they laughed at their own silliness.

"If we get through with this before it gets too late, maybe we can walk to the store," Anna suggested.

That set Grace's mind in motion again about the young man she had met.

She wanted to go back to the store, so she sped up the washing process as much as possible. The clothes were soon hanging on the line with still plenty of time.

"Anna, you ready to go?"

"I'm ready."

The two hurried down the street, calculating verbally what they could afford to purchase before they arrived and then entered through the screen door.

"I'm gonna get a soda pop and some cheese crackers for my break tomorrow," said Grace.

"I think I'll get the same thing," replied Anna, as they picked up the items and started to the counter with their selection. Grace glanced over to the next aisle and couldn't help thinking of the last time she saw the mysterious handsome guy standing there. The screen door opened from time to time as customers entered, but Grace was not particularly noticing who came in.

As Anna looked across the room, she whispered, "Grace, I think that's him over there looking at those knives."

Grace looked that way and saw him admiring a pocket knife.

"Let's just pretend we're looking at something," Anna whispered.

"Like what?" Grace asked, as she cautiously glanced his way.

"Anything! Just look."

He put the knife back in the case and sauntered over to the drink box, got a soda and caught sight of Grace as he turned around. He coyly worked his way closer to the girls, pretending to be interested in something on the shelf nearby.

"Hey! Haven't I seen you girls before?" he said, sporting a sly grin.

"Yes, we saw you walking down the street awhile back," Anna replied, while gently nudging Grace to speak.

"And I believe I saw you in here awhile back," he said to Grace.

"I saw you, but I was in such a hurry that day …" Grace replied nervously.

By that time, Anna had slipped around the other side of the aisle to allow them to talk.

"Do you live around here?" he asked.

"I work here in town and stay at one of the boardin' houses for now," she quickly replied, noticing his strikingly white teeth as he smiled.

"What's your name?" he pressed.

"Grace. Grace Grubb."

"I'm Allen Scarlett. I live down in the Petree Field area."

"Oh, I've heard mention of that place," Grace responded, as she searched for words.

He has nice eyes, she thought to herself. And she observed his black, wavy hair when he wasn't looking directly at her. She stood there, enamored, feeling a strange, warm flush spread over her body, which she desperately hoped didn't show on her face.

"Where you from?" he inquired.

"I grew up in the Cid community down toward Denton."

"Is that close to Silver Valley? I have kin folk that live there," he continued.

"It's just a mile or two down the road from there. Our house is back in the country right close to Randolph County."

"Are you headin' back to where you stay?" he asked.

"As soon as we pay for our things," she replied.

"You mind if I walk you back as far as your house?"

"That'd be fine," Grace assured him, as her heart beat faster and she found it a little harder to breathe.

Grace and Anna completed their purchases as Allen stood waiting near the front. He then followed them out the door and toward Nellie's, with Anna giving Grace mischievous eye jestures all the way. They talked and laughed as he joked with them, and Grace began to feel surprisingly comfortable. As they got closer to the boarding house, Grace was certain she didn't want to lose touch again, but didn't have the nerve to ask him to stay.

"Which one do you live in?" he asked.

Anna devilishly blurted, "It's the white house right down there. You want to come and sit on the porch?"

Grace was taken aback with her forwardness, but deep down she was thankful that Anna had opened up the opportunity.

"Is that alright with you, Grace?" Allen asked.

"Sure," Grace beamed.

Anna scurried off through the front door to ensure their privacy, looking back once to smile as they stepped up on the porch. They both sat down possessing a look of infatuation with each other while they began to gently sway on the porch swing in the balmy, late summer breeze.

"Do you have brothers or sisters?" Grace inquired.

"I have four brothers and two sisters. I'm the second oldest. What about you?"

"I'm the third oldest. There are two boys and seven girls," Grace answered.

"My, that's a lot of sisters," Allen exclaimed.

"There would have been eight girls but one died at birth a couple years ago," she added. "My youngest sister, Ora, is now four."

"Well, how about that. My little sister is also four. Her name is Alma."

"That's a pretty name, Alma Scarlett," Grace replied. "I'll have to say, Scarlett is one of the prettiest names I've ever heard."

"Thank you. I think Grace is a very pretty name, too," he returned. "How long you been stayin' up here?"

"I got my job and moved here back in the early summer," said Grace.

"I went to work for the railroad last year," Allen said. "It's hard work puttin' in crossties but it pays a fair wage."

"It does sound like hard work," Grace agreed.

As they sat and talked, the sun began to set on the back side of the house, and it would soon be getting dark.

"I've enjoyed talkin' with you, but I need to get home. Another workday tomorrow," said Allen.

"I've enjoyed talkin' to you, too," she replied.

"Can I stop by to see you again sometime?

"Yeah, that'd be nice."

"Do you have plans Friday evenin'? I'll be gettin' off work early, and if you don't mind, I'd like to come by."

"That'd be fine. We should be through with supper dishes by six."

"Good. See you around six thirty."

Grace was wishing she could invite him to the evening meal on Friday, but knew she should ask Nellie first.

She didn't want their conversation to end, but understood that he had to get home, and she also had to get ready for work the next day.

"Bye, Grace. See you Friday."

"Bye, Allen. Have a good night."

Chapter 14
The First Date

Grace spent the next few days daydreaming and wishing time forward, just to Friday, anyway. There were moments she wondered if their meeting had actually happened, and if he could really be coming to call on her. She could hardly contain her excitement, and everyone could tell.

"You seem so happy this week," Claire commented. "It's good to see you smiling so much."

"Oh, I just enjoy bein' on my own and havin' a job."

"I remember my first job," Claire recalled. "It was good to be making my own way."

"It was hard to imagine what leavin' home and movin' up here would be like," Grace added. "I didn't think I'd ever have the confidence to make that first step. But here I am," she said, pausing with a smile.

"Well, you have a good heart, Grace, and I trust God has something special in store for you down the road."

"I hope so," she answered.

On Friday, Grace was experiencing nervous energy from all the anticipation. Allen was different than any boy she had ever known. Sometimes he seemed mysterious, and she was intrigued by him. Although her head told her to not get so excited, her heart felt otherwise. After all, this was the first time she had actually been interested in someone and, more important, she felt his affections were mutual.

She couldn't wait to get home to her room. What shall I wear? If I wear my Sunday best, they'll probably pick on me here for days, she thought. I'll wear the new, blue summer dress we made at home back during the winter. But I shouldn't change until after we eat. What if I was to spill somethin' on it? Thoughts raced through her mind like never before.

Nellie was bringing the food to the table, and as Grace and Anna came in and sat down to eat, Anna immediately proclaimed, "Nellie, Grace's beau is coming to call on her today."

"Anna…," Grace scolded, with a grin. "I'm gonna get you, girl."

"Haven't you learned by now not to tell her anything you don't want repeated?" Nellie stated, prompting laughter from all three.

"I'm beginnin' to find that out," Grace quipped, although she was actually pleased that Anna brought the subject up.

"Is it the boy that's been eyein' you for a while?" Nellie pressed.

Trying to appear coy, Grace answered, "Oh, he's just a boy I've talked to a couple of times."

"Don't let her kid you, Nellie," Anna added slyly, "They're struck on each other." Grace felt her face getting a little hot and hoped they didn't notice.

"Well, you'll have to invite him over for a meal sometime," Nellie offered.

Collecting herself, Grace said, "You wouldn't mind? I'd be glad to pay for extra food."

"The first one'll be on me. Just give me fair warnin'," she answered.

"Well, at least you can offer him some of this lemonade today," Anna suggested.

They finished up their meal and Grace proceeded to help with the dishes as Nellie stated, "Grace, we'll take care of the dishes tonight. You go on and get ready for your friend."

"Nellie, I don't want to leave you two with all the dishes."

"Now, I've said my peace. Go!" she said, with a laugh.

"Yes, you go on and get ready for that fine, young boy," Anna added, with a wink, as Grace walked off shaking her head but smiling to herself.

It was around ten after six and she figured she had just enough time to change and spruce up a bit before he arrived. At twenty-five after, she went back down the stairs to wait for her visitor. She thought of going out on the porch and sitting in the swing, but she didn't want to come across as eager. She stepped to the kitchen door and thanked Nellie and Anna again as they finished up, and they complimented her on how nice she looked. She then decided to wait in the front sitting room, for surely he would come to the door and knock. It was now six thirty. She peered out the window but Allen was nowhere in sight. She wondered if maybe he had forgotten which house it was.

Anna walked through the room to go upstairs. "Is he not here yet, Grace?"

"Not yet."

"Well, I'm sure he'll be here soon. He's probably just running late for some reason," Anna assured.

"It's no big deal," replied Grace, trying not to appear concerned. "He may have changed his mind."

"I don't think so. Just give him a little more time. He's not very late," Anna offered, as she proceeded up to her room.

It was now twenty to seven, and at this point Grace's heart sank as she wondered what could have happened. She figured he probably was not interested in seeing her again. She had such mixed emotions now. Here she had finally met someone interesting and he doesn't show up.

Another lengthy stare out the window produced nothing.

At fifteen 'til, Anna walked back down to check on Grace.

"Maybe something came up that he couldn't help," she offered.

Anna sensed her obvious disappointment as Grace answered, "I guess so."

Glancing down the street again, she caught sight of someone walking her way and immediately heaved a sigh of relief when she realized it was Allen. Her smile was hard to suppress as she whispered, "Here he comes now."

Anna strained to look around Grace for a glimpse, and then ran off to her room, stating, "Tell me all about it later, Grace!"

Grace sat down and grabbed up a book, pretending to read, not wanting to appear anxious, then thinking how obvious that would look since she realized the book was upside down.

After only a minute or so, she heard his footsteps coming up onto the porch, and there was a knock at the door.

Grace walked over and opened it.

"Hi Grace, I'm sorry for bein' late. I tried to get here at six thirty, but we didn't get off as early as I thought. Then when I got home, there was some things that had to be done before I could leave," he explained.

"It's okay, Allen. I thought nothin' of it. I had plenty to do, anyway. You wanna sit on the porch or in here?"

"The porch is fine," he answered.

"Go ahead and make yourself at home, and I'll get us somethin' to drink. Do you like lemonade?"

"That sounds pretty good. That long walk sure worked up a thirst."

He sat down in the swing and waited as Grace rushed to the kitchen, filled two glasses, and hurriedly made her way back to the porch.

She handed him the glass and he took a sip.

"Mmmm…, that's the best lemonade I think I ever had."

"Everything Nellie makes is good," she stated as a fact.

"Well, if her food is as good as this," pausing to take another drink, "this is perfect after workin' in the heat all day."

"What do you do with the railroad?" Grace inquired.

"Right now they got me puttin' in crossties. I've only been there a little over a year."

"Where'd you work before this job?"

"I did odd jobs 'til I was old enough to go to work. This is the first real job I've had."

Grace mentally calculated, trying to figure his age. If he did odd jobs until he was old enough to take this job just over a year ago, how old is he? But she was afraid to ask. Eventually she would find out, after they had gotten to know each other a little better.

"This my first job, too," Grace added. "With my family livin' on a farm, I was needed at home until now. And now I'm cleanin' houses on the weekends to help pay for my room."

"I guess that's the good thing about livin' close to town. I can still live at home while I work," he added. "I don't have a car yet so one of the crew comes by to pick me up. I should have enough money to get one soon. Have you ever driven a car?"

"No," she quickly answered. "Well, my daddy has a truck that I tried to drive once — only a few feet. Couldn't remember which pedal to use. Don't think I'd have enough nerve to try it again."

"Do you think you'd have the nerve to ride with me when I get one?" he asked.

"I probably would. Your drivin' couldn't be as bad as mine."

"Well, I guess we'll see, and I'm gonna hold you to it," he said, with a grin.

As the day's heat subsided and the house began to cool, Grace invited Allen into the living room. She turned on the radio and waited for it to warm up. After searching the dial, an announcer said, "And now, Dreamy Melody, by Art Landry and his Orchestra."

It was the perfect music as they continued to talk until almost dark. Grace remembered the last time he was there that he had to get home early and wondered if he needed to leave. But tonight he didn't mention it and neither did she. The music played on, setting the mood for an ideal evening.

After a while, Allen said, "I guess I best be goin'. Can I see you next week?"

"If you'd like. Would you like to come for supper Friday evenin'?"

"I think I could manage that," he replied.

As Grace followed him to the door, he turned around and looked at her for a moment as if he wanted to say something. He then just assured her that he would see her on Friday and wished her a good night.

She hurried upstairs smiling while anticipating Anna's barrage of questions, to which she was all too willing to oblige with the answers.

Chapter 15
The Visit Back Home

On Monday evening, Grace went straight to the boarding house and scurried around to gather her night clothes and something to wear for work the next day. She didn't want to keep Luke waiting when he arrived to take her home.

Luke was there promptly, not giving her time for anything else. She didn't see Nellie anywhere as she came down, but yelled goodbye through the hall while she was leaving.

"Have a good time and tell your folks I said hello," Nellie echoed back, as Grace sprinted out the door.

"Hey, Grace," Luke greeted. "Am I too early?"

"No. You're fine," she answered. "How are you doin'?"

"Doin' pretty good. Just glad this day is done. Our plant has more work than we can get done. Been that way the past couple years now. But I'm glad to get it," Luke exclaimed.

"The mill seems to be runnin' full steam, too," Grace added. "I'm certainly glad to have a job."

"I bet everybody at home's gonna be glad to see you."

"I'm lookin' forward to seein' all of them, too," Grace replied, although she had reservations about leaving. She especially hesitated to go overnight now that she had met Allen.

All at once a frightening thought crossed her mind. The sight of her in a car with another young man would be so embarrassing if Allen were to see them. And they would be going right in the direction he lived. Luke was a wonderful person and friend, but she hadn't thought to tell Allen about going home and that she would be riding with someone else. They hadn't known each other very long, but she wanted to protect the budding relationship they had formed and didn't want anything to jeopardize it. What if he happened to be walking close by and saw her leaving with Luke? What would he think? She worried.

When they were finally out of the area and on the main highway, she felt relieved.

"Grace, you're awfully quiet," Luke remarked.

"I was just thinkin' about all the things I gotta do this week. I feel like I need to stay here, but I know I need to go home and see how all the family's doin'."

As she neared home, Grace began to think on the warm and familiar comforts there. She then resigned within her heart to give them her undivided attention and devote this time to her family.

As she entered, the younger ones ran up for hugs, telling her how much they missed her. Dora came through the kitchen door and embraced Grace with a hug and kiss.

"We all missed you," Dora exclaimed.

"I missed y'all, too," she replied. "Somethin' smells good."

"Supper's about ready. Are you hungry?" Dora asked.

"Yeah, I'm starvin'. My lunch didn't last long today," she said. "Where's daddy?"

"He's finishin' up down by the pasture. He should be in directly."

Grace followed Dora into the kitchen, greeting the others as they began asking what had been going on as they finished preparing the meal. She soon heard the door close and someone say, "Is that workin' girl here?"

"I'm here, Daddy," Grace answered, as she embraced him with a long hug.

"How you been, Grace?"

"I been doin' good, Daddy."

"Well, let's get ready to eat and you can tell me all about it."

It seemed like old times as they all sat around the table and discussed the events of city life Grace was now experiencing.

Grace had almost forgotten how the girls would all try to talk at the same time. It used to be slightly annoying, but it now seemed quite comical. Being away from it for a while and adapting to the quieter surroundings at Nellie's just brought a smile to her face as she enjoyed all the chatter.

After supper, Walter and Dora suggested that Grace join them on the front porch where they could talk without interruptions as the girls cleaned up the kitchen.

"Are you managin' alright with the job and rent?" Walter asked.

"Everything's workin' out good, Daddy. They say there's plenty of work comin' in, and I'm able to save a little, even after the rent's paid. I met some really nice people at work and I enjoy stayin' with Nellie."

"Are you goin' to church anywhere while you there?" Dora inquired.

"I been goin' with Nellie to her church some, but it's a far cry from church here. I miss all the folks at Walter's Grove."

"Does Luke stop by to see you much?" Walter continued, eyeing her carefully.

"He's been by a couple of times," she replied, as she pondered the thought of mentioning Allen.

"I guess there ain't much time for him to linger in town with the work at home," Walter reasoned. "Maybe he won't be so busy when summer's over."

Attempting to lead the subject back to her life in town, Grace stated, "I made friends with a girl named Anna that lives at the boardin' house. She's been there a while longer'n I have."

"Does she work where you do?" Dora asked.

"No, she works at another plant nearby. We walk to the store and do things around the house together. By the way, have you ever heard of a Scarlett family?"

"Can't say as I have," Dora replied. "How 'bout you, Walter?"

"I remember some folks by that name up above the valley toward Lexington. Why you ask?"

"I met someone by that name who lives down Fisher Ferry Street in a place called Petree Field. He says he has relatives somewhere down this way."

"Where'd you meet him?" Dora inquired.

"Oh, me and Anna met him while walkin' to the store one day. He walked us back to the house and we chatted for a while.

And then he came for a visit Friday night."

"Well… for a date?" Dora asked, with a smile. She knew how trepidation and anxiety had always played a big part in her staying single and close to home in the past, and she was visibly pleased that she was finally opening up to people outside of her own family.

"Well, I guess that's what it was," Grace returned, with a slight smile. "We mostly just sat and talked all evenin'."

"Well, we'd like to meet him sometime," Dora said.

"He's savin' his money for a car and when he's got enough to buy it, maybe we can come down," explained Grace.

"So, he's got a job?" Walter asked.

"Yeah, Daddy, he works with the railroad puttin' in crossties."

"Well, just be sure you don't get mixed up with somebody that won't work," he advised. "I think a man needs to make an honest livin' if he intends to have a family someday. Some of those city-grown kids ain't like the farm-raised ones, you know. How old is he?"

"I don't know. I just met him. I guess he's about my age," Grace answered, feeling disquieted as he pressed.

"But he's been workin' a lot from what he tells me and he seems really nice."

"Well, just bring him down when you can," Dora said, reassuringly.

Grace decided it would be best to change the subject while in the presence of her dad. Maybe he would approve after he met him, she thought.

After chatting awhile, she got up to go inside and spend time with the sisters who were finishing the dishes.

"Grace, are they hirin' at the mill?" Maggie asked.

"Not sure, but I have seen a few new faces lately. Who's lookin' for work?"

"I've been talkin' to mama and daddy about goin' to work after the fields are done," she replied. "They said to ask you if Nellie has any room at the boardin' house there."

"I want to go, too," Tura exclaimed. "But I don't know if they gonna let me. I'm tired a-workin' in that field."

"Yeah, she's been havin' a fit to go to work, too, but I keep tellin' her she ain't old enough. I'd have to watch after her if she did go," Maggie quipped.

"I can take care of myself, Maggie. And I'm 'bout old enough to get a job," Tura retorted. "I'm fifteen, you know."

"What'll they do about the fields next spring?" Grace asked, posing her concern.

"Times are gettin' better, and Daddy says he's cuttin' back and won't be plantin' as much next year," Maggie informed.

"I can check and see if there's any job openin's tomorrow," offered Grace.

"Do you think Nellie would mind me comin' up to stay? We could share the room you got."

With a look of apprehension, Grace responded, "I guess we could do that for a while. I'll ask Nellie about it."

"Well, send word back by Luke as soon as you find out if they're a-hirin', and tell him to stop by here so I can arrange for him to bring me up," Maggie demanded, as she walked out of the room.

"That Maggie thinks she's the only one that can do anything," complained Tura.

"Pay her no mind. It's just her way," consoled Grace. "For my part, you're welcome to come up and get a job if mama and daddy don't mind."

As everyone got ready for bed, Ora walked up to Grace and asked, "Can I sleep with you tonight?"

"Sure you can. Let me get my things and we'll go on up. Goodnight, everybody."

As they slipped under the cover and snuggled into bed, Ora whispered, "I missed you, Grace."

"I missed you, too, sweetie."

Chapter 16
A Budding Romance

Her visit home was pleasant and time there savored, but the next morning, Grace was eager to be on her way back to the city. She'd been away for only one night, but there was such a nagging feeling of having missed something important while she was gone, even though she knew it just to be her imagination.

Throughout the following week, she couldn't get Allen off her mind and keenly anticipated seeing him again as she and Anna walked in town, or maybe even a possible unannounced visit. She realized he would be there on Friday evening, but a week is a long time when the heart desires the company of its captor.

She wanted it to be a special evening and couldn't get home from work fast enough to help Nellie with the meal. After all, if Nellie was gracious enough to let her invite him, she wanted to contribute in any way she could.

"Oh, by the way, Nellie, my sister Maggie had me to ask at the mill if they're hirin'. They want her to come in and apply closer to fall. She also wants to stay here. Will you have an extra room?"

"They're all taken for now, but if you wanna let her stay in your room for a while, one may open up eventually. I have an extra bed we can put in there."

Accustomed to having her own space now, Grace had hoped Maggie would have her own room. But she decided it wouldn't hurt to share for a while.

"I'll tell her when I get back home," Grace said.

The time for Allen's arrival was near. Grace and Anna were setting the dishes and silverware on the table when they heard a knock.

"Grace, you wanna get the door? It's probably your friend. We'll finish up here. You entertain him 'til it's ready," Nellie advised.

Grace was just relieved that he was on time today. She opened the door and said, "Come in, Allen. Supper's almost ready. We can sit in here while they're finishin' up."

"Boy, somethin' sure smells good," Allen remarked.

"How was your day?" Grace asked.

"Pretty fair. It's not as hot, but we still need some rain."

"We sure do. I noticed things around here are lookin' a little wilted," she added.

"My mama says even her tomatoes done poorly this year," Allen stated.

Grace felt a little awkward, not sure what to say, so to elude a void in conversation, she suggested they listen to the radio as they waited but Allen had no trouble taking up the slack and keeping the conversation going.

"Supper's ready!" Nellie exclaimed. "Come on in and be seated."

Everyone took their places, and after it was blessed, the food was passed around and they began to eat. Allen raved about how delicious everything was. As he talked, Grace subconsciously envisioned herself serving and sharing meals with him in their own home. She hadn't cooked a lot in the past, but now she felt more compelled to hone her skills. Although seriously attracted to him, she was very careful not to appear overly disposed.

Upon finishing, Nellie and Anna sent the couple into the parlor while they cleaned the kitchen. Grace turned the radio's volume low as they sat next to one another on the sofa to chat, both attentive to every word.

"Thank you for havin' me over for supper, Grace. I really enjoy spendin' time with you."

"I've been lookin' forward to seein' you today, too," she replied.

They were oblivious to the fleeting time, and as the evening gradually deepened, he began showering her with expressions of affection that she had never been accustomed to. It was abundantly clear that he was romantically interested in her, and she was just as overwhelmed by his romantic charm.

Only days later, there was an unexpected knock at the door. Nellie stepped from the kitchen to see who the visitor was.

"Well, hey, Mr. Scarlett," Nellie greeted. "What brings you this way today?"

"Oh, I have a little surprise for Grace. Is she here?"

"Grace! Somebody here to see you!"

Grace peeped around from the top of the stairs just enough to see Allen on the other side of the screen door. She ducked back and ran to her room to freshen up.

"Be right down," she exclaimed.

She hurriedly combed her hair and checked her dress, all the while curious about his unannounced visit. Although not feeling completely confident that she looked presentable, she chose to appear and walked over to the door.

"Grace, sorry to drop in like this, but I'd like to show you somethin' if you have time."

"What is it?" she asked.

"You'll have to come outside."

She opened the door and stepped out on the porch.

"There it is," he said proudly, pointing to an old, black T-Model on the street.

"Is that yours?" asked Grace, excitedly.

"Yep. That's what I've been savin' my money for. I finally had enough to buy it. You said you'd take a ride with me when I got it. How about it?"

"Let me tell Nellie," she informed him quickly, and she was back in a flash.

"Oh, Allen, it's a nice car," she remarked, as they walked toward the street.

The color was supposed to be black, but it had mostly faded into a dark gray, with some rust and paint peeling off in a few spots. Grace noticed, but she didn't care. She had ridden in much worse than that back home.

"Well, it's not new," he allowed. "But hopefully it'll get us where we need to go."

He opened the door of the single-seat Model T to let Grace in. She placed a foot on the running board and then stepped inside and sat down as Allen walked to the front and gave the crank two turns. The engine started and Allen climbed in and pulled out into the street, cruising along proudly with a cool evening breeze flowing through the windows. They looked at each other and smiled.

"It sure rides smoother'n daddy's truck," observed Grace.

"Now I can take you anywhere you need to go. I know you been wantin' to go home for a visit so that's what we'll do whenever you ready."

"Everybody does wanna meet you," Grace said.

"Well, why don't I take you down there Sunday?"

"Alright, we could have dinner and spend the evenin' with 'em if you want to."

"I'll get to try some of that good country home cookin' I've heard you talk about."

After circling the town, Allen said, "I probably should get this machine back home. After payin' for it, there ain't much gas money 'til I get paid Friday."

He pulled back up in front of the house and stopped. He sat there for a moment, and as she looked his way, he leaned over and kissed her precisely on the lips. For an instant she was taken by surprise, but she was more spellbound than anything.

"Can I see you Friday evenin'?" he asked. "Maybe we can ride somewhere again and talk more about Sunday."

After collecting her head and recovering her heart, she replied, "I'd love to."

Feeling a bit mesmerized as she walked toward the porch, Grace stopped at the door and turned, pulling her sweater around her shoulders in the cool evening air and raised her hand to wave, watching as he pulled out into the street and drove out of sight. Grace walked inside as if in a sweet, fragrant fog, and walked straight past Nellie, oblivious to her presence. Nellie just smiled in amusement.

On Friday evening, Allen came by and asked, "Grace, wanna

ride to my house and meet my folks?"

"I… guess so. Yeah, that'd be fine," she agreed, feeling anxious about meeting his parents for the first time.

When they arrived at his parents' house, there were two young boys out in the side yard.

"They your brothers?" Grace asked.

"Yeah. The younger one is Thurman and the other one is Richard. Not sure where Luther is. My oldest brother Lola's married. We call him Lo for short."

The boys leaned around the corner of the house to get a better look, and then carried on with what they were doing as Allen accompanied Grace through the front door and introduced her to the others inside.

"This is my mom, Ada."

"Hey, Mrs. Scarlett," Grace said, timidly.

"Mama, this is Grace."

"Yes, I've been hearin' about you," Ada greeted her, with a smile.

"I bet you're Alma," Grace said, leaning around to get a better look at the little girl peeping from behind her mother with arms wrapped around her legs. "You sure are pretty. I got a little sister the same age as you."

"Can't you speak to Grace, Alma?" Ada pressed.

"Hey, Grace," Alma finally said.

"This is my sister, Clara Lee," Allen continued.

"Hey, Clara Lee."

"Hey, Grace," she returned.

"Where's daddy?" Allen asked.

"He walked over to see one of the neighbors," Ada replied.

They hadn't been there long until Alma opened up as she and Grace began chatting as if they had known each other all their lives and both loving every minute.

After a short visit, Allen announced they had to leave.

"You bring her back again now, Allen," said his mother.

"I'll do that, Mama."

On their way back up the street, Allen announced, "Mama's

gonna have another baby."

"Really? You wouldn't know it."

"I think she just found out," he replied.

They drove around a little longer, taking in the sights and having fun like two kids just out of school. Before he dropped Grace off at Nellie's, they made arrangements to leave before noon on Sunday to arrive in time for dinner with her family. He pulled up to the curb and stopped the car as Grace prepared to get out — but not before he kissed her goodbye, and this time a little more prolonged and passionate than the last.

She had never been kissed by anyone, and as she was becoming more receptive, she felt consumed by a fire of emotions and feelings she had never before experienced until now.

Sunday was two days away, but it may as well have been two weeks. It seemed her every thought was occupied with the passion she was now feeling for Allen, and she was entirely smitten with this dark-haired, young man she still knew very little about.

At times she would wonder if it was all a dream and she would soon wake up in her bed back home as if none of it had happened. There was also a part of her that wondered if anyone should be this happy and if it might end suddenly.

House cleaning on Saturday seemed to occupy her mind slightly and make the time go faster, but by early afternoon her mind swirled with too many thoughts as she began to have doubts that their romance was even for real. Would he really come back? If he didn't show up Sunday morning, she felt she would be absolutely crushed. The unrelenting thoughts would creep into her mind throughout the day, causing her heart to ache and feel empty. If only he would come by for a moment so she could see him for reassurance…

She returned home and started up the stairway, realizing the emotional and physical exhaustion her imagination had created.

Anna walked through the hall as Grace reached her door, noticing the dejected look on her face.

"Grace, is anything wrong?"

"No, not really," she sighed, as she walked into her room with Anna following.

"Okay, I've known you long enough to tell when something's bothering you. Just tell me what it is," Anna pressed.

"Really, I'm fine. I'm just tired."

Finally, after Anna's persistence, Grace confided in her.

"Grace," Anna consoled, "you absolutely worry too much. You need to get that out of your head. He'll be here tomorrow and everything will be fine. After a good night's sleep, you'll feel much different. Trust me."

"I guess you're right. I feel better talkin' to you already."

"Now…," Anna continued, "Nellie has supper ready. Let's go down and eat. Then we'll sit on the porch and have some more girl talk."

Nellie was her jovial, happy self during the meal, which was more instrumental in helping to lift Grace's spirits. Afterward, Grace and Anna escaped to the front porch to talk as they had many times since she had moved there. Although Grace and Allen had made no plans to see one another that day, she couldn't help secretly glancing at each car that passed to see if by chance it might be Allen. By bedtime she was feeling a great deal better and was ready for rest, as she inwardly prayed for guidance and direction before retiring. As they all retreated to their own rooms, one by one the lights faded into the darkness of a late September night.

Chapter 17
He meets Walter

Nellie always allowed Anna and Grace to sleep in a little longer on Sunday mornings until time for church if they preferred. Anna usually went home on weekends but stayed at Nellie's on occasion. Being accustomed to waking early when back home, Grace was up awhile before Anna. She heard sounds in the kitchen and soon the aroma of breakfast was drifting up the stairs. She sat quietly in her room, reflecting on the many changes in her life through the recent months and the difference that moving there had made.

Soon she heard sounds of life in Anna's room, so she decided to start getting ready for the highly anticipated day. She was hopeful her mama and daddy would like Allen. She couldn't imagine why they wouldn't. He had been a perfect gentleman in every way, although her daddy could have preconceived notions at times. Grace was all ready, but she had something on her mind to ask Anna this morning. She heard Anna walk out of her room and toward the stairway. Grace opened her door and whispered, "Anna."

"What?" Anna whispered back.

"I need to ask you somethin'."

Anna stopped. "Why are we whispering?"

"You know that rouge stuff you use on your face?"

"Yes."

"Do you think I could use a little of it today?"

"Why, sure. Let me go get it."

Just then, Nellie called from the kitchen door, "Girls, breakfast is almost ready. You up?"

"Be right down," Anna exclaimed.

She grabbed the rouge off of her dresser and scurried into Grace's room.

"Sit down," she instructed.

"Just do it fast," said Grace. "And not too much."

After a few feathery brushes to the cheeks, Anna proclaimed, "There, you look ravishing!"

"It's not too much, is it?" she asked.

"It's just right. Take a look."

Grace stood, leaning in toward the mirror, turning her face from side to side. It did look pretty good. Not too obvious. Just enough to give her cheeks a little blush.

"Thank you, Anna."

"Think nothing of it. Let's go eat."

As they entered and sat down at the table, Grace looked at Nellie to see if she would notice the difference. Nellie gave a curious look back but did not comment as she continued placing the eggs, bacon, and biscuits on the table. She walked behind Grace to go back for the gravy, and as she came back, while Grace was not looking, Anna motioned to Nellie with her hands, rubbing circular motions on each cheek. Nellie furrowed her brow with a puzzled expression until she looked straight at Grace and instantly understood.

"Grace," Nellie said, with a smile, "you look different today. You lookin' sorta rosy."

Grace smiled and answered, "Had a little help from Anna."

"Well, I'll tell you one thing. Allen might have to fight off all the other men you run into today."

"He's the only man I plan to be around today," Grace replied, and quickly added, "other'n my daddy!"

Grace decided to wait for Allen in the porch swing after Nellie and Anna left for church. She hadn't sat there very long before he pulled up in front of the house, getting out and starting up the walk as Grace met him halfway.

"Hey, Grace. Looks like you're all ready to go?"

"I figure they should be home from church by the time we get there," Grace stated. "I'll have time to help 'em get dinner ready."

Actually, she was thinking she didn't want to be there waiting with all eyes on them when the family arrived home.

As he eased away from the curb and started down the street, she was feeling enthusiastic about introducing her new beau to her family. He was so courteous and seemed that he sincerely cared for her, and the feeling was mutual.

The trip seemed shorter than usual as her attention was focused entirely on their conversation.

"I'm lookin' forward to meetin' your family," Allen said.

"You'll just have to overlook the girls," Grace warned. "They tend to bicker and be a bit dramatic at times."

"Well, I imagine that's prob'ly pretty typical when you get a bunch of young girls together," he said, with a chuckle.

"It's the next house up there on the right at the top of the hill," Grace pointed out, as they got closer.

As they reached the driveway, Grace saw her father sitting on the front porch, giving her slight reservations about Allen meeting the family now. They pulled up into the side yard, parked, and got out.

Grace could hear voices as they neared the side door. As they entered, Bessie was walking through the dining room and halfway to the kitchen before she noticed Grace.

"Grace! You're hom…," and after seeing Allen, sheepishly scurried on through.

"I think she was a little embarrassed," revealed Grace, with a laugh. "She'll eventually get used to bein' around you."

It wasn't long until curious eyes were peeping around the doorway as Dora entered the room. They huddled around her like little peeps to a mother hen.

"Well, Grace, what a nice surprise. Didn't know you was comin' home today."

"Hope you don't mind we came down for dinner," she said.

"Law, no. We got plenty, and you know you can come anytime."

"Mama, this is Allen."

"Hey, Allen," Dora greeted. "Grace told us about you. Good to finally meet you."

"Good to meet you, Mrs. Grubb," he returned.

"Hope you young'uns are hungry," she said. "We got a mess o' food cooked and no church company a-comin' today."

Just then Maggie appeared, wiping her flour-dusted hands on the front of her apron.

"This is Grace's friend, Allen," stated Dora.

"Howdy do, sir," Maggie exclaimed, in her subtle disapproving manner that Grace hoped Allen didn't detect.

"Your daddy is out on the porch. Take Allen out and introduce him," Dora urged.

Well, this is it, Grace thought, as she led him through the front room and out the door onto the porch.

"Daddy, this is Allen."

Walter just looked up at him for a moment and said, "Have a seat, son."

"Allen, I'm gonna help get dinner ready. If you want, you can set out here and talk with daddy."

"Sure, that'll be fine," he answered.

As Grace re-entered the room, she hoped she hadn't made a mistake.

"How you been doin', Mr. Grubb?" Allen asked.

"Fair, I guess, how 'bout you?"

"Real good."

"Grace tells me you workin' with the railroad these days."

"Yes, sir. Been a hot job this summer, but I finally saved enough to get a car. Glad it's finally coolin' off now. I guess the crops are 'bout ready to start harvestin'."

"Won't be long. You folks have a garden?"

"My mama plants a few things ever year. I helped her with it some 'til I went to work. I don't think I ever want to farm for a livin'. I want to get a public job when I get older," Allen informed.

"How old are you now?"

"I'll be eighteen in November."

"You only seventeen?"

"Yes, sir."

"Well, let me tell you son, you got a lot a years ahead of you. You might have to do a lot of things you don't like down the road.

Especially if you aim on gettin' married and havin' a family."

"Well, Mr. Grubb, the economy has gotten real good the past few years, and I think a lot more people will be gettin' jobs in town. They say local farmin's on its way out," Allen reasoned.

"Well, that can change in a hurry," Walter warned. "You have to be sure a family can be provided for, just in case. What's your intentions?"

"You mean about Grace?" Allen asked, as Walter just looked and didn't answer.

"I'm really fond of her and I hope you approve of me seein' her. We ain't talked about marriage or anything. We've only known each other for a short while, but I can see maybe somethin' more serious down the road."

"Do you know how old she is?"

"Well, no sir, I've never asked."

Allen sat wondering why he thought that would matter to him. He had assumed they were not far apart in age, as Walter continued to inform him of the life he desired for his daughter.

Someone inside called for all to come in for dinner, and as far as Allen was concerned, not a minute too soon.

Grace met him at the door, detecting a look of "get me outta here" as she accompanied him to the dining table. After everyone was seated and the blessing offered, they passed the fried chicken and then the bowls of vegetables. Allen was just glad to join the group and be back by Grace's side.

As soon as the meal was over, Grace suggested she and Allen go out for a walk. Cletie, Ruth, and Ora filed in behind them as they started out the door until Dora intervened.

"Girls, let 'em be. They'll be back directly, and you'll have plenty a time to spend with 'em."

Even though her life had, in a sense, evolved from the country life she once knew, Grace was proud to show Allen around the farm while they walked. The pear tree in the backyard still had a pear or two, however shriveled, still hanging on. Allen wanted to see the barn and the animals it housed. George was receptive to having his long, white mane and face rubbed, but stubborn ol'

Bob cowered in the stall corner with his face hidden. The chickens ran freely through the barn, scratching in the dirt and straw, as the now half-grown chicks still scampered around the mother hen pecking for food. They could smell the pungent hog pen enclosed with rough lumber that Walter had attached to the end of the barn. She took him to the grain bin and showed him where they all played when they were younger. And then she introduced him to the big rock she would hide behind as a child, sometimes not answering when her mother would call.

"Your folks have a really nice place here," Allen said.

"I think so. Mama and daddy work hard to provide for everbody."

"Grace, I know I haven't known you very long, but it would be nice for us to have a place like this someday."

"That would be nice," was her only response to the sudden remark. She smiled, assuming what he was implying.

As they strolled around the home place, they decided to go back in and spend a little time with family before returning home.

"Grace, did you ask Nellie if I can stay there when I go to work?" Maggie asked.

"She said you could stay in my room 'til one comes open," Grace answered. "When you comin' up to apply?"

"I'm gonna ride up with Luke in about two weeks."

"I'll let everbody know you'll be there soon," Grace assured. "Well, I guess we'd better head up the road before it gets too late. I'm gonna step out on the porch to tell daddy bye," she said, making her way to the front.

"Daddy, we're ready to go back. Just wanted to tell you bye," she said, as she hugged him.

"Grace, I hope you don't intend on marryin' that fellow," he stated.

"Daddy, he's really nice."

"I'm afraid you'll have a heap of grief with him," he replied. "He don't seem too keen on workin'."

"Well, I'm not makin' any hasty decisions, so don't worry."

"I hope not. Y'all be careful goin' back now."

"We will, Daddy."

She felt disappointment with her daddy's response to Allen as she walked back through the house to join him and the others before leaving.

"You come back to see us, Allen," Dora requested.

"Thank you for the meal and good to meet you all," he replied.

Grace hugged everyone and said goodbye as she and Allen made their way back to the car and started back to Thomasville.

"He's a handsome boy," Dora said, as Walter entered from the porch.

"Well, looks ain't everything. Do you know he's only seventeen years old?" Walter grunted. "He don't know how old Grace is, and I don't think she knows how old he is, either."

"He seems like a pretty nice boy, though," she added.

"I tell ya, he's got some learnin' and a-growin' up to do, by jacks."

About halfway back to town, Allen said, "Grace, I don't think your daddy approves of me."

"What makes you say that?"

"He gave me a lecture about providin' for a family. I think we have different views on a few things."

"Oh, you can't take everything he says to heart. He's a bit protective and comes across a bit gruff."

"When I told him I wanted to get a public job when I get older, he asked me how old I was. And then he asked if I knew how old you was."

Grace turned and looked straight ahead, and he immediately realized he had touched on something that was sensitive.

"What is it, Grace?"

"How old are you?" Grace asked.

"I'll be eighteen in November. Why?"

She didn't speak as she looked down, feeling embarrassed.

"There's a bit of a difference in our age. I'm a little bit older than you. I didn't know. It never came up."

"Grace, that don't matter to me and I told him that. I figured we were about the same age. You can't be much older."

After a moment of silence, Grace figured she might as well tell him. He would eventually find out, anyway. She was just hoping it wouldn't change the way he felt about her.

"I'm twenty. I'll be twenty-one in March," she revealed.

"Well, I don't care. That's not much, and it's nobody's business but ours," he declared.

"You sure it don't bother you?"

"Sure. I sorta like older women, anyway," he said, smiling.

Grace wasn't sure how to respond for the next mile or two until Allen broke the silence.

"Your daddy also asked me my intentions."

Grace glanced over at him in dismay, but not surprised as he continued.

"I told him I was very fond of you and that I could see a future for us. I do love you, Grace."

Tears welled up in her eyes, and she wasn't sure if it was the embarrassing, awkward moments earlier, combined with the stress of having her family meet him for the first time, or the fact that he finally admitted that he loved her.

"You okay, Grace?"

She just nodded yes as he continued to speak.

"I love you and hope we can get married someday."

She swallowed hard and managed to utter, "I love you, too."

"Now that that's out on the table, let's move on and just enjoy bein' together," Allen suggested.

"Okay," Grace said softly, sensing a great weight beginning to lift from her shoulders as she wiped her eyes.

He had made her feel comfortable enough to slip over and sit a little closer to him.

They were both all smiles now as they talked for the remainder of the trip home. Once there, they greeted Nellie and then spent most of the evening in the front porch swing, affectionately talking. Nellie suggested they come in and fix a sandwich from the leftovers, and then they retreated back to the swing, huddling together in the fading light of dusk, on past time for either of them to have stayed up on a work night.

The October nights were now getting cooler, and ordinarily it would have been too chilly to sit outside, but she knew she wouldn't have any trouble staying warm with Allen by her side.

Chapter 18
The Picnic

Allen had begun to show up nearly every other day, but as the weekend approached, Grace knew her house cleaning obligations had to be met. As soon as they were finished and she was home, he was at her door.

When she arrived home Monday evening from work and stepped inside, out walked Maggie.

"What are you doin' here?" Grace asked, somewhat puzzled.

"I decided to come up early. Luke dropped me off this mornin' right after you left for work. I met Nellie and just been hangin' out with her today."

"They ain't expectin' you at the mill 'til next week. You gonna go on and apply tomorrow?"

"I reckon so. If they don't need me yet, I can just hang around here for a few days."

"Maybe they'll go ahead and put you on," Grace said. "They did say they'd let you start as soon as you got here."

Allen had told Grace over the weekend that he wouldn't be able to come by on Monday, and she figured now that maybe it would be for the best, considering Maggie might need some help getting settled in.

"Where's your things?" Grace asked.

"Nellie showed me to your room and I took 'em on up and put 'em in some of the empty drawers. I had to move some of your things," Maggie replied.

Ordinarily, her imposition may have been annoying to Grace, but now that she had met Allen, she was not going to allow anyone to diminish her joy. Predicting that she herself would not be in the room as much now anyway, she decided to be the gracious host for the evening, but Maggie would be on her own thereafter.

Maggie went to the mill the next morning, applied, and they

put her right to work.

"What do they have you doin'?" Grace asked, as they walked home that evening.

"I'm trainin' to be a winder. It looks a lot harder than what you're doing."

Well, of course, Grace thought to herself. Her work's always just a little harder.

"Well," Grace replied, "none of it's easy. Let's get home and eat, I'm famished."

After the evening meal with Nellie and Anna, Grace and Maggie went to the front porch. Maggie sat down in the rocker, so Grace took the swing.

"Seen that fellow, Allen, lately?" Maggie asked.

"Yeah. He came by yesterday."

"Is he comin' by today?"

"No, he had things to do today."

"I don't think daddy likes him very much."

"Why?" Grace asked, already aware of his feelings, but interested in hearing Maggie's reasoning.

"Daddy says he's not very responsible."

"Oh, Maggie, daddy wouldn't approve of anybody that payed attention to any of us."

"Well, I'm just tellin' you what he said. He says he's got a lot a-growin' up to do. Didn't you know how young that boy was before you started a-courtin' him?"

"Yeah, I know how old he is and it don't matter," Grace replied. "And he's not exactly a boy."

Searching for a way to change the subject, Grace said, "What'd you think of Anna?"

"She looks like a real city girl to me, but she seems sweet," Maggie allowed.

"She is a sweet person and we've become good friends. You need to be careful not to offend people that seem different than us. We might seem odd to them, too. And you need to know, Allen's gonna be comin' by here a lot."

"I ain't a-gonna say nothin' out of the way," Maggie assured.

"Well, things are a little different here than back home. Some people here know nothin' of the country life, just as we don't know too much about their ways."

Anna stepped to the front door, "Mind if I come out and join you?"

"Be glad for you to," Grace invited. "Sit here with me. There's a nice autumn breeze this evenin'."

Anna sat down and as the three talked awhile, Grace began to feel more confident they might all get along just fine.

When Allen returned to visit the next evening, Maggie appeared to be keeping in mind the discussion she and Grace had had the day before and allowed them uninterrupted time together. As the weeks passed, it was apparent the two were growing closer with each date. Grace knew November was just around the corner and Allen's birthday was on the sixth. The idea of him turning eighteen made her feel somewhat better about the age gap. She studied for days trying to figure out what to do for his special day.

"Nellie, what would you do for Allen's birthday if you was in my shoes?" Grace asked.

"Law, child. You might not want my advice on romance." She paused. "But I guess we could bake him a pie or fix him a dinner or somethin'."

"That's a thought. I'm not real good with pies, but you 'n Maggie could show me."

"Well, honey, between the three of us, we oughta come up with somethin'. You know, if it's not too chilly, the two of you could have a picnic out there on the table. You could make sandwiches with tea or lemonade. And there's still a few apples put back for a pie."

"That's a good idea. Thanks."

Grace spent the week planning, and informed Allen to be there Thursday evening for supper around six.

On Wednesday evening, Maggie and Nellie helped her with baking the pie. Anna made lemonade and helped get things ready to prepare sandwiches for the next day.

"Will sandwiches be alright with the rest of you girls for tomorrow since that's what we'll already be makin'?" Nellie asked.

"Fine with us," they exclaimed.

"Then, Grace, we'll fix the sandwiches tomorrow evenin' as soon as you get home."

It had been warm around midday Thursday, but as they got home from work, it had gotten much cooler and a light rain had begun to fall.

"Grace, I believe your picnic's gonna have to be inside," Nellie informed her. "November is unpredictable."

"I was sorta thinkin' the same," she said, disappointed.

"You could have a cozy date on a quilt in front of the fireplace," Nellie suggested. "We'll all eat in the kitchen."

"Why don't you all join in and eat with us?" Grace asked.

"Oh, no, we couldn't intrude that way," Nellie replied. "This is Allen's evenin'."

"I insist. And I think Allen would love it," she said. "It'd be fun with everbody together."

"Yeah," they all said. "That would be fun."

"Now, are you sure?" prodded Nellie. "Havin' an old woman in the room would probably kill all the romance," she said, with a hearty laugh.

"Yes. I'm sure."

"Well, if you're sure he won't mind, then you girls get a big quilt and lay it out on the floor. We can still put everything in the basket just like it was gonna be outside."

When Allen finally arrived, they were ready as he walked in.

"Happy Birthday!" they all shouted.

"What you all up to?" Allen scolded, in fun.

"Come on," Grace said, taking him by the hand. "You'll see," as she led him to a full basket, resting on the patchwork quilt with the others following close behind.

"We gonna have to sit on the floor," she said, somewhat apologetically.

"That's no problem for me," Allen assured her.

"Might not be for you young'uns," Nellie hooted. "But somebody might have to help get me back up!"

They all laughed as they knelt down and sat on the quilt, while Grace squatted down beside the basket and began to set the food out for serving.

"My, you thought of everything, didn't you?" Allen commended. "You even made that lemonade I like so good."

"Oh, I had some help," Grace replied. "I hope this is okay."

"This is great. And it's so nice of you all to do this," he responded.

They all sat like school children, still laughing and eating their sandwiches. Grace then brought out the apple pie with the crisscross crust she had mastered with a little help, sprinkled with sparkly sugar and a fragrant spiced fruit aroma that made its presence known.

"Mmmm, that smells yummy," Allen said. "And it looks like somethin' that oughta be in a contest somewhere."

After they sat talking for a while, Nellie said, "Well girls, let's take a few things to the kitchen and let these two court a spell."

When they were finally alone, Grace reached into her dress pocket and brought out a small, wrapped box.

"This is for you, Allen. Happy Birthday."

"Grace, you didn't have to get me anything."

"Hope you like it."

He tore into the box, and as he opened it, a huge smile spread across his face.

"How'd you know I had my eye on this knife?"

"I wasn't sure if this was the one you looked at that day we met at the store. I went back and bought the one I thought was it when I found out your birthday was comin' up. I was afraid it would already be gone."

"This is the exact one, and, it's one of the nicest gifts I ever got. Thank you, Grace," he exclaimed, as he leaned over and gave her a kiss, which was the perfect ending to a perfect day.

The next evening, Nellie responded to a knock at the front

door.

"Well, hey. It's Luke, right?"

"Yes, ma'am. Is Grace or Maggie here?"

"Grace! Maggie! Luke's here."

After a moment, Grace appeared at the door. "Hey, Luke," she greeted, as she stepped out.

"Tura wanted me to stop by and let you know she's wantin' to come up and get a job now."

"Did she say when?" Grace inquired.

"Your folks say she can come up next week. She just wanted you to see if you could make arrangements for her, and then I can let her know."

Maggie walked to the door and spoke to Luke as Grace announced, "Tura wants to come up and get a job."

"Well, they must've finally give in," Maggie retorted.

"I'll have to check with Nellie and at the mill tomorrow," Grace replied to Luke.

"Okay, I'll stop back by in a couple days to find out."

Allen had just pulled up and parked and was coming up the walkway, watching curiously as Luke was saying goodbye to Grace. He eyed Luke suspiciously as Luke passed him to leave. Allen proceeded onto the porch, offering a short "hey" to Grace that made her feel uncomfortable. He sat down in the swing just in time for them to hear Maggie tell Nellie in the next room that Luke had always been sweet on Grace.

Grace felt appalling shock and embarrassment as she stared through the door at Maggie, not believing her ears. She looked back to see Allen's reaction as he fumed and deliberately looked away.

Searching for something to say, she replied, "Allen, pay her no mind, that's not true. He's just a family friend. Don't be upset about what she said."

"I'm not!" Allen snapped, his face turning dark and foreign.

"What is it?" she pressed, as she sat down beside him almost in tears, puzzled at a reaction that she had not encountered before. She wasn't quite sure of his response, but wondered if he felt threatened by her just talking to another man.

Grace kept pressing him to communicate until he finally asked, "Who was that you was talkin' to?"

"That was Luke. He's the one I used to ride to work with. He just came by to tell us our sister wants to come up and get a job."

He still seemed upset for a while, but as Grace continued to reassure him that he had nothing to worry about and that there was never anything between her and Luke, his mood gradually improved. The remainder of his visit turned more pleasant, and eventually, affectionate by night's end.

"Grace, I'm sorry for actin' so jealous. Sometimes I feel like you might meet somebody else and like them better."

"Allen, you ain't got nothin' to worry about," she asserted, as she held his hand.

They parted with a goodnight kiss, and Grace went back into the house. Just wait 'til I get a hold of that Maggie, she thought. She marched upstairs to their room clad in armor for war.

"Maggie Grubb, you had no business sayin' what you did where Allen could hear it."

"Well, I didn't know he was out there."

"Oh, yes you did!"

"No, I didn't, and besides, it ain't no big deal. He shouldn't let a little thing like that bother him."

"Well, it did, and it bothered me, too. From now on, you need to keep quiet."

"Okay, I'll not say another word."

Grace bathed and put her night clothes on, slipping into bed without speaking, hoping that she had gotten through to Maggie. But even as she lay there, she knew everything would be amended the next day, as her siblings had always spoken their minds, not staying upset with each other long.

"Night, Maggie."

"Night, Grace."

Chapter 19
The Proposal

Luke stopped by a couple of days later as planned to find out when he could bring Tura up. Grace had gotten the mill's approval for Tura to come in on Monday. To avoid another misunderstanding, Grace instructed Maggie to give Luke the message that Tura was to come up before the weekend so she could go to work with them on Monday.

"By the way, Luke, would you mind givin' us a ride down the road with you on Christmas Eve?" Maggie asked. "We want to go home and spend the night."

"I don't mind one bit. I'll be by to pick you all up after work that day," he obliged. "And I'll have Tura up here Friday mornin'."

Ordinarily, Nellie wouldn't have had a vacant room, but someone decided not to take a room that she had been holding for them. Tura and Maggie would share that room now. Grace was glad to have her quiet space back, but a little concerned that Maggie might try to supervise Tura too much.

Tura arrived on Friday and introduced herself to Nellie. When everyone got home from work, she met Anna and they helped her get her things put away. Then the girls decided to show her around the neighborhood.

"Tura, you can help me clean houses tomorrow," Grace offered. "I have another one I can take on now that I got you to help. Maggie's got one she's startin' tomorrow, too."

"Good. I'd druther help you, Grace. I probably couldn't do it to please her, anyway."

They got started early the next day and cleaned all morning.

"It doesn't seem so tirin' when you got help," Grace said.

"It's a lot more fun than at home," Tura said, with a big smile. "And you get to see other people's pretty things."

"And you're makin' money, to boot," Grace added.

"Thank you for lettin' me come up here and stay, Grace."

They finished and started on their way home as Grace's thoughts were of getting back and ready for Allen's visit.

"Grace, you like that Allen, don't you?" Tura asked.

"Yeah, pretty much."

"Think you might marry him someday?"

"Never know. He did mention it awhile back."

"Well, Grace, that's for you to decide. It's always somebody a-sayin' somethin'."

"I know. I'm the one that has to live with my decision. Nobody else."

They were all up early Monday morning as Tura was to experience her first working day at the Amazon Cotton Mill. Grace and Maggie walked with her through the crisp, cold, morning air and into the office, stopping by to check her in with Eva, and then on into the plant. At noon, the three met back together to have lunch.

"What they got you a-doin'?" asked Maggie.

"They trainin' me to spool," Tura said, proudly.

"Well, between the three of us, we'll know how to do it all now," said Maggie, chuckling.

The young girls worked persistently for the next few weeks, realizing Christmas was getting closer. They were all determined to buy something, however modest, for the family.

"Grace, you think Allen would take us to town one day to shop?" Tura asked. "We don't have much time left."

"I don't know. I imagine he would. We'd have to do it on Saturday after we get through with our cleanin'. I'll ask him when he comes tonight."

"Let's see, we only have two more Saturdays 'til Christmas," Tura counted in her mind.

As Maggie walked in the room, Tura said, "Grace is gonna ask Allen to take us to town the next Saturday or so to shop for Christmas. You wanna go, don't you?"

"Does a donkey have a tail?" she remarked. "Oh, and I went ahead and asked Luke to come by and get us Christmas Eve to go home for the night."

"I'm askin' Allen to come to mama and daddy's on Christmas mornin'." Grace informed them. "If he goes, then I'll be ridin' with him," asserted Grace.

"You mean you ain't goin' home and spend the night on Christmas Eve?" Maggie chided. "We ain't ever missed Christmas Eve at home. Mama and daddy are really gonna be upset, Grace."

"Mama and daddy are not gonna be upset. Bud ain't been there on Christmas Eve for three years now. They understand when one of us gets married or ain't livin' there no more."

"But you ain't married, Grace."

"Well, I might not be. But for now, I'm stayin' here and I'm a-ridin' down with Allen. They'll understand."

Maggie quickly appeared to remember the little talk she and Grace recently had and decided maybe she ought to abandon the subject, realizing Grace had made her choice.

During his evening visit, she said, "Allen, Tura wants to go to town one Saturday soon to do some Christmas shoppin'. Would you mind takin' us if you don't have anything to do?"

"Why, Grace, you know I'd take you anytime I can. I don't know of anything I have to do in the afternoons. When you wanna go?"

"We'll have to go either this Saturday or the next."

"We can go this Saturday if you like," he offered.

"I'm sure that'd be fine with both of 'em," she replied.

The girls hurried home through the chilly December air as soon as they had finished all their work on Saturday.

When Allen arrived, they eagerly ran out to his car as Allen was opening the rumble seat. Just then, Maggie and Tura realized they would be the ones riding in it.

"You girls might wanna put somethin' else on," suggested Allen. "It's a might chilly back there."

"We ain't got time for that now, so just drive slow," ordered Maggie. "Besides, it ain't that far."

"Well, suit yourself, then. Let's go."

The girls jumped in the car and were off on their shopping

excursion.

He pulled the car up to the curb on Main Street and the girls proceeded to get out, pulling their coats tighter around them in the cold wind.

"My face is about froze," said Tura, "Wish I'd a grabbed a scarf."

"Oh, Tura, it watn't that bad," Maggie scoffed, even though her own face was getting numb.

"You wanna go with us, Allen?" Grace asked.

"No, y'all go ahead. I might go in that hardware store over there and look around."

"Okay, we'll try not to be long," Grace assured him.

"Don't worry, take all the time you need. I'll be fine," he said.

"Love you."

"Love you," he returned.

They took off to the stores as if they were in a marathon. Although it didn't take a great deal of time to shop, Grace felt guilty leaving Allen to wait.

After a while, they returned with arms full of bags. Allen got out of the car to help place bags in any spot they could find. Grace folded the top down on one particular bag to prevent Allen from seeing inside. She had found a gift for him and very much wanted to keep it a secret. As they were all finally seated with expressions of delight , Maggie said, "Thank you for bringin' us up here today, Allen."

"No need to thank me. Glad to do it."

It was now Christmas Eve and Luke stopped by after work to take Maggie and Tura home for the holiday. Grace did not come down to say hello to Luke or goodbye to her sisters, and Luke knew he and Grace would be distant friends from now on.

Grace stayed behind, waiting for Allen to show up, planning for a special, quiet evening alone. He soon arrived and they enjoyed a simple meal, then relaxed in the parlor, enjoying one another's company with a bowl of Nellie's Christmas goodies. It was quite a romantic evening for the two as they exchanged gifts they each had expressly selected for one another.

Grace persuaded Allen to open his first. When he untied the ribbon on the solid green box and opened it, he smiled broadly as he pulled out a fine-looking plaid fleece shirt and held it up to his chest for fitting approval.

"I've never had a shirt this nice," he said. He leaned over to give her a kiss and said, "Thank you, Grace."

Grace then opened her small black box to find a shiny silver watch with a brown leather band.

"I'll have to be on time from now on, won't I?" Allen joked.

"I love it!" Grace exclaimed, as she gave him a hug. With a broad smile, she took it out and let Allen help fasten it around her wrist.

When it was time for him to leave, they embraced at the front door and kissed goodnight.

Allen and Grace spent the next day having a pleasant Christmas dinner with her family. Not accustomed to receiving many presents in the past, the younger siblings were excited with their gifts, however modest, that the older ones could now afford, and Grace, Maggie, and Tura beamed with pride from their ability to provide for them. As the evening neared, Grace announced that she and Allen should return to town. Hugs and kisses were exchanged as they made their way out the door to the car. He wasn't sure if it was because of the holiday or not, but Allen felt fortunate to have escaped the scrutiny that Walter frequently offered. Just maybe it was the beginning of being accepted, he thought. What he didn't know was that, Walter, being alone with Grace for a moment, once again reiterated his disapproval of marriage to him.

Walter had told her hurriedly, "You mark my word, you'll see nothin' but trouble with that boy." And his words echoed troublesome in her ears.

The days grew colder during the next couple of months, but Grace and Allen didn't notice it so much. The love they felt in their hearts could ward off any icy blizzard to come their way as long as they were together, and they were together every chance they could find.

Allen was late arriving on Sunday, February 8, but had exciting news from home.

"Grace, mama had a little boy. That's why I'm late. I stayed for a while to make sure they were gonna be alright."

"That's fine. You needed to be there," she said. "What'd they name him?"

"William. He sure is a cute little fellow."

"I sure would love to see him," Grace replied.

"We'll go when mama's feelin' better."

The next week, Allen took Grace to see the new family member. She held and rocked him with a contented smile the entire time they were there.

On their way back, Allen said, "Grace, you looked like you enjoyed holdin' little Will."

"I just love little babies," Grace stated, with a smile. "I've looked after several in my day."

"Well, maybe one day we might have one of those," he suggested.

"You never know. I'd love to have one of my own someday," Grace replied.

It was now the middle of March 1925, and Grace's birthday was approaching. Maggie had mentioned it to Anna, who in turn asked Allen if he knew.

"We're fixing a birthday supper for her, and I know she'd want you to come."

"What day is it?" he asked. "I remember her tellin' me back last year, but I forget."

"It's next Saturday, the twenty-seventh," she informed him.

"I'm glad you told me, and thank you for invitin' me, Anna."

"I thought you might like to know," she replied, with a smile.

An early spring rain was falling the morning of her birthday, and although Grace feared thunderstorms, she loved the tranquil, soft rains that early summer could bring.

Grace and Tura finished their cleaning and went back to Nellie's to get ready for the evening meal. When Allen arrived, Nellie and the other girls presented Grace with a cake and birthday greetings before the meal.

After they finished, the sun peeked from behind the last, lingering cloud in time for Allen to invite her on a walk with him.

"Grace, I got you somethin' for your birthday," Allen announced. "It's not exactly what I had planned, though. That'll have to come later."

With eyes sparkling, she asked, "What is it?"

She enthusiastically took the small, tin box as he handed it to her and opened it, finding a gold-colored pin for her dress.

"Oh, it's beautiful, Allen."

"It's not really what I wanted to get you, but I didn't have enough money for that right yet," he said, apologetically.

"I don't care, I love it," she replied.

Allen had brought up the subject of marriage once, and she wondered if an engagement ring was what he had intended since he mentioned not having enough money.

On Monday afternoon, Allen was waiting at the mill as Grace walked out the door with the others to go home.

"Hop in, Grace. Got somethin' to ask you."

"Y'all go on. I'll be there directly," she told the girls.

He was all smiles as she slid in close to him.

"What you a-grinnin' about?" she asked.

"Whatta ya say we go get married?"

"What?" she responded, with a confused grin, thinking he was just teasing.

"Yeah. Let's get married."

"Really?" she asked. "When?"

"We could go tomorrow."

"Are you serious?"

"Never been more serious," beamed Allen.

After absorbing the information, she finally replied, "But, don't we need to make some plans? We don't even have a place to live."

"We can find a house," Allen assured her. "I've seen several of 'em right around here. I saw one on Hinkle Street the other day.

We can go check it out and see if it's still for rent."

"Where would we get married at?"

"We can go to South Carolina. That's where a lot of people go."

"What about work?" she pressed.

"Surely they won't mind you bein' off one day. You're never out for anything."

She was feeling dizzy from the sudden decisions she had been confronted with, as she asked, "Where did you say the house was?"

"I'll take you there to see it now," he replied.

As they pulled up and parked, Allen was disappointed to see someone already carrying furniture in. Grace was not quite sure about all this, as she tried to grasp the reality of his sudden proposal.

"I'll go ask if they're movin' in," said Allen.

He came back shortly and told her that it had already been taken, but they told him of another one on Pine Street that was thought to be vacant and told him who to see about it.

Can he be serious? she thought.

They then left to find and check out this house on Pine Street. When they got there, it looked empty, so they got out and walked around, peering in windows and then checking the door. Finding it open, they stepped inside and looked around. It wasn't as nice as Nellie's house, but Grace felt it had potential.

Still reeling, Grace exclaimed, "I can't believe we're doin' this."

"Let's go talk to the owner and find out what the rent is," Allen said.

They pulled up to the house where the landlord lived and Allen got out. There was a man on the porch in a rocker as he approached.

"Hello, sir. I'm here about the house on Pine Street. Wonderin' if it's still for rent."

"It's available. You look awfully young. You got a job to pay for it?" the man inquired.

"Yes, sir," Allen replied. "I'm gonna be gettin' married this week and my future bride, well, she's got a job, too."

"When you want it, son?"

"We'll take it now if that's alright," replied Allen.

"Well, let's step inside and let Ma get you fixed up," he said.

When he finished, Allen walked quickly back to an anxiously awaiting bride to be with a gleam in his eye.

"It's ours!" he stated proudly, looking satisfied as he got in.

"We're really gonna get it?" Grace asked, still looking surprised while realizing the events unfolding were real.

"Now, when can we go get married?" he asked.

"I really need to let 'em know at work before I stay out. I could tell 'em tomorrow and then we could go Wednesday," she suggested.

"That'll give us some time to get furniture and other things together," Allen offered. "Mama's got a few things she can give us."

"I've got a little money put aside to buy some other things we need," Grace replied, smiling now as reality finally started setting in and she began to get excited.

Grace felt exhilarated to think she would have her own house now to do as she pleased.

"Oh, Allen, I sure do love you!"

"I love you too, Grace," he said, as they embraced with a kiss before pulling out of the landlord's driveway.

As he backed out into the street, she wrapped her arm tightly around his. She could hardly wait to tell the others. She wished she could share the news with her parents, but she presumed her daddy would only try to talk her out of it. Although she knew he didn't approve, her feelings for Allen overruled logic.

Grace waited until Allen left before telling anyone about their plans, wondering how Maggie would react. They all began to congratulate her after the announcement, except Maggie. She just stood there subdued and expressionless, as Grace had expected.

Grace loved Allen very much, and even though her family's actions caused her to ponder the decision at that moment, it all seemed so right within her heart. She reasoned that after all of the loneliness she had experienced in the past, surely God would want her to be happy now.

When Grace arrived at work the next morning, she informed her supervisor that she would not be in the following day. The good news brought a smile and hugs when she shared with Claire. Grace could hardly contain her excitement, but the thought of how her daddy would react still hung in the back of her mind.

Sensing her reserve, Claire asked, "Grace, is there anything bothering you today?"

"I just wish daddy liked him better. He gets so protective of all us girls. I'd never do anything to hurt 'em, but they don't know him like I do, and I love him."

"Well, sometimes parents have a hard time letting their children make their own choices. From what you've told me about your parents, I'm sure they want the best for you. Just listen to your heart. We all come to crossroads and have to decide which way to go. Only God knows what's down the road. You're young, honey, just seek His help to make the right decisions," Claire encouraged.

"I always try to. Sometimes it's just hard to know when so many are tellin' me what to do. But thank you for always listenin', Claire."

After work, the evening was spent shopping for a few household items and delivering them to their new home as Grace and Allen discussed their plans for the next day. When they told friends close by of their upcoming marriage, they offered odd pieces of furniture, towels, and any other articles they could spare to hold them over until they could do better. Grace and Allen thoughtfully placed each item, stepping back and admiring it with a smile until they no longer had anything else to arrange in the house.

As they were about to leave, Allen remarked, "Just think, Grace. Tomorrow we'll be married and we can come back to our own place."

She slipped her arm around his and laid her head on his

shoulder saying, "I still can't believe we're really doin' this. It all seems like a dream."

"Well, it'll all be real tomorrow," he assured her.

Chapter 20
The Marriage

She could hardly sleep that night for anticipation of all the next day's events swirling in her mind. Waking early, she got up to prepare for the trip. It would be awhile before Allen would arrive, but there was no staying in bed even a minute longer.

Soon, the others were up and getting ready for work. As Maggie walked in, she asked, "Are you sure you wanna do this?"

"Yes, I'm sure."

"Okay," she said, with a voice full of warning.

The girls were ready to leave for work when Allen arrived. Grace hurried through the house and bolted out the front door to meet him, hugging each one on the way as they all wished her well.

Grace felt overwhelmed with excitement as they drove south to their destination. The rising sun shimmered and danced through the trees into Allen's side window as they discussed their plans for the upcoming days.

"You know, they're gonna put our ages on the marriage license. Why don't we put down we're the same age?" Allen suggested.

"Oh. That hadn't crossed my mind," Grace replied. "Can we do that?"

"I guess we can put anything we want. Who's gonna know the difference?" he said.

"What age are we gonna put? Are we gonna use your age or mine?" she asked.

"How about we go in between and we both put twenty?" he suggested.

"Okay, I like that idea," she said. "How long will it take us to get there?"

"I was told about three hours."

"I've never been this far from home. There's a lot to see out on the road," she said. "Do you know where we need to go when we get there?"

"I talked to some folks that told me about a Mr. Houston who is a probate judge there. We'll have to stop and ask somebody when we get to York."

It hadn't seemed like a three-hour trip as they arrived. Allen pulled up to a storefront in town and went in to ask where the courthouse was. They found it on the next street over and entered the large, stately front doors. They were anxious, not knowing what to expect but ecstatic to be getting married.

Together, they walked up to the receptionist at the wooden counter.

"We're here to see Judge Houston, ma'am," Allen stated.

"May I tell him your reason?"

"Yes, ma'am. We wanna get married."

"Okay. Let's see, we need this form right here. I'll need to ask you a few questions for the license application. What is your name?"

"Allen Scarlett."

"And, what is your age?"

"Um, I just turned twenty, four months ago," he said, as he glanced at Grace and gave a wink.

Where is your place of residence?"

"Thomasville, North Carolina."

"You both are Americans, I presume?"

"Yes, ma'am."

"And Miss, what is your name?"

"Grace Grubb."

"And what is your age?"

Grace paused and gave an anxious look Allen's way.

He nodded to continue and she nervously said, "Twenty." She was now feeling a little guilty for not being truthful.

"And your place of residence?"

"I live in Thomasville, too."

"Alright, I'll get this typed up while you wait. He's with a client right now, but it shouldn't be long if you'd like to have a seat," she explained.

"Thank you," they both said, as Grace turned and exhaled.

As they waited, Grace became tense and Allen a bit fidgety. He sat bouncing his knees nervously up and down. For the first time she realized this was her wedding — in a courthouse by a judge, with a stranger for a witness, not in Walter's Grove Baptist Church with her parents and sisters for support.

"I'll be glad when he gets through with whatever he's doin' so we can be on our way." Allen's voice brought her focus back to the hard bench and the echoing hallway of the large, stone building.

"Me, too," Grace replied.

Fifteen minutes passed, and Judge Houston, a man of large stature, opened a side office door and bid his client goodbye. Then, he asked, "Who's next?"

"Mr. Scarlett, you and Miss Grubb may go in now," said the receptionist.

They arose and preceded to his door, feeling slightly intimidated.

"So, you folks are getting married today, are you?" asked the judge.

"Yes, sir. I'm Allen, and this is Grace."

"Well, come right on in and we'll get this matter taken care of," he said, with a broad smile.

Mr. Houston closed the door and picked up his booklet to start the ceremony legalities as his assistant stood by as the witness. He went through all the formalities, pronounced them man and wife, and said, "You may now kiss your bride," as they both readily obliged.

"Now, what we all have to do is sign this marriage license and you're ready to be on you way."

They each took turns signing after the judge, and they were now officially husband and wife.

Allen said, "Thank you, sir."

Grace just smiled as they hurried out the door to the car.

"We did it, we did it!" Allen exclaimed, on the way to the car.

As they quickly got in, Allen asked, "Grace, are you hungry?"

"Just a little," she replied.

"I saw a diner on the way into town. We can stop there on the way back."

When they arrived, Allen pulled up in front of the diner and parked. Grace marveled at the passenger-car-type structure that looked to her as if a train had pulled up and unhitched it where it sat. They walked in and saw round stools at the counter and square tables to each side in front of the small, square windows.

"Where do you wanna sit, Grace, at the counter, or at one of these tables?"

"One of those tables will be fine, Allen."

Soon after they were seated, a waitress came to the table with menus and offered to bring them something to drink. When she left, they opened their menus, scanned the items, and then the prices.

Allen and Grace both agreed that maybe they should order only coffee and hot dogs. They realized they would need all their extra money for new living expenses they had now acquired.

After the waitress brought their food, they began to eat as they smiled at each other throughout the entire meal.

When they finished, Grace said, "You know, for a hot dog, that was really good."

"And the coffee wasn't bad, either," replied Allen, with a grin.

Allen paid for their lunch and they were back in the car, pulling out in the street, eager to return home.

Arriving back late in the evening, they decided to go straight home to their new residence without stopping anywhere to announce their news. Grace reasoned in her mind that telling her family later would just be better anyway.

Once inside the house, Grace began to get her things to wear for the next workday and lay them on the chair, while Allen sat on the edge of bed watching. She poured herself a pan of water and began to freshen up, and he got up to undress and do the same.

"You gonna get your clothes out tonight?" Grace asked.

"I'll just get 'em in the mornin'… it won't take me long," he replied. "You ready for bed, Mrs. Scarlett?" he said, with a grin, after they finished.

"Yes, Mr. Scarlett."

Grace's past fears vanished while in the arms of someone she had waited for so long, and she truly felt they had been blessed by God as her anticipated dream had become reality.

She did not recall drifting off to sleep that night, but awoke early to find Allen gazing at her. They held each other, smiling passionately for a moment, and then kissed good morning.

"Grace, why don't we stay home today?"

"But, I only asked off for one day," she reminded him.

"One more day won't hurt," he replied.

"I guess it won't," she said, as she lay there in thought. "They do have somebody else that can do my job 'til I get back. This evenin' I'll need to let Maggie and Tura know I'm alright, though. They'll be worried."

Although she felt bad not contacting someone at work, she relented and stayed home with Allen, spending an affectionate day together in their new home.

"I guess we're gonna have to go tell mama and daddy," Grace said, as she fixed them both some lunch.

"How safe will that be for me?" Allen asked, with a chuckled.

"They'll be alright after they get to know you."

"Guess they don't have much choice now," he said. "You wanna go down Sunday?"

"Yeah, I guess we could go have dinner with 'em again and break the news."

Grace began to experience butterflies in her stomach as they drove down Cid Road, wondering what her daddy's reaction would be. But her happiness outweighed the concern she had about anybody objecting to their marriage. They pulled up in the yard next to the cedar tree and parked. Everyone was surprised at their visit and asked where Maggie and Tura were.

"They're back at the boardin' house," Grace answered.

"Why didn't they come with you?" all the girls asked, just as Walter and Dora entered the room from opposite directions.

Grace hugged one and then the other before answering.

"Well," she continued, with Allen by her side, figuring this was as good a time as any, "I ain't seen 'em in a couple of days. Me and Allen got married, and I don't live there anymore."

Eyes grew big as they all glanced toward Walter. After everyone recovered from the initial shock, her sisters pressed for all the details. Dora's demeanor changed to pleasantry more quickly than Walter's, while his sternness went unchanged. She told them about the trip to South Carolina where they had gotten married, and all about the house they rented on Pine Street near the hospital. While she enlightened them with all there was left to tell, Dora said, "The Hopkins' are eatin' dinner with us today and I hear 'em comin' in now. Let's get dinner finished and then we can talk about it more."

During dinner, Grace would occasionally glance her daddy's way trying to analize his demeanor. He didn't appear that upset, but he seemed moderately subdued as he talked to their visitors.

Walter and his church guests later advanced to the front porch while Dora graciously excused herself for a few minutes to speak with Grace alone. To allow them their privacy, Allen took a leisurely stroll through the backyard, teasing Ora, Ruth, and Cletie as they followed.

"Grace, I'm gonna get a few things together for you and Allen to use in your new house. She proceeded to box up some towels and sheets as she asked, "How are the girls doin' at the mill?"

"They're doin' good. I think they like makin' that money," she answered.

"You plannin' to make Thomasville your home?" Dora inquired.

"I don't know right now, but we will for a while."

Grace noticed the twinkle in her mama's eyes as she revealed her own news. "Grace, I think I'm expectin'."

"Really!" Grace replied, with a smile and hug, recollecting the last baby being stillborn.

Pensively, Dora stated, "I hope this one is alright."

"Oh, I'm sure it will be, Mama. Do you know when it's due?"

"From the best I can figure, it should be here sometime in November."

"I'll keep a check on you, Mama. I guess we'd better get back home. Send word if you need anything."

"Okay, bye, honey," Dora said. "I hope you and Allen make a good start."

"Thank you, Mama."

She went to tell her daddy goodbye, as Dora followed.

"Goodbye, everybody. Bye, Daddy. We gotta go," Grace announced.

Walter rose from his chair and excused himself as he followed Grace into the front room.

"Well, Grace, you're already married, so they ain't much I can say. You made your bed, now you gotta lay in it. I hoped you wouldn't marry him. I trust he'll treat you alright."

"He does, Daddy. You take good care of Mama while she's in the family way," she said, with a hug.

As Grace and Allen started back home, she said, "Mama thinks she's expectin."

"Sakes alive. Country people sure have a lot of young'uns don't they?" Allen remarked. "Wonder how many we'll wind up with?"

"However many the good Lord sees fit, I guess," Grace answered.

Chapter 21
The Firstborn Son

As the months passed, Grace and Allen settled into married life and their new relationship was affectionate and peaceful, although he still showed tendencies toward jealousy and often voiced to Grace that he didn't want her working at that old mill.

By August, she suspected she might be pregnant and told Allen so.

"We're gonna have a baby?" he asked, with obvious excitement.

"I think so."

"Oh, boy! Do you know when it'll be here?

"I don't know for sure," she said. "But mama can probably help me figure it out when I go back home."

To the best of their ability, Dora and Grace figured it would most likely be March or April. Everyone back home was so excited and could hardly wait for the arrival of her first baby.

Grace was feeling more at ease about her pregnancy after Allen's mother told her of her niece, Minnie, who would stay with her when the time gets close and help with the birth of the baby. She had been concerned about not knowing anyone there and being so far from her mama and family to rely on.

"Now, you can't work in this condition, Grace," Allen advised.

"I'll still be able to work for a while," she replied. "My nerves would be frazzled just settin' home and waitin'. You don't mind if I work a little longer, do you?"

"I guess not for a little longer, but it's not good for you or the baby to be in a place like that."

"I promise I'll quit before I get too far along," she assured him.

Allen was so persistent for the next two months that finally Grace decided to give her notice. On her last day at work, she re-

135

gretfully said her goodbyes to Claire and her other friends at the mill and walked back to Nellie's with Maggie and Tura for Allen to pick her up after he got off work.

She was beginning to show some, but she would have still been quite able to continue working. She knew she would now have to keep herself busy around home for the next few months until her baby was born.

By November, she was beginning to get restless, running out of things to do, when she heard a familiar voice calling out.

"Grace, it's Tura and Maggie!"

"I'm here," Grace replied. "Come on in."

When Maggie and Tura stepped in, Grace asked, "What brings you two here?"

"Daddy sent word that mama had a little girl yesterday," Maggie said.

"Are they alright?" Grace asked.

"They both fine," Tura said.

"What's her name?

"They named her Arlene," Maggie said. "We're goin' down Sunday. You gonna be able to go?"

"I'll get Allen to bring me down."

"How you been feelin', Grace?" Tura asked.

"I'm doin' too good to be a-settin' here ever day, but Allen don't wont me a-workin'."

"Well, I'm here to tell you," Maggie interjected. "Ain't no man gonna tell me what to do."

Well, if she ever does get married, she might change her mind, Grace thought to herself, noticing Tura roll her eyes when Maggie turned to leave.

Allen arrived home from work early, and Grace told him the news of her new baby sister.

"Do you wanna go have dinner with mama and daddy on Sunday or wait and go later?"

"I'd just as soon eat a bite here and go later," he answered.

"By the way, why are you home so early?" Grace asked.

"Well, I got some news, too. But, it's not so good," Allen

replied. "Several of us got laid off today, but I think I found work somewhere else. We might have to move to a cheaper place for a while. In fact, I checked out a house on Oak Street across town. We'll go look at it tomorrow."

Grace felt troubled at the news, especially as she was further along in her pregnancy. She would not be able to lift anything very heavy, and having just gotten adjusted to their first home together, they were now to be uprooted. But Allen had always worked from the first day she met him, and she trusted that he'd look after her now.

After lunch on Sunday, they set out for the country to meet Grace's new little sister.

When they walked in, the proud sisters quickly grabbed Grace's hand as Allen followed, and led them to the front bedroom where their mother was sitting up in bed with their new baby sister. A couple of the neighbors had stopped by earlier and were now leaving as they spoke to Grace on the way out.

"How are you, Mama?" Grace asked, as she entered and leaned down to hug her.

"I'm fine, honey," Dora answered. "You wanna hold her?"

"Yeah, let me have her," Grace said. "She's so tiny."

"Won't be long 'til you two'll have one of these," Dora replied to the smiling couple.

"Her name is Arlene," Ruth said.

"Oh, that's so pretty. And she's such a pretty baby," Grace said. "What's daddy think about her?"

"I don't know," Ruth answered,with such a serious look.

"Oh, he's happy," Dora stated, with a chuckle. "But he's probably tuckered out with girls about now. He was hopin' for another boy to help out around here."

About an hour later, more Sunday company arrived. Grace figured her mama had plenty of visitors and decided they should leave.

"Mama, we're gonna head back home. Glad you're doin' good."

"You take care, too, Grace. Good to see you, Allen," Dora

said.

"You, too, Mrs. Grubb. Take care now."

The following week, Grace helped Allen move to the new house as best she could before the winter months set in, and they soon had their belongings in place once again.

They were getting excited as the New Year passed, knowing they would soon have their first child. It was obvious Grace's time of delivery was getting closer, as she became more uncomfortable with each passing day.

"Grace, you think we need to get Minnie to come on up and stay some now?" Allen asked.

"Probably not yet. It's just the first of March. I'll let you know if I think I need her," replied Grace.

The next week Grace noticed subtle changes but didn't mention it to Allen. She kept it to herself and decided to just wait awhile longer.

On Sunday night when Grace went to bed, things felt different. She couldn't put her finger on it, but it was definitely something she had never experienced before. She regarded it as maybe something she had eaten. She really wasn't sure, but she didn't think the baby was due yet.

In the early morning hours, she awoke.

"Allen, my water just broke! I think it's time for the baby to come!" Grace exclaimed. "I need somebody here to help!"

Allen jumped up and quickly got dressed.

"It'll take too long to get your mama. I'll go get Minnie. Are you okay?"

"I don't know. Just hurry and get her," said Grace, with urgency.

After Allen left, Grace became very anxious at the thought of being alone. She wasn't in distress yet but kept pondering what to do if he didn't make it back in time. She remembered all the encouragement in the past and began to pray for the protection of her and her unborn baby.

She had witnessed all the babies born to her mother and to

other family, but the reality of her own labor was much different, and she was now wishing she lived closer to her family.

Much to her relief, Allen soon returned with Minnie. She got Grace situated and comfortable so she could evaluate her.

"I don't think you're quite ready yet, honey, but it probably won't be real long. Allen, start some water boilin' on the stove and get some towels so we'll be ready."

Allen escaped to the porch afterward and sat while Minnie tended to Grace.

Around mid morning, Grace felt a piercing pain and let out a cry as Minnie coached her through the contractions.

"Is she alright?" Allen yelled, jumping up to look through the door.

"She's fine."

The contractions lasted until Grace felt she couldn't handle any more, when Minnie said, "We're just about there. You need to push whenever your contractions start again."

Pretty soon she was instructing Grace to push hard as the miracle of a new life entered the world with a boisterous scream.

"You got a big boy with one set of lungs!" Minnie announced, as Grace collapsed in relief.

Although exhausted and drenched, Grace managed a weary smile while Allen stood there beaming with pride.

"Have you picked out a name?" Minnie asked.

"Yeah," Allen said. "We decided on Clyde Walter. I'm namin' him Clyde, after an old buddy of mine, and both of our dads are named Walter."

"Okay, Mama Grace," Minnie replied. "Here's Clyde Walter."

Grace began to comprehend what she had always heard about motherhood as Minnie put the baby boy in her arms. The joy and warmth she felt as she held him and gazed upon the little pink face erased all the pain she had endured.

"Allen, you wanna hold him?" Grace asked.

"I'm afraid I'll hurt him."

"You won't hurt him. Here," she said.

Allen sat smiling with wonder at the new person that had

only been imagined earlier that day.

After a while, Minnie interrupted, "Okay, folks, the new mama has had a long, hard day and needs some rest. Allen, you find somethin' to do while she gets some sleep."

"Now that you're here, Minnie, I think I'll go to mom's and give her the news," he said.

The job Allen had hoped to get did not materialize, so he went looking for work the next few days while Minnie continued to stay on with them at least until Grace could comfortably take care of things on her own.

After Minnie went home, it was just Grace and her baby boy while Allen was out during the day.

Walter and Dora soon came for a visit to see little Clyde, along with their now four-month-old baby, Arlene, and the other girls who were still at home.

"Grace, the old Jones place is empty," Walter informed. "Y'all oughta move down there. You'll be closer."

"Really? We ain't hardly got settled in here yet, but I'll mention it to Allen."

When Allen got home, she told him of the old Jones place.

"Where's that?" Allen asked.

"It's not far from their house. I used to go over there with mama and daddy to pick pears," Grace replied.

"It'll be a further drive when I find work," said Allen. "But then, maybe I could get a job at one of the sawmills down there."

They rode down to the country when Grace felt strong enough and looked it over.

"What you think about it?" Allen asked.

"I'm not sure. I'd like to get closer to mama and daddy, but this is so far off the road."

"Well, it's a lot cheaper'n where we're at," Allen said. "We could save a lot of money. Especially while I'm out of work."

"I'm just not up to movin' stuff yet."

"I'll get some help with that if you wanna move here," assured Allen.

By the end of the week, Allen had persuaded Grace to pack

up most of their things in boxes. Allen recruited his brothers to help with moving the heavy things, and by Saturday evening Grace was faced with the task of sorting all their belongings that were stacked in a single room.

Grace was still uncomfortable when she was home alone, and felt too secluded back in the woods at the old Jones place, but she was pleased that living here now afforded her more time with her family as well as help with the baby.

Chapter 22
Blessed With a Girl

The early part of 1927 brought the realization that Grace was pregnant again.

"Allen, how would you feel about us havin' another baby?"

"You expectin' again?" he asked, with a look of surprise.

"Pretty sure. Looks like maybe in August."

"Hope it's a girl. Wouldn't it be nice to have a girl this time," he said, smiling.

"That'd be nice," Grace replied. "Just as long as it's okay."

"And little Clyde would have a playmate."

They were both thrilled to be adding another member to the family, although Grace was not sure how they would make it since Allen had not found work other than a few odd jobs from time to time. She felt ashamed to impose on her family, but luckily they were close to her parents now and her mother insisted they come eat with them at times.

The hot summer months created a less comfortable pregnancy for Grace than with her first child. But, she was able to get out in the sunshine with Clyde through the day, making it more bearable for her to live there when Allen was not home. Clyde, who was only a little more than a year old, kept his mother busy since learning to walk, not leaving her much time for relaxing.

It was a humid August 4th morning and the mugginess had lingered throughout the night. When Grace and Allen awoke, she got up to get breakfast started. As she pulled out the frying pan, her water broke.

"Allen! You need to go get mama!" she cried.

"What's wrong?"

"I think it's time for the baby."

He left in a hurry as Grace managed to check on Clyde, still asleep in his bed.

It took only minutes for Allen to get back with Dora and Bessie.

"Bessie, you help me with Grace until Clyde wakes up. You'll need to feed and change him when he does," Dora instructed.

Grace was having contractions much closer than when Clyde was born, and realized that sometimes the following births might occur faster.

They had everything prepared for the delivery as the contractions began to get closer over the next hour.

"I believe it's about time," Dora said, as Bessie stood by.

Clyde remained asleep as Allen stayed close for any assistance they might need.

A few pushes more and another precious life entered the world and into the hearts of all who witnessed the event on August 4, 1927.

"It's a girl!" Dora proclaimed, as Bessie squealed with joy.

"I'm gonna name her Gladys," Grace said, wearily. "Gladys Leona."

She was such a beautiful baby, with a little round face and features much resembling Grace's.

Allen and Grace were so proud of their family. He had just recently found a job, and life seemed to be improving for them while treasuring all the changes and experiences of observing Clyde and Gladys grow throughout the following year.

Grace was still adjusting to living in the backwoods, though. She had always been accustomed to living near other people, but knowing her family was just up the road lessened her uneasiness.

Soon afterward, Allen came home and mentioned a house he found for rent on Jarrell Road and asked her to go see it. He felt it would be better than the one they were in and had already told the owner he would take it.

"It costs a little more, but we can make it. And you'll still be fairly close to your family," Allen said.

So they put Clyde and Gladys in the car to go see if it was what they wanted. As they drove up the road, the car began to sputter and then make a buzzing noise.

"This darned ol' car," Allen muttered.

"What's wrong with it?" Grace asked, nervously.

"It's on its last leg."

"Are we gonna make it?"

"It's been actin' up for a while," Allen said. "It'll clear up in a minute, but I'm gonna have to get a new car soon. Do you know how long we been drivin' this ol' thing?"

"Can't you fix it?" asked Grace.

"It's patched up 'bout as much as it can be."

"Well, I guess you better get another one while work is good. We could use the money for somethin' else, but I sure don't want to be on the side of the road with these young'uns when it breaks down."

"See, it's already clearin' up," Allen said. "But who knows when it'll happen again. I'm goin' tomorrow to look for one."

They arrived to look at the house and Grace said, "I already know I'm gonna like this place better."

The next evening, a navy blue Pontiac two-door sedan pulled up the driveway. Grace walked to the door and realized it was Allen, stepping outside to meet him as he got out.

"Oh, Allen. Did you go an' buy a new car?" she asked, as her heart sank.

"No. Don't worry, it's not new. It's a '26 model. I got a good deal on it. And they even allowed me some on the old clunker."

"It sure looks new. And it's so big," Grace exclaimed.

"I like a big car. They just drive better. Let's take a ride," said Allen, cheerfully.

Grace went back inside to get Clyde and Gladys and put them in the car for their short trip. They started down the road as Clyde stuck his head out the window in the breeze.

"Well, it does ride a might good," Grace admitted. "And it sure looks a lot nicer than our old one."

They returned home and Allen arranged for moving their belongings that week. Even though it was a lot of work, Grace was relieved to just be closer to the road where she could see signs of human life again.

Bessie still occasionally stayed with her through the end of the summer to help out after Gladys was born, but now, fall was coming and she, too, was planning to join Maggie and Tura at the boarding house to work at the mill. At times, Grace still thought about the good times that she experienced at the boarding house and working at the mill, but she loved her family and knew where she belonged.

As the next two years passed, Grace settled into the home life of being a wife and mother, while Allen now worked and provided for his family.

Gladys was rather helpful for a little girl of her age, wanting to help Grace with the chores, especially the dishes. She was quite adorable as she stood in a chair with her hands in a pan of sudsy water like a little lady, often causing Grace to chuckle and smile.

Grace felt that she and Allen had as much as they needed, and she was happy with the way things had turned out for them.

Late that summer, there were rumors that there might be a downturn in the economy and that it could become severe. Allen listened to the folks in town with dread as the news spread of a possible depression.

"Grace, a depression's comin' and I'm afraid it's gonna be bad," Allen warned.

"Do you think you'll still have work?" asked Grace, worriedly.

"I don't know. I hope so. If I lose my job, I don't know what we'll do," he sighed.

"Maybe we shouldn't have moved here. It was a lot cheaper at the other place," Grace said.

"Well, we can still move somewhere else if we need to," he replied.

The thought of moving again and getting even further from family without any help brought back a recurring dread.

As October 1929 arrived, there were definite signs of a worsening depression. People began to lose their jobs, their property, and families were being displaced with no place to live at all.

"Grace," said Allen hesitantly, as he arrived home a little earlier than usual. "Afraid I got bad news again."

"What?" asked Grace, with a sense of alarm.

"I lost my job today," he finally said.

Grace stood there in the kitchen feeling numb, as what she had hoped would not happen began to soak in.

"What are we gonna do?" Grace implored.

"I don't know. Looks like everybody's losin' their jobs," he explained.

"I'll just have to try and find work somewhere else. If it gets real bad, mama will let us eat with her some if we need to."

The year was ending badly, and Allen had not found a job. The economy rapidly declined going into 1930 and was not looking hopeful. Although they had a small supply of food stored to last for a short while, there probably wouldn't be as much as there had been in the past. They were feeling discouraged and the whole family was experiencing the agonizing hardships. As days went by, Allen would snap at little things Clyde would do or say, and he appeared to get mad at Grace for any advice she offered or when she voiced concern. With each day that followed, when he left the house he would stay out longer, and eventually he came home with what Grace detected as the smell of alcohol. Grace realized he was worried, but she was concerned by the behavior he now displayed, and if he didn't get a grip on the situation, she feared he would eventually get worse.

"Allen, why are you doin' this?" she questioned, one night after he had finally gotten home late and reeking of alcohol.

"We gonna wind up with nothin'." he growled. "I ain't got no job. How we gonna survive?"

Grace walked to the kitchen chair where he sat and put her hands on his shoulders, pleading, "Allen, please don't do this. We'll make it somehow if we just have faith."

"I'm sorry, but I can't seem to find much of that right now," he said, his eyes becoming reddened, as he turned away.

Feeling distressed, he said, "I'm sorry, Grace. Sometimes I just can't deal with all this."

"You wanna ride up to your mama's for supper?" Grace said. "Might make you feel better."

They gathered the children in the car and headed that way.

They parked and got out with Clyde running ahead as Allen carried Gladys. While starting up the steps, Grace noticed movement over by the steps.

She screamed and ran through the kitchen door, grabbing a chair to stand on. Everyone rushed in to see what was going on as Allen began to laugh hysterically.

"It's gonna come in the door!" Grace screamed.

"What is it?" Ada asked.

"There's a snake tryin' to come in the door!" cried Grace.

"It's not comin' in, Grace. And besides, a black snake ain't gonna hurt you," Allen said, laughing again.

"Boys, you go take care of that black snake," Ada ordered.

After being assured that the snake had been removed, Grace finally came down from the chair as Allen still laughed.

"Allen, you just an ol' goat," Grace exclaimed, and then half chuckled herself. "But, I guess at least somethin' got your mind off your troubles for a few minutes."

"You been worried about work again, Allen?" Ada asked.

"Yeah, Mama. I don't know what we're gonna do."

"It's been bad, but it'll eventually get better. We just gotta get through it," Ada said.

And things seemed a little better as Allen convinced Grace that maybe he would have a better chance at finding a job if they moved back to town.

On a Saturday in late May 1931, Allen found an empty house for rent on Cunningham Road near Thomasville.

"I know you want to be close to your mama and daddy, but maybe it'll be for the best."

"I really don't care to move again, but if it's gonna be easier for you to find a job, I guess we need to," Grace said, with resignation.

Grace dreaded yet again all the packing and unpacking, for Allen apparently didn't realize how much of a burden it was for her, especially with tending two children.

For a moment, she resented the fact that all he had to do was move the boxes and crates but she had the task of putting it all back in order.

"Well, I guess we need to go soon and tell mama and daddy we're movin'." she told Allen.

"Alright, we better go down there and tell 'em now," said Allen.

"We don't have to go today."

"Yeah, I think we need to."

He then added, "besides, we'll have to move when I can get the help, and it might be in only a day or so."

"Well, let's go then so I can get back and fix supper," Grace said.

She set out a jar of the canned vegetable soup her mother had given her last fall. She could heat it up when they got back and add some of the ham her dad had sliced from the smoke-house.

As they pulled up at Walter and Dora's, Clyde and Gladys were on their feet, standing just inside the car door ready to get out.

"Y'all go on in. I'm goin' over to Ray's for a few minutes," Allen said.

"You ain't goin' in?" Grace asked.

"I'll be right back," he answered.

The kids ran to the house ahead of Grace, with Clyde trying to pull Gladys up the steps by her hand.

"Hey, Paw Paw Grubb," Clyde said to Walter.

Gladys grabbed Dora around the legs and exclaimed, "Hey, Maw Maw Gwubb."

"Well, hey there, Gladys. Hey, Clyde," they both greeted.

"I'm goin' in the yard to play, Mama," Clyde said.

"You stay close," ordered Grace.

"I found somethin' for you, Gladys," Dora said. "Come to the kitchen with me."

Gladys followed Dora to the sink as Dora picked up a little silver tin pitcher and handed it to her. Gladys's mouth flew opened and her eyes widened with surprise.

"I found this in town the other day and I thought about you." Gladys held it tightly as she looked at Grace and smiled.

"Say thank you to Maw Maw, Gladys," Grace instructed.

"Tank you, Maw Maw."

"You're welcome, sweetie."

Grace helped her mother and sisters with things around the house as the afternoon slipped away, and she wondered where Allen could be for so long.

Her family began to start supper as Grace walked to the door to check for his car. The food began to cook, and the aroma made their mouths water.

When Clyde came in, he announced, "I'm hungry!"

"Well, it's about ready, so y'all come on in and set down," Dora invited.

"No, Mama. Y'all go ahead. We can eat when we get back home," said Grace.

"But these babies are hungry," Dora urged.

She had tried to keep the worst of their situation from her parents, but unknown to Grace, Walter and Dora were already aware of their plight.

"They ain't no need in standin' there," Walter stated. "Your mama's gonna have the last word."

Grace felt they were taking advantage of her parents under the circumstances, but she decided to take them up on their offer, especially since it would be awhile now before the children would get to eat.

"Where's Allen?" they asked.

"He said he was goin' over to see somebody called Ray."

"What's he goin' to see him for? Ain't he a bootlegger?" Cletie asked.

With a sinking feeling in the pit of her stomach, Grace just looked down at her plate without commenting, hoping it wasn't the reason for his going there.

As soon as she had a chance to speak, Grace announced,

"Looks like we're gonna have to move back to town."

"Awww, I'm not gonna get to see the babies much if y'all move," Dora said, plaintively.

"Allen can't find work and he thinks he'll find somethin' there if we move back," she said.

"I sure hate to see you leave, but I know you have to do what's best," Dora said, trying to encourage her.

"Well, it ain't gonna be any better in the city," Walter remarked. "If anything, it's gonna be even tougher on folks there. We're just fortunate to have a farm where we got plenty to eat."

Grace wasn't sure if he was being concerned or merely cueing the conversation he had had with Allen before they married.

When they finished the meal, Dora asked, "Walter, do we have a box around here that I can put some canned food in for Grace to take home?"

"I think there's one out on the side porch. I'll go see."

"Grace, fix Allen a plate of food to take home so you won't have to cook somethin' when you get there," urged Dora.

"Mama, I'm goin' back out to play," Clyde stated.

"Can I go out, too?" Arlene asked.

"Alright, but don't you young'uns get into nothin'." Dora warned.

As Dora's girls cleared the table and headed to the sink, Gladys pushed a chair up to the cabinet to help.

Dora laughed and said, "Just look at that! I've never seen a three-year-old child so sweet. She's gonna be one smart girl."

After helping with the dishes, Grace began untying her apron and went to the den to talk with Walter and Dora while she listened for Allen's car, worried and hoping to prevent them from discovering the condition in which he might return.

At that moment, they heard Clyde and Arlene screaming. Everyone ran to the door to see what was happening. Arlene was desperately grasping for the screen door to get in, as Clyde was spinning and swatting with all his might.

"The bees are gettin' him!" Arlene shouted.

When Grace got to him, she could see wasps swarming and

diving to sting him. She quickly took off the apron and started swatting them away with it. She finally got them off and got Clyde into the house somehow without getting stung herself. Clyde was crying hard but she managed to examine him, finding red spots covering any bare skin on him and even some under his shirt.

"What happened?" implored Grace.

"He grabbed the nest. He just reached up there and pulled it down," Arlene replied.

"Clyde, don't you know better than to do that?" Grace asked.

"Bring him here," Walter instructed. "We'll put some snuff on 'em."

When he got through, Clyde had little wet brown spots all over him.

"Well, that'll take care of the swellin'." said Walter.

Gladys, still clutching her little tin pitcher, had already fallen asleep while Dora rocked her, and Clyde had calmed down but was moving cautiously as he played on the floor with two small blocks of wood from the woodbox. Enough time had passed that Grace was becoming quite concerned, and soon she heard Allen's car pull in.

She immediately stood up, saying "Let me take this stuff to the car, and I'll come back for Gladys. Clyde, do you think you can carry this plate for me?"

"I'll carry the box out for you," Walter offered.

"No, Daddy, I've got it. I'll be right back in."

As soon as she opened the car door, the odor was overwhelming and she knew he had been drinking.

"Allen, where have you been?"

"Never mind. Just get them kids in the car and let's go."

She felt as if her heart was about to break, trying to mask her feelings as she returned for Gladys.

"Everything okay?" Dora asked.

"Everything's fine, Mama. I'll see you and daddy soon. Love you," Grace replied, as she left with the children and the box of food.

She put Clyde in the back seat and held Gladys, as she sat

silent all the way home, with the exception of when Allen was driving too close to the edge of the road.

"Watch out, Allen. You're gonna run off the road."

"Yeah, Daddy, you gonna run off the road and kill us all dead," Clyde added.

"You better hush your mouth, boy, and mind your own business!" Allen snapped. "I'm nowhere close to the ditch, Grace. You worry too much."

She kept thinking how glad she was that they didn't have far to go.

Once home, she asked Allen to carry the box in and noticed him slipping a bottle in it before picking it up.

Grace was amazed that the wasp stings had not made Clyde sick. After putting him and Gladys to bed and then getting ready herself, she went to bed, with Allen following shortly afterward.

"I don't like the thought of bringin' liquor in the house around the young'uns," Grace said, as she lay in the dark.

"It ain't hurtin' the young'uns," he retorted.

"Well, it ain't right. And you said you wouldn't do this anymore."

"Well, you don't know what I'm goin' through," he said. "And, I've heard all about Willie Ervin and Matt Corbin."

"What do you mean?" she asked, confused.

"Oh, I've heard all about them."

"I don't know what you're talkin' about, Allen."

"Ray told me all about how they liked you. They better never show up around here or they'll be sorry they did."

"Well, the Lord… Allen Scarlett! I've never heard such!"

She felt embarrassed that anyone would tell such things, knowing that both of them had been family friends for many years.

Grace was emotionally and physically exhausted and knew whatever he drank earlier that evening was making him irrational, so she decided against arguing further. She lay there as her heart raced, unable to sleep with the thoughts of what was happening and what they might face ahead.

Chapter 23
A Tragic Loss

The next morning Allen asked, "What in the world happened to Clyde? His eyes are almost swelled shut. And what's all those little brown spots?"

"He got in a wasp nest at daddy's. They got him good. He's runnin' a little fever. I hope it don't get worse."

"Ah, he'll be alright. I guess he'll learn to stay away from 'em now," Allen said, offering no pity.

Clyde moved slowly through the room and didn't seem to want to do much as Grace continued to treat his discomforts with concern.

The next day, once again, Allen recruited help to load up everything they owned in order to move to the house on Cunningham Road and be closer to town.

The little house sat up on a hill in the curve of the road.

Even with the endless tasks of keeping house and looking after the children, Grace eventually got everything put away and in its new place.

Since the move they were now seeing more of Allen's family. Ada would ask them to let Clyde and Gladys come for visits, and on occasion they would all be there for dinner.

Allen was only able to find part-time work through the summer months, which barely supplied them with the necessities, but it seemed to keep him from being so pessimistic. He now only drank on occasion.

"I can go back to work if we can find somebody to keep Clyde and Gladys," Grace offered.

"No," Allen replied bluntly. "You ain't got no business goin' back to work."

"Well, I'm gonna have to 'til you find steady work. Jobs are scarce, but I can get on second shift at the mill since I'm experienced."

"I'll find a full-time job soon and everything'll be fine," he said.

That night, Grace repeated, "I really need to go to work for a while. We need the money. You think your mama might look after the kids in the evenins'?"

"I guess so, but it's only 'til I get a full-time job," he replied, finally resigned to his wife's practicality.

It was the end of July and Grace had now been working at the mill for a couple of months. Allen was still able to find odd jobs to help them get by.

"Mama said to bring the kids over on Saturday so you can get some things done here," Allen said, when he arrived home. "She mentioned that she'd like to take the kids to church with her sometime. They could spend Saturday with her and then I could take y'all back over there Sunday mornin' so you could go with her," he suggested.

"I don't know, I guess I could," Grace said. "You're not goin'?"

"Nah. I'll just let y'all go this time. I'll let her know tomor-row."

On Saturday morning, Grace kissed Gladys and Clyde good-bye as Allen drove them up to his mother's house for the day.

He dropped them off and said he would be back that evening to pick them up.

Grace enjoyed the quiet while she stayed home cleaning and straightening up, although she missed the little feet that were always scampering under hers.

Late in the afternoon, Allen came home to see if she wanted to ride along to get the kids.

"Have you already cooked?" he asked.

"I've got a pot of beans on," she replied.

"Why don't we take 'em down to mama's and have supper with 'em?"

"Well, I'll need to fix a little somethin' else. It won't take long."

"I got some things to do to the car 'til you get through," he said.

When both were finished, they loaded the food in the car and headed to Ada's.

As they arrived, Clyde and Allen's younger brother, Will, were playing cowboys, and Alma was carrying Gladys around the yard.

"She's a little big for you to be luggin' around like that, ain't she?" Allen said, laughing as he walked by.

"She's not heavy at all. I'm almost eleven now, Allen," Alma informed him.

"Hey, Daddy," Allen said, as they passed by him sitting on the porch.

"Hey, Mr. Scarlett," Grace greeted.

"Hey, young'uns. Somethin' you got there smells good," he replied, with a smile.

They carried the food in and Allen said, "Mama, we brought some extra food and thought we'd just eat with you all this evenin'."

"That's fine," Ada said, as she walked in the room. "But you didn't have to bring anything, we got plenty enough."

"Oh, we're not gonna come and eat without bringin' somethin'," Grace replied.

"Well, everything's ready, so call 'em all in," Ada said.

As they all sat around the table, it brought thoughts of home to Grace, with the exception of her sisters' loud chattering.

Once they finished their meal, the kids made a straight line outdoors again.

"Tell them boys not to wander off too far, Alma," instructed Ada.

"I'll tell 'em, Mama. But I don't know if they'll listen."

"Grace, you and the kids goin' to church with us tomorrow?" Ada asked, as they washed the dishes.

"We plannin' to if nothin' happens. I tried to talk Allen into goin' with us."

"Maybe he'll come back around," Ada said.

Just then they heard a lumbering sound of something falling outside, followed by a scream. Everyone ran toward the commotion to hear Alma say, "The garage door fell on Gladys. She just

157

touched it and it fell on her."

Grace rushed to her as Allen lifted the door and Grace picked her up.

"Are you okay, honey?" she asked, as Gladys cried and wrapped her arms around her mother's neck.

Grace took her to a chair on the porch and sat down to check her over as Gladys whimpered and held tightly onto her mother.

After a few moments she quieted down and Grace said, "I believe she's alright. I think she's just scared."

Grace carried her inside and put her on the sofa where she sat timidly until it was time for them to leave. She whimpered once again when Grace picked her up to go.

"You think she's alright, Grace?" Ada asked, concerned. Alma reflected her expression as she awaited Grace's response.

"She's probably just sore."

"Well, if you don't get to go to church in the mornin', y'all be sure and let me know she's alright tomorrow, now," Ada said.

Gladys was sore when Grace got her up the next morning, so she decided against visiting church with Ada that day. They stopped by later with Gladys to assure them that she was alright, although she still whimpered when Alma picked her up, as she continued to do during their visits the next two weeks.

Gladys seemed to improve and asked to go pick muscadines growing at the edge of the woods next to their house.

Grace took her out to the vine as Clyde played close in the yard.

As they picked the grapes and put them in the pan, Gladys started eating them and ate almost as many as they picked.

"Little girl, you eat many more of those and you gonna have a tummy ache," Grace warned.

"Dey good, Mama," she said sweetly, warming Grace's heart to a smile.

"Okay, but just a few more."

Grace eventually managed to fill a pan and take it back to the house to eat later.

By the next morning, Gladys had developed a slight cough,

and each time she did, she would whimper.

"Allen, we might need to take her to the doctor," Grace suggested.

"You think she's gettin' sick?" he asked.

"She just ain't been right lately, and now this cough. I know we don't have the money, but I'm worried."

"Let's get 'em in the car," Allen said. "Maybe he'll work with us."

They were soon on their way, with Grace holding Gladys in the front seat, and Clyde in the back. They had passed the doctor's office in town many times but never had a need to stop until now.

They didn't have to wait long to get her checked.

"There has been a lot of whooping cough the past few years, but this looks more like a cold or mild cough at the present," the doctor informed them. "Just call me if she gets worse."

Grace shuddered at the thought of her getting the whooping cough. She knew of many neighbors and friends who had lost children to that in the past. They drove back home and Grace kept a watchful eye on Gladys throughout the day and night.

Grace had not been able to go back to work since Gladys was not well, and with work scarce, Allen usually got home early. Grace always tried to have supper ready, but the next day he was running a little late. Gladys appeared tired and had crawled up on the sofa to take a nap, and Clyde played in the kitchen floor as Grace worked.

When Allen came home, it was obvious by his speech and actions that he had been drinking again.

"I've got a gun and I'm a-gonna shoot any man that comes around here," he slurred.

"Allen, you been drinkin' again. How do you think that's gonna help our problems? You gonna have to start thinkin' about these children. And there ain't been any men here today or any other day."

"And they better not!" he shouted.

"Gladys is asleep. If you wake her up, you gonna scare her."

He slowly made his way to the bed and sprawled out across it sideways. Grace assumed he was asleep so she kept Clyde as quiet as possible and decided against waking Allen for supper. She then decided to feed the kids and get them to bed early in case he woke up in a bad mood.

"Hop up here and eat, Clyde."

She put his food on the plate and went over to the sofa to rouse Gladys from her nap.

"Wake up honey, it's time to eat."

She opened her eyes when Grace touched her, but she appeared so drowsy and wasn't fully awake until she picked her up.

Her cough had not progressed, and that gave Grace some comfort, but she whimpered as Grace carried her to the table and sat down to feed her.

"You hungry?" Grace asked.

"Uh, uh," she responded.

"Well, you need to eat a little bit."

She ate only a small amount from the spoon, and was not alert enough to finish.

"You feel alright, honey?" Grace pressed, as Gladys just laid her head against her mother. "Please try to eat a little more."

"I hope she's not gettin' sick," Grace said to Clyde, as she felt her forehead.

After unsuccessfully coaxing her to eat a little more, Grace put her to bed in hopes that maybe she would wake up later and want to eat.

Meanwhile, Grace heard something fall on the floor from Clyde's direction.

"Mama, I dropped my spoon," he called.

"Shhhh," she gestured, with a finger to her lips. "Daddy's asleep. Let's not wake him."

After Clyde finished eating, Grace washed the dishes and checked on Gladys.

Can she be dreaming? Grace wondered, as Gladys twitched and whined in her sleep each time she checked on her.

Allen awoke and sat up on the side of the bed, rubbing his

face.

"Your supper's still on the stove. I been tryin' to keep it warm," Grace said. "Clyde, you jump on in bed now."

Allen was now much quieter as he got up and went to the kitchen. He sat down in the straight-back chair and began to rub his eyes and face.

"Gladys don't seem right, Allen. I don't know if she's sick or what. She wouldn't eat anything and she seems restless while she sleeps."

"Maybe it's just a stomachache or somethin'." he said, wearily.

"She did eat a mess of muscadines earlier today. I shouldn't a let her had so many. Maybe it is a tummy ache."

"Don't you still have some paregoric? That oughta help," Allen said.

As he ate and they talked, they heard Gladys cry.

Grace immediately went to pick her up and brought her back to the table.

"Mama's here, I got you, sweetie. You feel like eatin' somethin' now?"

But as Grace sat holding her, Gladys would only softly whine and cry in her mother's arms.

"Maybe she shouldn't eat anything," Grace reasoned. "I'll just give her the paregoric and rock her awhile."

Grace eventually coaxed Gladys to sip some and it eventually eased her discomfort as she rocked and hummed to her softly.

Gladys was sleeping peacefully when Grace put her to bed. She felt relieved that she was now resting and more assured that is was most likely the grapes upsetting her stomach.

Grace had been so concerned and preoccupied with Gladys, that at this point Allen's previous bad behavior seemed irrelevant.

As they all went to bed that Wednesday night, Grace left a lamp burning low as she lay there attentive to any sound Gladys made, checking on her periodically during the next few hours.

Grace finally dozed off sometime after midnight, only to be awakened a short time later by a faint sound.

She woke abruptly and jumped up to check on Gladys, find-

161

ing her moaning in her sleep.

"What is it, sweetie?" Grace asked, quickly picking her up.

Gladys partially opened her eyes and looked at her mother with an expression of pain.

Grace felt helpless as she debated whether to wake Allen.

She gave her a little more paregoric as she sat in the rocker trying to soothe her by any means she could think of.

As Gladys would get quiet, Grace would drift off until a whimper would awaken her.

Grace wasn't sure how long she had sat there when she awoke in the quiet of the dim, predawn hours.

As she shifted Gladys to her other arm, she seemed much too limp. Her breathing was a little more rapid than usual and she seemed unresponsive to Grace's voice and touch as she rubbed her feverish face. She then gently patted her face but her movements were weak, and Grace could not fully awaken her.

A chilling wave of panic and fear struck Grace's every nerve.

"Allen!" she screamed. "Allen! Get up! Somethin's wrong with Gladys. I can't get her awake!"

He quickly jumped up and rushed over to Grace's side.

"What's wrong?" he asked.

"I don't know," Grace cried. "Do somethin'!"

"What should I do?" he implored.

"Go get mama. She'll know what to do."

Allen hurriedly dressed and ran out the door, still buttoning his shirt.

"Please wake up, sweetie," Grace pleaded, through her tears.

"Dear God," she prayed. "Please help my baby. I can't bear to lose her."

To Grace it seemed an eternity before Walter and Dora got there.

"Mama, I don't know what to do. She won't wake up," Grace sobbed. They hurried in and Dora took Gladys from her, laying her on the bed as the others watched.

"Get some wet cloths," Dora said. "She feels hot."

Grace brought them and Dora began wiping her little face

and arms.

"Gladys, wake up, sweetie. Maw Maw's here," she said, with no response.

Dora tried to mask her concern, immediately aware that something was seriously wrong.

"Allen, you might need to get the doctor," Dora suggested.

"What's wrong with her, Mama?" cried Grace.

"I don't know. How long has she been this way?"

"She was restless all night but was like this when I woke up this mornin'. I thought she had a stomachache when she wouldn't eat last night so I gave her somethin' to settle her and then put her to bed. After midnight she woke me up whinin'. I rocked her the rest of the night."

Allen returned with his mother after summoning the doctor.

Ada stepped over to observe Gladys, and quietly asked Dora if she had any idea what was wrong, but Dora just shook her head.

Ada then looked around at Grace and then over at Allen, and they knew from the expression on her face that Gladys's condition was serious.

Allen could no longer bear it and walked outside as Grace wrapped her arms around her daddy and began to cry.

"Grace, honey, we're gonna do everything we can," Dora said. "Just pray for her."

The doctor arrived and began examining Gladys. Grace explained what she had told her mother earlier. He sat by Gladys's side for a while, checking her closely, and then turned to Grace and her family. "It's hard to say with her condition at this point. It could be Meningitis or a number of things. Just watch her and keep her as comfortable as possible through the day. If there's no change by this afternoon, let me know and I'll come back."

As they sat by her side through the early part of the day, they took turns rubbing her hair and talking to her, but with no response or visible improvement.

"She's not gettin' better, is she, Mama?" Grace tearfully asked, as the afternoon wore on.

Dora turned and observed Gladys's shallow breathing and finally replied, "Only God knows. She could come out of it, but it don't look good."

Walter decided to go home to tend to some things, and told Dora he would bring the girls back, realizing they would want to see Gladys if the worst happened.

"How about havin' the girls bring the supper up here," Dora requested. "Grace ain't had no chance to fix anything and we'll all eat here."

"Daddy," Grace said sadly, "will you go by and tell Maggie, Tura, and Bessie? They'd wanna know."

They kept watch through the early evening, taking turns holding Gladys.

"If only she would open her eyes and tell me she was hungry," wept Grace, softly.

As they talked quietly, Grace had been rocking her very slowly for a short while when Dora suddenly sat alert on the edge of her seat. With a furrowed brow, she leaned forward, observing Gladys.

Grace immediately looked down.

"She's not movin'. I don't think she's breathin'!" Dora said.

Grace stopped the rocker instantly and stared intently.

"Oh, no, Gladys, breathe! Breathe, honey!" Grace coaxed, as Dora and Ada jumped up and rushed to her side.

As Grace placed a hand on her chest and shook her gently, she started to breathe again.

"What's wrong?" Allen asked, stepping in after hearing the excitement.

"She stopped breathin' for a minute," Ada said. "But she's breathin' again now."

"Grace, do you need a break? One of us can hold her awhile," Dora offered.

Swallowing hard, she replied, "No, I'm okay, Mama."

Walter returned with all the girls as they quietly walked in and made their way to where Grace was holding Gladys. Grace looked up at them helplessly with tear-filled eyes as they each bent down and took turns kissing her through their stifled grief.

"Do you need one of us to hold her for you, Grace?" Tura asked.

"No. I can't bear to turn her loose," she replied, as she wept.

Her sisters put the food on the table and got plates out for everyone to eat.

Dora walked to the kitchen as Bessie whispered, "It's a good thing daddy brought the food. They ain't hardly got nothin' in here to eat."

"Times have really been hard. I didn't know they was havin' it this bad," Dora said.

"I told her not to marry him," Walter snapped. "I knew she was headed for trouble from day one."

"Fix me a plate for Grace," Dora said, ignoring Walter's remarks.

She took it to her and set it on a little table beside her chair.

"Let me hold her while you eat, Grace."

"I can't eat anything, Mama. Not right now."

"You gonna need your strength."

"I'm just not hungry. Maybe somethin' to drink."

Grace continued holding and whispering to Gladys as her tears fell on Gladys's little dress, while the rest of the family stood in different parts of the house to eat.

Dora and Ada were still staying close when Grace cried, "Mama, she's not breathin' again!" as everyone dropped what they were doing and rushed into the room.

Grace shook her, begging her to take another breath.

"She won't breathe!" she cried.

They all stood in a state of shock as Grace, with the help of Dora and Ada, desperately tried reviving her to no avail.

After working with her a few minutes longer, Dora tearfully said, "Grace, honey, I think she's gone," as Grace dropped her face on the small, limp body and sobbed.

The cries from Grace's sisters immediately grew with emotional intensity at their mother's confirmation.

"I always knew she was too precious to live," wept Maggie.

They all lingered around Grace and the child in utter despair. After a while, some of them began to return to the kitchen to discuss what should be done next.

Walter looked at Allen and said, "I think it's your place to get in touch with the funeral home. If you can't seem to do nothin' else, you can at least do that."

Allen narrowed his eyes and firmly pressed his lips together at Walter's remarks, then left without responding.

A half hour later Allen returned and informed everyone that the undertakers would be there shortly.

As Grace still held the child she had nurtured for three years, there was no one at that moment who could console her.

As she mourned and grieved, no one dared to take her child from her arms.

The undertakers finally arrived to transport the lifeless little body to the funeral home as Grace stood and held fast to her baby.

"Grace, honey, you gonna have to let her go," Dora finally said, as Grace hugged her and sobbed again.

After consoling her for a while, her family finally persuaded her to let Gladys go. When they removed the baby from her arms and started out the door, Grace felt an emptiness she had never experienced before, collapsing into the chair from grief and exhaustion.

Chapter 24
From Tragedy to Hope

Dora and Ada stayed and sat up through the night with Allen and Grace while Walter took the girls home to their own beds until time to return the next day.

Grace was still exhausted from the two previous nights of grief and despair, and slept for several hours after her mother persuaded her to lie down.

Upon waking, she numbly got up with an instant realization of her loss. She walked slowly over to the dresser and picked up one of Gladys's little dresses. Holding it to her face, she began to sob as Dora embraced and comforted her.

"What am I gonna do without her? I can't believe my baby's gone. What did I do wrong?"

"You didn't do anything wrong, Grace. Things happen that we'll never understand."

"I don't feel like I can bear to go through this, Mama."

"You have to ask God to give you strength. I know it's hard, but you'll get through it somehow." Dora knew well the pain of losing a child.

While Grace had been sleeping, family and friends delivered food. Dora took her to the kitchen to show what had been brought, hoping it would encourage and distract her mind, if only for a short time.

As they sat and discussed the arrangements, Grace said, "Mama, I don't know how we're gonna pay for all this. Allen's not workin' and we don't have any money right now."

"Honey, they'll let you make payments. And we'll help you what we can, so don't worry about it right now."

Grace somberly went through the motions, greeting guests until they delivered the little white felt-covered casket for the wake, and then the sobering truth returned once again.

The following days seemed a blur as they prepared and arrived at the church for the funeral.

"Grace, why don't you go home with us for the night?" Walter and Dora urged, after the final rites at the gravesite were said.

"I don't know," she whispered, as she stood there staring at the coffin.

"I think that might be a good idea, Grace," Allen said. "I'll be fine. You go on. I can come back and get you whenever you want me to."

After consideration, she decided to go with Walter and Dora as they led her and Clyde from the cemetery.

They knew the stay would not remedy the agony of losing her child, but they felt the sisters would help to distract her more than if she were at home alone.

Ora and Arlene kept Clyde occupied with some of their games while the others tried to keep Grace's attention as she sat silent in the rocker.

"She turned three only a month ago," Grace finally said, through tears, as she was hugged and comforted by the family.

When Grace went home, she was once again reminded of the emptiness Gladys's death had left in her heart as she held up to her face the little tin pitcher Gladys loved so much.

The funeral expenses soon had to be taken care of and even though Allen was working part of the week, he didn't seem to have money to help pay for it. Fortunately, the funeral home arranged payments for Grace, and it was several years before she would manage to pay it off with whatever means she could.

The grieving process was slow and difficult during the following months as Grace gradually began to recover, so Walter and Dora would send one of the girls to visit regularly and occasionally spend the night.

Ora, who was now ten was visiting Grace for a few days. "I told Allen I need new shoes," Grace told her. "I asked him to take me downtown one evenin'. This is the only pair of shoes I got and they plum wore out. It's been years since I got these. He got mad and said he'd just stay out of work if I want to go so bad."

"Ain't he got no money, Grace?" Ora asked.

"He's got money if it's for somethin' he wants."

The next morning after breakfast, Allen announced that he was not going to work and that Grace should go get in the car if she just had to have new shoes.

"I don't know why you need new shoes right now, anyway. They don't look all that bad," he grumbled.

"They wore out," Grace repeated. "But you don't need to stay out of work to go get 'em. I told you we could go one evenin'."

"Nope, we're goin' now," he insisted, as he headed to the door. "Come on now."

As they drove toward downtown, Allen said, "Looks like you could get a pair from one of your sisters."

"I'm not gonna ask my sisters for a pair of shoes," she replied. "And besides, I ain't had a new pair of shoes in I don't know how long."

"Well, the money could be used for somethin' better," he continued, as he pulled up in front of Effird's Department Store on Main Street in Thomasville.

"Well, what you losin' by stayin' out of work today would've paid for 'em."

"Well, here's the money," he said. "Go on and get 'em."

Grace was getting madder by the minute.

Ora sat nervously on the edge of the back seat next to Clyde as they continued to argue, and was thinking that if she ever got back home, she'd never come back and stay with them again.

"Well, ain't you gettin' out?"

"No!" she snapped. "Forget it. Just turn this car around and go back home!"

With that, Allen exploded out of the driver's door, cranked the engine, slammed the door and pulled out on the street toward home, with a wide-eyed Ora looking at him and then at Grace. Clyde just sat and played with rocks he had found, pretending not to notice.

By the end of that year Grace was pregnant, and felt encouraged that it might somehow improve the condition of their relationship.

As winter began to break in March, Minnie stopped by to see how Allen, Grace, and Clyde were getting on. Allen was in the yard swing, so she sat down with him and chatted for a while before going in the house.

"I just love that Allen," Minnie chirped, when she entered the house. "He is so sweet."

She ain't had to live with him and she just don't know, Grace thought to herself.

"I hear you in the family way again, Grace. When you due?"

"I think about the middle of the year."

"Send for me when it gets close, now."

"Oh, we will, Minnie. We couldn't do without you."

Minnie leaned in close to Grace and asked, "You and Allen gettin' along any better?"

"Well, maybe a little. I know you think I fuss a lot. But he just won't work. It worries me when we can't get by. Sometimes now I think he was too young when we got married."

"Just be patient with him and he'll be alright."

On the twenty-third day of June 1931, Grace gave birth to Marie, a beautiful baby girl with thick, black hair.

She thought of Gladys often, but now felt God had given her this child to help fill the empty hole in her heart.

Allen, who had always appeared more receptive to Gladys, also seemed to dote on this new baby girl, giving renewed hope to Grace. His attention had waned toward Clyde, though, so Grace made a special effort to give him extra attention. Allen often became irritated and complained that he was too mischievous, threatening Clyde when he bothered any of his belongings. He had spanked him a few times, a little too aggressively, Grace felt.

Clyde would soon start school and Grace felt relieved that this might lessen his boundless energy and perhaps not disturb Allen as much.

The Great Depression still had its immense hold on them throughout the following year, allowing them to barely get by, and sometimes the money Allen earned was spent on unnecessary things for the car or things he wanted for himself. The amount left over was inadequate for their basic needs, which caused conflict between the two of them. Grace would worry and then confront him on the matter, which in turn provoked an angry response from Allen. Financially, and, increasingly in their marriage, Grace felt stagnant and Allen felt trapped.

Months later, on their way to visit Allen's parents, Grace again confronted him about their financial situation and other matters on her mind. When they arrived, Allen exited the car and walked briskly ahead, leaving Grace to bring the children in.

He shook his head in disgust upon greeting his mother at the door. Grace approached just in time to hear him say, "That woman's gonna drive me crazy."

Ada just looked at one and then the other, wondering what was going on.

Everyone sensed the tension as Grace and Allen each took opportunities to be defensive.

Afterward, they carried their subtle discussion outside to the porch for most of the afternoon, where Allen sat quietly stewing as Grace continued to confront him with their problems, due to what she perceived as inadequate concern on his part.

Ada stepped out on the porch as Allen bolted out of his chair toward the woods spouting, "I can't take any more of this!"

Grace attempted to follow when Ada intervened.

"Grace, just leave him be and come on back. You've said enough." She stopped at Ada's request as Allen stormed off alone.

Grace sat back down with Ada for the remainder of the visit as Ada kindly recommended remedies for their disagreements.

That year, 1933, became an economic nightmare, and Grace prayed that things would somehow get better. They, among many others, had suffered greatly for such a long time, but there didn't seem to be any relief in sight. Allen became more despondent and more physically aggressive with Clyde, blaming him for anything that went wrong.

As the next New Year passed, the Depression was predicted to ease through the upcoming months. It caused Grace to feel a little more secure and some feeling of relief, but now she was wondering if she might be pregnant again. Another month of being late would confirm it.

I should have been more careful, she thought. How did my life get like this? She felt depressed and alone and that no one cared as she sat on the porch, rocking Marie and watching Clyde as he played in the yard.

Clyde walked up to the edge of the porch and asked, "Mama, can I walk to the store?"

"All the way to Hepler's? You'll have to go through the woods, and that's a long way for you to be a-goin' off by yourself," Grace said.

"Mama, I'm eight years old now. I know the way. I'll stay on the path. I heard you say you needed some salt this mornin'. I can get it. I'll be fine, I promise."

"Let me get some change, but you better be careful," Grace warned, handing Clyde the money.

"I will!" he replied, as he set off across the dirt road and into the woods.

An hour and a half passed and Clyde still had not returned home. Grace began to worry.

Allen arrived home, but to avoid conflict, she didn't mention how long Clyde had been gone.

When Clyde walked out of the woods shortly afterward, he appeared nervous as he approached Allen and Grace.

"Mama, I dropped the salt and spilled some of it, but I scooped up all I could. Here it is."

With a concerned expression, he handed it to Grace, glancing timidly toward his dad.

Allen then walked around the corner of the house, broke off a branch from the bush, walked up to Clyde and grabbed him by the arm, striking him anywhere he could.

Clyde shrieked from the first lash, followed by a sharp cry of pain as Allen continued, ignoring Grace's intervention and pleas to stop.

When he finally stopped, Clyde ran off and hid as Grace scolded Allen for his angry outburst.

"What is wrong with you?! He just spilt some salt! You ain't got no business hittin' him like that," she cried.

"He'll learn to be more careful and not waste my money!" Allen growled.

"I paid for the salt with my own money. Not yours," Grace informed.

"I don't care. He needs to learn!" he yelled, as he stormed off, grumbling.

The economy was slowly getting better, but their relationship was still very strained. Grace felt Allen drank too much and didn't seem very concerned, which caused her to worry for her and her children.

If he don't go back to work, we'll be no better off than we've been through the hard times, she fretted, and here I am, gonna have another child.

The summer months seemed a trifle hotter than usual, and when August arrived, Grace had not gone into labor when she had expected. Maybe she just figured wrong, but she was ready to have this child and get it over with.

She had heard women talk about taking castor oil or mineral oil and certain teas to help induce labor. Even a bit of turpentine mixed in a drink was mentioned. She had no castor oil or any of the others, but Allen had some turpentine in the cabinet that he had used to treat a cut to his hand once. She decided she might try that, as it was already the ninth day of August, which seemed way over the due date. It was about time for Allen to get home as Clyde played in the yard and Marie slept.

She nervously poured herself a glass of tea and measured out what she thought was a reasonable amount of turpentine into a teaspoon. She stirred it well and drank it as she held her nose. Even though it wasn't much, she thought it was utterly awful, and grimaced.

Allen arrived home shortly afterward while she anxiously waited through the evening with not much more than an uneasy moment before eating supper.

Grace slept through most of the night, waking occasionally, and anticipating labor to begin at any moment.

Chapter 25
Heartbreak and Guilt

Grace awoke the next morning and started her day as usual, but within an hour she felt the pain.

"Allen, you might better go get Minnie. I think the baby's gonna be born today," Grace said. "And take Clyde and Marie to your mama's."

When Allen returned with Minnie, she began getting things ready for the birth.

"Did your water break?" she asked.

"No, not yet, but I feel like I'm beginnin' to have contractions."

"Well, that's sorta odd," Minnie said, with a furrowed brow.

"I thought so, too. I feel alright except for the pain."

"Well, let's see what happens in the next while," suggested Minnie.

Grace sipped on thin soup as noon passed with no change, and then waited through the next few hours with Minnie.

Allen supposed that it would still be a while before the baby would be born, so he decided to make a quick trip to the store. But as soon as he left, her water broke and it was just a matter of time before a new life would enter their lives once again.

Contractions were getting closer as Minnie coached Grace to push, and then, again, much quicker than the previous births, there she was, another beautiful baby girl.

As Minnie cleaned her up, Grace noticed she didn't cry as the others did at birth.

Minnie didn't say much, other than to ask if she had a name picked out for her.

"I'm gonna name her Peggy Lee," Grace said, wearily. "Is she alright, Minnie?"

"Yeah. She's shakin' quite a bit, but maybe she's just chilled."

Bundled in a soft, off-white blanket, Minnie placed her in Grace's arms.

After she held and nursed her for about five minutes, Grace pulled the blanket back to examine her newest wonder, noticing that she was still shaking.

"You need to get some rest," Minnie said, as she took the baby from Grace's arms. "I'll look after Peggy while you sleep."

Grace tried to stay awake. but she was overcome with exhaustion and soon dozed off.

When she awoke, she immediately asked, "Minnie, is she alright?"

"She's still shakin'," Minnie replied.

"What could be causin' it?" Grace asked, with tears in her eyes.

"Just give her a little more time and see if it stops," assured Minnie, realizing there might be a problem, but trying to avoid upsetting Grace.

Grace occasionally glanced at Minnie, attempting to read her expressions.

As time passed, they noticed the symptoms got worse.

"She's shakin' so bad," Grace cried.

Minnie figured she might as well be honest with her at this point.

"Grace, I'm not sure what's wrong but it could be serious. You might wanna have Allen get the doctor to come check her."

Grace sat stunned, as tears began to flow.

"Am I gonna lose this one, too?"

"I hope not, Grace."

Allen walked up on the porch as Minnie met him at the door. She spoke quietly.

"Allen, you've got a little girl, but there's somethin' wrong with her. She needs to see the doctor. I think she might have meningitis."

Allen walked over to the bed and looked down as Grace sat silent, caressing Peggy's tiny little head.

"I'll go get him," said Allen, as he quickly departed.

It was getting late when the doctor arrived. He wasn't certain if it was meningitis, but after observing her for a while, he gave them little hope of her recovery. Allen paid the doctor for his visit and he left.

Grace and Minnie awoke numerous times through the night to check on Peggy, and by daylight her condition had only changed for the worse. She trembled more severely than the day before.

Allen had slept through the night, but Grace asked Minnie to wake him and send him after Dora.

After Allen left and she was alone with Minnie, Grace said, "I wonder if I caused this."

"Whatever do you mean?"

As Grace began to cry, she said, "Minnie, I heard that if you took a little turpentine, it would help you go into labor. It was only a little bit in a teaspoon. I shoulda never done it."

"Grace, that watn't enough to hurt anything. You quit frettin' about that now. It's not your fault."

Dora arrived later in the morning and Minnie explained to her that Grace felt responsible for Peggy's illness. Grace still felt brokenhearted, but less distraught as they both tried their best to comfort and assure her.

Minnie decided she would stay on for a while, and one or more of Grace's family members came nearly every day to help and give support.

And then, only twenty-four days later, baby Peggy stopped shaking as she took her last breath.

All along Grace had known in her heart that she would not survive, but that knowledge did nothing to ease the pain of losing yet another child.

Still harboring guilt of the possibility that she could have caused her death, Grace became stricken with a deep and agonizing grief beyond what she could have ever imagined.

Their steps took them numbly through the cemetery once again, to a grassy spot beside the place where Gladys lay.

Back home, day after day, she would sit in the rocker and

cry or stand by the window, staring off into the distance. And as winter approached, the shorter days gradually intensified her sadness.

When Walter and Dora came by to check on her, they realized she was deeply depressed.

"Grace," Walter said, as he sat down across from her. "You can't go on like this. If you don't soon get a hold of yourself, you're gonna be down sick."

"I can't help it," she said, through her tears. "I just can't deal with this anymore. Sometimes I wish I was back home again, like I used to be."

"I tell you what. I'll give you a piece of land if you can get that husband of yours to build a house, and you'll be closer," Walter offered.

"I'll mention it to him, Daddy" she said, weakly.

Grace just didn't have the will or energy to discuss the matter with Allen that night, but when she was feeling better the next morning, she told him of her daddy's offer.

"You said yeah, didn't you?" Allen asked.

"Not yet. I said we'd talk about it. After thinkin' about it last night, I'm not sure it's the best thing."

"Grace, if he's gonna give you some land, you take it!"

She withheld her response, concerned how Allen would manage to build a house without a steady job. Grace knew she would have to pay for most of the extras even if he cut all the lumber himself. She was also afraid there would likely be conflict between Allen and her family with his behavior and their constant advice if they moved there.

"We can finally have a house of our own. I can take timber to the saw mill and get lumber to build it myself," he pressed.

Grace deliberated throughout the day and finally decided maybe the move would be the best decision. She hoped this would help Allen regain the fortitude and confidence he had lost.

That evening, she told him they would move down there if that's what he wanted to do. They would need to go and ask her daddy to show them the plot of land where they could build.

The next day, Allen was so eager that he persuaded Grace to get ready so they could go to her parents and start planning their new home.

As Walter walked with them across the field toward the church, he said, "You can put your house anywhere from here to the field next to our house, and Bud said you can get water from his well."

Grace liked the meadow with the small pine trees that were a little closer to the church, and Allen agreed. They would be just over the road from her brother, Bud, and his wife, Grace.

As they stood there in view of both her infants' graves in the nearby cemetery of Walter's Grove Baptist Church, it was a bittersweet feeling. She felt somehow closer to them, but she also realized, even more brutally, that they were forever gone from her in this life. Grace just stood there and stared across the cemetery.

"I want the house away from the road, next to the trees," Allen continued.

"That's fine if that's what Grace wants," Walter said. "That alright with you, Grace?"

"What?" she uttered, as she turned back around. "Oh, yeah. That'll be fine, Daddy."

Her heart was still heavy, and although she continued to battle the nerve problem from all the heartache she had been through, she felt a small, new spark of life as they began to discuss plans for their new house.

The following week, Allen started cutting timber for the project.

Walter agreed to help him take timber to the sawmill so he could cut it to frame the two-room house. In the spring, everything was ready to get started.

As Allen framed the structure, occasionally someone would ask, "Why are you building it with such a low ceiling?"

"To keep Willie Ervin and Matt Corbin out of it," he groused. "They both tall and I know they got their eye on Grace."

As Allen's jealousy continued, Grace felt anxious thinking about how her family would react to Allen's occasional odd behavior. But even through her doubts and uncertainty, Grace felt content to be coming back home and close to family once again.

With help, by the middle of summer, the two-room house was finished and they moved in.

The Great Depression dragged on, and although its effects were especially troublesome for Grace, she felt it might be easier now that they no longer had a rent expense.

Allen still only managed to find part-time work, but he had also found alcohol more readily available from the local moonshiners since moving to the country.

He would soon be thirty and had retained much of his youthful appearance. But it seemed his emotional maturity had aligned itself with that as well.

His being at home more often generated friction, especially with Clyde, and it seemed that Allen's harshness became more frequent with him. The slightest of Clyde's actions would cause Allen's temper to flare, which in turn caused him to get physically abusive and strike him with anything he could get his hands on.

Grace felt trapped and helpless and too ashamed to tell her family, knowing they would cause disruption beyond what her frayed and timid nerves could stand.

When Clyde got home from school the next day, he entered the front door with a broad smile as he clutched a shiny object in his hand. He held it up with pride.

"What you got there?" Allen asked.

"It's a knife, Daddy. I traded for it today with a friend at school," Clyde boasted.

"Let me see it," Allen demanded.

"Ain't it a nice one?" Clyde stated, as he still smiled.

Allen opened it and then closed it. He slipped it in his pocket as he turned to walked away and said, "This is mine."

Clyde stood there in bewilderment. His smile slowly fading, as feelings of disbelief soon turned to inward anger.

As the weeks passed, Clyde befriended Jack Hill, his Great Aunt Allie's son, who lived just on the other side of the church beyond Ernest and Lilly Pierce's little log store. He and Clyde were both ten years old and their friendship provided an escape from the abusive hand of his father. They spent their summer days scouring the woods, looking for treasures, slaying mythical creatures in the creek and fighting evil tyrants to prevent them from taking over their territory.

By fall, Allen drank more, and would occasionally wake Clyde abruptly very early in the morning. He would beat him until the sheets were bloody, for no apparent reason that Clyde could identify.

Eventually, realizing he had to protect himself in any manner he could, Clyde would somehow wake up upon hearing his dad approach, and crawl out the window to avoid his certain fate.

Clyde's behavior at school was typically normal under the circumstances, although he displayed moments of stubbornness and at times became restless. He would attend school for a few weeks but then be absent for several days.

When he returned to class, he would have a black eye or bruises, but he would remain quiet about the truth, telling any who asked that he fell down the steps. Most people, however, somehow knew and suspected what was going on at home.

Grace's family also began to suspect Allen's mistreatment of Clyde. Walter happened to be out in the yard and saw Allen chasing Clyde through the adjacent field with a small tree limb.

"Allen, if you lay another hand on him, I'll come over there and take care of you," he yelled.

Allen backed off at Walter's warning, allowing Clyde time to escape into the nearby woods.

Later that day, Clyde slipped back into the house to pack a few things to eat and then decided to go see if Jack wanted to run away with him. Clyde told Jack that he was going to kill his dad someday if he continued beating him.

Jack was in agreement to run away, as he felt his dad was too strict on him also, so they set out to make a new life for themselves.

When Clyde did not come home that night, Grace became

very worried, and all through a sleepless night she wondered if he might have gotten hurt somewhere and couldn't get home. Allen had already assured her that he would "take care of him, but good," when he came home.

Early the next morning, Grace was about to go looking for Clyde when she heard a knock at the door. When Grace answered, Jack's mother, Allie, was there.

"Grace, have you seen Jack?"

"Didn't he come home last night either, Aunt Allie?" Grace asked.

"No. Clyde came by the house yesterday evenin' to see Jack and then they were gone."

"Well, Allen got after Clyde yesterday and he ran off into the woods. I figured he was too scared to come back home."

"If you hear from either of them, let me know," Allie said. "And I'll do the same."

Three worrisome days passed before they came dragging back home, hungry and dirty.

Allen kept his word, and Clyde, unable to avoid his wrath, eventually got another severe beating. Allen would often wait to punish Clyde when Grace was gone, now with her reproach becoming more frequent as time passed. Clyde secretly and helplessly endured the abuse when he was unable to escape in time, but he was becoming a little more effective at avoiding future encounters with his father.

Chapter 26
It's Still Money

It was time for prayer meetings to begin in the spring of 1936, and some of Walter and Dora's friends asked if they would plan a meeting at their home.

The church members had all taken turns holding the event at one another's home and most families hosted them outdoors during the warm months.

Walter and Dora agreed and set their appointed time in the summer.

When Grace came to visit, Dora made a point of inviting her and Allen, hoping it might help them with some of their problems that she was more aware of than Grace knew.

"Grace, we're havin' a prayer meetin' in a couple months. Why don't you see if you can get Allen to come?"

"I don't know if he will, Mama, but we certainly need it. I'll mention it to him."

After returning home, she brought up the matter, but he didn't seem interested. He wouldn't even remotely answer, so Grace decided not to press him until the time got closer.

When Grace visited her mother again the next day, Dora questioned whether she had asked him.

"I don't think he's interested, Mama. I think he'd be more likely to go if somebody else asked him."

"Well, maybe I could get one of the preachers to stop by sometime. We still got time," Dora assured her.

A few days before the meeting, a car pulled up. Allen was in the yard as Grace peered out the window.

It was Albert Gourley. Grace figured her mama must have sent him over and hoped Allen would agree to go.

They talked for a while, and Albert shook his hand as he left.

When Allen come inside, Grace inconspicuous asked, "Who

stopped by?"

"It was Albert Gourley. He invited me to the prayer meetin' at your mama and daddy's next week,"

"What'd you tell him?"

"Told him I'd try to come if I could."

I just hope he keeps his word, Grace thought to herself.

When the time finally arrived, Grace said, "Are you goin' to the meetin' this evenin'?"

"I got a lot to do… I don't think so."

"Allen, you told Albert you'd try to come."

"I told him I'd try. Didn't say for sure I would."

"Well, you oughta go. Mama's lookin' for you to be there."

"You just sayin' that. Your mama don't care if I'm there or not."

"She does, too," Grace insisted. "She told me so."

That seemed to have some impact. Grace reminded him of her mama's concern during the evening meal, and finally he relented and agreed to go.

The people were gathering in the side yard as Allen, Grace, and the kids began walking from their house. As they got closer, Allen noticed several younger men in the group outside. He didn't say anything until they got to the front yard and then escorted Grace into the house and said, "We're stayin' in here."

"Why?" Grace asked.

"We just are. The windows are raised and we can hear everything they say from in here. You can sit right here in this rocker."

"Hey, Allen," Dora greeted, as she came through on her way outside. "Glad you came. Y'all comin' on out?"

"No, he wants to stay in here," Grace mumbled.

"Well, that's alright. Long as you're here," she replied.

Grace sat with arms crossed, hardly hearing anything that was going on in the yard as she inwardly fumed. She knew if she dared step outside it would be an exasperating ordeal when they got home, and she knew exactly why he didn't want her out there.

Once the meeting was over, she wanted nothing more than to go home. She felt embarrassed when others asked why she didn't come outside. She rounded up Clyde and Marie and directed them out the path toward home.

"You beat all, Allen Scarlett," Grace exclaimed, as they walked back home.

"Well, was there somebody out there you wanted to see?" he asked, with mock concern.

"I'm a-gettin' tired of your old queer ways," she replied.

He didn't respond to her comments or try to rationalize his actions further.

Later that night after they had gone to bed, Allen attempted to be affectionate with Grace, but she was still angry.

"I'm tired and sleepy," she said. "I just wanna go to sleep."

He turned the other way and soon was sound asleep.

At that moment, she felt as if she wanted nothing more to do with him ever again.

Allen began to take less and less interest in the family, and Grace was beginning to suffer extreme feelings of frustration and dejection. Allen would occasionally take time to play with Marie, but still displayed his intolerance for Clyde during the rare moments they were together.

Walter and Dora were becoming concerned about Grace's rapidly deteriorating situation. Cletie was twenty-three and was still living at home, so Walter occasionally sent her to stay with Grace during the day.

Allen kept taking walks through the woods and Grace wondered why he would stay away so long. Sometimes he would come back and then leave again, carrying tools.

Soon, various men were pulling up in the drive and walking into the woods with empty quart jars. They would soon come back out with their jars full, confirming her suspicions.

"Are you makin' liquor back on daddy's land?" Grace asked.

"It's makin' us some money," he said, with a rising pitch.

"Daddy's gonna have a fit when he finds out."

"He already knows. He's been over there and seen it. He even tried a little of it."

During the next few weeks of making daily transactions,

Allen would come back to the house and test some of the spirits first hand, eventually consuming too much as Grace feared he would.

Allen slumped in his chair, thoroughly drunk, fidgeting with a matchbox until he finally got a match lit.

"I'm gonna burn this house down!" he blurted. "If there's anything you want you better get it out!"

Grace was terrified as she grabbed the kids and ran to her parents.

"He's gonna burn the house down!" she cried, as she burst through the door.

They all ran to the window facing her house and watched intently, expecting to see a blaze at any moment. Marie was crying and Grace was shaking so badly that she sat down and pulled Marie close to her. Clyde just stood quietly, leaning against the arm of the sofa.

"Grace, I don't know what to do," Dora said. "Your daddy rode off with his brother, Frank, and the boys. What happened?"

"He's been a-drinkin' that brew he made back in the woods. He says he's gonna burn up everything we got."

As they kept watching, nothing happened.

"Y'all stayin' here tonight. You ain't a-goin' back over there with him like that. It's too dangerous. Them young'uns don't need to be around that," Dora stated firmly.

When Walter came in and they informed him of the eventful evening, he promised Grace he would go back with her the next day to make sure everything was alright and set him straight.

They finally all got to sleep, and as if Grace had not already been through enough distress for one day, she was suddenly awakened by a scream which caused her to sit straight up in the darkness.

Ora's voice was heard saying, "Ruth, wake up. You're dreamin' again."

"Is she havin' those bad dreams again?" Grace asked, from the next room.

"Yeah," Ora answered. "Seems like they come more often."

"Ohhh…it was awful!" Ruth exclaimed, after recovering her wits.

"It watn't real, Ruth. You alright now. Go back to sleep," Ora told her.

The following morning, Grace and Walter walked over to check on her house and found everything as she had left it the evening before.

Allen was gone, apparently back at the still, so Grace got the children ready and off to school.

"Grace, you wanna move back to the house?" Walter asked. "He's dangerous and he ain't never gonna amount to nothin'."

"No, Daddy. I'll be alright. I imagine he just drunk too much of that stuff last night. He's probably alright now."

"Well, you come on back if you need to."

She felt she was about to collapse from nerves, and she dreaded for Allen to return, not sure what to expect.

"Where was you when I woke up this mornin'?" he asked, as he came in.

"Don't you remember anything about last night?"

"No…, not really," he answered.

"You threatened to burn down the house last night, so I went to mama's."

Allen laughed and said, "I don't remember anything 'til I woke up this mornin' and you was gone. I ain't gonna burn the house down."

"You better leave that stuff alone and get rid of that thing in the woods or you gonna wind up doin' somethin' you'll regret," she warned.

"I guess I might've had a little too much. But I can handle it."

"Well, apparently not," she scoffed.

The next day, Bessie decided to pay Allen a visit with a stern message.

"If you make any more liquor back there on my daddy's land, I'm a-callin' the sheriff down here and they'll put a stop to it. So you better get rid of that still if you know what's good for you. Daddy didn't let you move down here to make liquor."

He knew Bessie meant what she said, so he decided to get rid of it before it caused him more trouble than he had bargained for.

Grace was relieved and thankful that Bessie stepped in and faced him square on.

As time went by, Grace seemed to accept her fate with Allen. She attempted to dismiss the frustration she felt, hoping to make their marriage and life together just a little more peaceful.

By December, Grace, now thirty-three, had become nauseous nearly every morning and she was recognizing the symptoms of pregnancy once again.

As she reflected on the past, she wept, wondering how she could manage another child with a distressed marriage and the instability of her nerves.

Cletie was staying with them more often, even though at times it appeared Allen was making her uncomfortable. But Grace felt she needed her and having her there was a tremendous comfort.

Chapter 27
A Change Of Heart?

The economic depression appeared to be easing up around the first part of 1937, and everyone hoped that the difficult times would finally be turning around. There were a few jobs available that had not been there before, and talk that things might be getting better.

A pain had been developing in Allen's side for the past several days that wouldn't subside, and Grace tried to convince him to go to the doctor. It was the dead of winter, but there had been no substantial amount of snow to date. Everyone talked about how it was too cold to snow.

After the pain had gotten severe, he had no other option but to wrap up and drive himself to the doctor's office.

"Allen, are you sure you don't want somebody around here to take you?" Grace asked. "You not really able to be drivin'."

"No, I'll be fine," he insisted.

Grace assumed he must have been feeling better, figuring he had stopped somewhere on the way back because he still had not returned home later that evening.

Hearing someone call her name, Grace stepped to the door to see who it was. Arlene was coming from across the field.

"Grace, mama says somebody stopped out here lookin' for you. They came to let you know the doctor put Allen in the hospital. She says to come on out to the house for the night."

She got some things together and headed out with the kids.

"What'd they say was wrong with him?" Grace asked Dora, when she walked in.

"They said the doctor thinks it's side pleurisy, and Allen sent word he needs some bed clothes."

"Oh, my, Daddy, can you take me up there?"

"I can't go this late. He'll be alright 'til tomorrow."

"The weather might turn bad by then. What if we can't get there?" she implored.

"We'll just have to wait and see," Walter said. "I ain't a-goin' up that road today."

During the night it began to snow, and by morning it was so deep that no one was able to get out, and it was still snowing.

"What am I to do, Mama? He ain't got no bed clothes and they ain't no way to get in touch with him. He's probably wonderin' where I am."

"Grace, I'm sure he realizes you can't get there in this storm. There's nothin' to do but wait. They'll give him somethin' to wear 'til you get there."

It had snowed more than two and a half feet and was one of the biggest snows that had fallen in the past few years. It took a couple of days to even begin to melt enough to attempt the trip. By the time Grace arrived at the hospital, Allen had been there four days.

Grace was shocked when she and Walter walked into Allen's room and saw how pale he looked.

"Are you alright?" Grace asked, as she leaned over the bed.

"I don't know. Where you been?"

"I'm sorry. I couldn't get here, Allen. It snowed so much, we couldn't get the car out," Grace explained.

"Did it snow?" he asked, sounding weak and muddled.

"You didn't see it snow this week?"

"I couldn't get up. I been in the bed for days. Nobody's been here."

He appeared tired, so Grace sat down in the chair beside the bed while Walter stood at her side.

"If he dies, I'll help you raise the kids, Grace," Walter remarked.

Grace quickly turned and looked at her dad in shocked, dismayed at his remark, especially in front of Allen, although she knew in the back of her mind that when it came down to it, Walter would be the one she might have to depend on.

Grace kissed Allen on the face before they left and assured

him that she would be back.

Before she had a chance make another trip to the hospital, Allen's brother, Richard, pulled into the driveway with Allen.

"They already let you out?" Grace asked.

"Yeah, I got to doin' much better after you came up, and the doctor said I could go home, so I sent word to Richard."

After several days of resting at home, Allen recovered and decided to drive to Denton after hearing there were job openings at the Denton Chair Factory.

Grace felt more confident when he didn't return home right away, and although she was hopeful he would be hired, she still felt a little uneasy at the thought of being alone all day. So she walked over to her parents and asked Cletie to come back with her.

Later in the evening, Allen drove up to the door and strolled into the house.

"Did you get on?" Grace asked.

"Yep. Start tomorrow," he said, with a smile and a wink at Cletie.

"Now I can buy you girls somethin' pretty."

Maybe we can afford a little food now, Grace thought, and he won't be home all day.

After just a few weeks on the new job, Allen got up early on Saturday morning and informed Grace that he was going to town and would be back later. She did not think much about it, but right after lunch he returned with a new car.

"Whose car you drivin'?" Grace intently asked, as she stood at the door.

"It's mine," he boasted, with a grin.

"You traded cars?!" she asked, in disbelief.

"Yeah. I got a job now, and that ol' thing I had watn't gonna last much longer."

"Allen, why would you buy a new car when we ain't hardly been able to get by?"

"Ah, Grace, you worry too much. Hard times are 'bout over."

"Here I am pregnant and you do a thing like that!" she reprimanded.

He threw a big sigh, then opened the car door and got in, mumbling that nothin' makes her happy, and drove off.

Eventually Grace resigned herself to the fact that he made a bad decision and she might as well deal with it, figuring there was not much she could do about it, anyway.

The next day, Allen mentioned that the factory commissioned out chair-caning jobs to individuals at their homes.

"Can you bring caning jobs home for mama and the girls?" Grace asked. "They did those once."

"I can get all they want. There's a lot of 'em to be done," he replied. And since Cletie is so good to stay and help you out, I'll be more than glad to. Who's gonna help your mama with 'em?"

"Ora, Ruth, and Bessie, mostly."

"Okay, then, I'll tell 'em to fetch up some seats and canes first thing tomorrow," promised Allen.

When Grace relayed his message, they were all eager to get whatever work he could bring them.

The next day he came home with a car load of seats for them to cane, and they were all delighted to be earning extra money.

Day after day as they finished what he had brought them, Allen would take the work back to the factory, collect their money and bring more home.

On Saturday, Grace asked Cletie if she would keep an eye on Marie outside playng while she walked over to their parents.

"Allen, I'm walkin' over to see mama for a while," Grace said, as he worked on the car outside.

Ora was in the front room alone when Grace walked in, and she had an important question she hoped Ora could answer.

"Cletie seemed upset when she came over yesterday. Do you know why?"

"Well, for some reason, she wanted to stay home and when daddy told her to go on over to your house, she cried, and asked him not to send her back."

Grace stood, puzzled, trying to figure out what could have caused her to react that way.

"Why would she not want to come back?"

"I have no Idea."

"What did daddy say then?" Grace asked.

"He told Cletie if she'd go on back over there, then Allen would keep bringin' the chair bottoms to us."

Grace pondered Cletie's reaction as she made her way back home.

Marie met her mother by the edge of the yard where she was still playing.

"Mama," Marie began, "when I walked up and looked through the front door, Daddy and Cletie was layin' on a quilt right at the door."

Grace felt flushed for an instant, considering the recent circumstances, but she rationalized that surely there wasn't anything to it. She knew Allen was a little flirty with Cletie. She didn't think anything of it. And, after all, she reasoned, Cletie's my sister and didn't figure she would put up with any foolishness from him or anyone else, for that matter.

When she walked in, Allen was in the kitchen as Cletie sat by the door looking out.

Grace didn't mention what Marie had told her, but she observed their interactions throughout the day, trying to dismiss any suspicions she had.

As Cletie continued staying with Grace, Allen would often come home after work with a bag of candy for Marie and Cletie. Clyde was never allowed to have any. He was only allowed to watch as they ate it.

Grace was six months pregnant now and battling more anxiety with all the swirling hormones and emotions inside of her.

Cletie would show up most every morning to keep her company throughout the day while Allen worked.

The days were warming up now and winter had given way to spring, so when Cletie didn't show up one morning, Grace decided to walk next door to her mother's and check on her.

"Somethin's made her sick, Grace," Ora said. "She was out in the back yard throwin' up this mornin'."

"Where's she at now?" Grace asked.

"I think she went back upstairs to lay down," Dora replied. "Since you here, why don't you just stay 'til Clyde and Marie get home from school. No use in stayin' over there by yourself all day."

Cletie soon came back to stay with Grace but appeared tired in the days that followed and napped occasionally, always leaving just before Allen got home.

"Cletie, you must not be over whatever was ailin' you," Grace said.

"I guess not," she answered, quietly.

Cletie appeared to regain her energy over the next few days, but seemed more subdued than usual.

Some time later, on an early summer afternoon as she and Cletie were hanging out clothes, Grace heard a terrible scream.

"Who in the world is that screamin'?" said Grace.

As they stepped to the edge of the yard, Cletie exclaimed, "It sounds like it's comin' from over at the house."

"Run on and see," Grace urged. "I'll make my way on over there."

Grace couldn't move very fast in her condition, but Bud was in his yard across the road and also ran to find out what the commotion was about.

By the time Grace arrived, Bud had both arms locked around Ruth to restrain her and quiet her down. She finally began to calm as he held her.

"We couldn't do a thing with her," Dora explained. "She's been havin' them nightmares more often lately, and she just fell apart today. I don't know what we'd a done if Bud hadn't come. She's strong as an ox."

"She just snapped," Arlene said.

"You know she's gonna have to have some kind of help, Mama," Bud advised.

"I know, Bud," Dora cried. "Can you take her to the hospital?"

"Now that she's calmed down I'll go get my car, and we'll take her to see what the doctor thinks," Bud replied.

Cletie followed Grace back home as soon as Bud got Ruth in the car and left.

They tried to compose themselves after the excitement as they discussed Ruth's behavior.

"She's been havin' them nightmares for a long time," Cletie said. "She'd wake us all up screamin' through the night. I guess we all was just blessed with the nerves."

"And I must've got a heapin' of 'em," Grace said.

"Speakin' of nerves," Grace added, "Clyde just about worries me to death. He wanders off and don't let nobody know where he's at. Sometimes, not comin' back 'til way after dark, and it really gets Allen riled up.

"Marie," Grace began, "step outside and call Clyde to see if he's come back around here yet."

It was too late to inform anyone about Ruth when Bud returned from the hospital, so he waited until the next morning to let Grace know of Ruth's condition.

"They kept her," Bud informed them. "They said she needed to be put in an institution for a while. She has to have special treatment. Somebody needs to go fill out papers. I watn't even sure how old she is now."

"She's twenty," Arlene said.

"And here it is garden time," added Ora. "It's a good thing daddy's not plantin' as much as he's been at."

Walter, Dora and the girls were not allowed to visit Ruth just yet, so they tried to complete as many chair bottoms as they could now while the factory work was picking up.

Lately, Grace noticed Allen seemed distracted and distant. He didn't talk as much and often wandered around outside late in the evenings.

"I been thinkin'." he said, as they ate supper one evening. "Maybe we need to go to some of the prayer meetin's they havin'."

"Where's the next one gonna be?" Grace asked, wondering why he was suddenly interested in going.

"I'm not sure, but I think I'll get with Albert and find out. In fact, I think I'll go see if I can find him now."

After he finished his meal, he left to find Albert, with Grace pondering the sudden change and wondering if maybe he was finally being convicted of his ways.

When Allen returned later, he informed Grace that he was planning to accompany Albert to the next meetings that were coming up.

Grace was relieved, finally feeling a bit more optimistic and encouraged about her husband and their marriage for the first time. He seemed so sincere and humble, and at times on the verge of tears.

He arrived home that day, a little earlier from work than usual, and Cletie hadn't left yet.

"We're gonna have a prayer meetin' at my mama's next month, Grace, and I want you to go. Cletie, you can go, too, if you want."

"Okay," she replied.

In June, Grace supposed she was around nine months pregnant and was anticipating the arrival of this new baby.

Soon, Grace's labor pains had Cletie calling for their mother to come over. By evening, Grace had a beautiful little baby boy with thick, curly, black hair. She had decided months earlier on the name, Clinard.

Allen sat watching through bleary eyes as Grace held their child with a loving gaze and heartfelt smile.

Dora had not been able to spend as much time with Grace as she normally did with all the work and visits to Ruth. Ruth was improving with the treatment, and they were allowed to visit now. They were hopeful that she could soon come home.

After a few weeks, Grace felt well enough to go to the prayer meeting at Ada's and asked her mother if the kids could stay with her and the girls while they were gone.

Cletie also went along but informed them that Tura wanted her to come to her house afterward to spend the night.

Tura was married now and lived on Summey Town Road in Randolph County in a little house her husband had built for them.

When they arrived at Ada's, Allen and Grace got out, but Cletie said she didn't feel good and remained in the car. Everyone kept looking out at the car, wondering why she didn't get out.

"Why didn't your sister come in?" Ada asked.

"I think she's feeling poorly and decided to stay out there," Grace replied.

The meeting started and after Albert had spoken for a while, Grace glanced toward Allen and realized he was crying. She was moved by his sudden humbleness and tears, but she still pondered his unusual behavior to herself as he continued to cry throughout the whole service.

On the way home, Allen asked Grace if she wanted to get out at home and get the kids to bed while he took Cletie to Tura's house.

He returned shortly afterward and explained to Grace that he was not working at the chair factory any longer and presented her with a request.

"Grace, why don't we just leave from around here and go where nobody knows where we are?"

"You want me to just up and leave my whole family?" she asked, puzzled.

"Why would you want to leave now with the prayer meetings and especially with a new baby? And, why ain't you workin' at the chair factory anymore?"

He did not give her an answer.

Now, she began to worry. Why would he want to move away just when things seemed to be getting better for them?

It was Friday morning. Allen got up early and started getting a few of his things together.

"What are you doin'?" Grace asked, groggily, as she sat up in the bed.

"I'm goin' off for a few days to see if I can find work," he answered, without looking directly at her.

As she got up, she asked, "Can't you find work somewhere close? I'm gonna be here alone at night with these children."

"I won't be gone long," he said.

"But, why don't you wait 'til Monday? You won't be able to find anything over the weekend, anyway."

"I have to go today. I can check out some places and be ready for Monday." He was to the point and his tone and demeanor told Grace his mind was made up.

He put his things in the car and started pulling out of the driveway, leaving Grace in a state of panic and fear. Cletie was the only one willing to stay with her, and she was at Tura's house with no way to let her know that she needed her.

She stood at the door watching and wringing her hands as Allen drove off. She turned around and stared at the little 1937 calendar on the wall near the door. It was the seventeenth day of September and she wondered how long he would leave her there alone.

Chapter 28
The Unthinkable

When Clyde and Marie came in from school that evening, Marie said, "Mama, daddy didn't pick me up at school today like he said he would."

"Marie, he went out of town this mornin' to see if he could find a job. He couldn't pick you up. He's already gone."

"But daddy told me to be standin' by the light pole in front of the school and he'd pick me up. I stood there 'til the bus started to leave, and Ora told me to come and get on."

"Well, go on and change out of your school clothes," Grace said. She pondered what Marie had just told her, but thought maybe she had misunderstood her dad.

Marie opened the dresser drawer to get out her play clothes but found something else.

"Mama, whose pocketbook is this?" she said, holding it up as she walked in the kitchen.

"Where'd you get that?" Grace asked.

"It was in the dresser drawer," she replied.

Grace walked over to look and began to feel faint, shocked at what she saw.

"Whose pocketbook is it, Mama?" Marie asked again.

Barely audible, Grace said, "It's your grandmaw's."

She looked inside and all the money she knew her mother had put back from her caning work was gone.

She now had the dreaded task of returning it to her mother with the humiliation of admitting that the only possible person responsible was Allen.

Walter had repeatedly voiced his disapproval of him, and Grace was not looking forward to his reaction.

Hurt and humiliated, she got up the courage to go over and face them.

Luckily, Walter was not at home when she arrived.

Feeling ashamed and dejected, she humbly handed the pocketbook to her mother with a tearful apology, trying to make amends for what Allen had done.

"Oh, my," was all Dora could say, as she attempted to console Grace.

"Where'd you find mama's pocketbook?" Maggie asked, upon entering the room. "We've all been lookin' everwhere for that today."

Noticing Grace's tears and her mother's expression, she asked, "What's wrong?"

They both were silent for a moment before Dora answered.

"Grace found it in her dresser drawer."

Bessie walked in upon hearing their conversation and asked, "How'd it get there?"

"Grace thinks Allen must've took it," Dora said, as Grace turned her face away.

A frenzy of accusations, questions, and intense ranting from all her sisters ensued until Grace felt she could take no more. She informed Dora she was going home, but stopped at the door for a moment.

"Mama, when's Cletie comin' back home?"

"I'll have somebody go to Tura's tomorrow and see why they ain't brought her home yet."

Grace left dejected and still in disbelief that Allen would do such a thing. She wondered if he took it for gas money to go looking for work. Why didn't he just ask, she wondered. She was also terribly uneasy now, with the house being so close to the woods, and she wondered why Tura and her husband, Lewis, had not brought Cletie back before now.

Bessie had been able to buy a car after going to work and had eventually moved back home after working at the mill, so Dora asked her to drive her to Tura's the next day to pick up Cletie. They stopped to see if Grace and the children would like to ride along, mainly just to get her out of the house after all the distress she had endured.

Tura smiled as they walked in.

"Well, hey, Mama. What brings y'all down this way?"

"We just came to see why Cletie ain't come home. Where's she at?"

Tura's smile turned to surprise and shock just as her husband, Lewis, walked in and joined the group.

"Allen didn't bring her home?" Tura asked.

They all appeared puzzled as they just stared at her.

"No!" Dora said. "When did he come and get her?"

"He came and picked her up yesterday mornin'. He said you and daddy sent him to get her and bring her home."

Grace suddenly turned pale as her heart sank. She was speechless as she tried to absorb what she had just heard, and now began to recall all the recent odd events at home. She was feeling only disbelief and dread, not quite knowing how to react at this point.

"What's he done with her?!" Bessie howled.

Everyone just stood there dumbfounded, staring at each other not sure what to think, trying to figure out what could possibly be going on.

Dora unsteadily sat down on the edge of the couch as she began to feel faint, and then finally said, "Where could they have possibly gone?"

"Grace, where's Allen?" Lewis and Tura asked.

"I don't know," Grace answered, as tears streamed down her face.

Her voice broke as she continued, "He said he was goin' to be gone for a few days to find a job. Why would Cletie go with him?"

"I don't know," Tura said. "I thought it was odd that he'd pull up in front of the house a couple days ago. Cletie stood out there and talked to him for a long time and when she came back in, she said she had left her pocketbook at home and had asked him to bring it back to her."

Clyde came through the front door as they were about to leave.

"Just let Clyde stay with us tonight, Grace," Lewis said. "You got enough to deal with at home."

Grace was too distraught to answer, but raised her head enough to nod.

"Where's your shoes, boy?" Lewis asked.

"Ain't got none," Clyde answered. "They tore up."

Grace, Dora, and Bessie rushed out the door and back home with the hope that Cletie would be there.

When they realized she was not there, Dora explained the present crisis to Walter, and all the fuming sisters became increasingly vocal.

"God help this world!" Maggie exclaimed. "That's a scandal and disgrace!"

Dora sat quietly as Walter's and the girls' ranting became increasingly louder.

Marie was already crying and Grace knew she needed to get her home as they both were very upset.

"Let's go Marie," Grace instructed, as she picked up Clinard to leave.

"Grace, don't go home," Dora pleaded. "You don't need to be out there by yourself. Stay here tonight."

"Mama, I gotta go and try to sort this all out."

She proceeded through the side door onto the porch and down the steps.

She was absolutely numb as she walked toward home, feeling as if she were in some horrible dream. She didn't feel she could take another step without collapsing, but realized she had to get her children home.

Bud was sitting out on his porch as Grace neared his driveway, and she knew she had to talk to him before going on home.

He could tell by the expression on her face that something was terribly wrong. As he met her in the yard, Grace broke down in tears again as she told him the news, and then, one by one, the rest of her family began to show up.

Marie was still upset and frightened by the uproar when they got to Bud's house. She slipped into their kitchen and crawled under the table and cried as Arlene followed, poking and hitting her with a stick, trying to get her out, not fully understanding Marie's sadness.

All of the adults present tried to comfort Grace as she started to leave. She just wanted to go home, put the children to bed, and grieve alone, but her family followed her there and would not leave until they were assured that she was alright.

Ordinarily, she would have welcomed their company, but right now she knew pretense was the only recourse if they were ever to go home. She bravely put up a front, although her heart felt torn apart and her head pounded.

The sun was beginning to set, so finally Dora and the girls hugged her and reluctantly said goodbye.

Grace put the kids to bed and soon they were asleep.

She now sat in the dark silence and cried as she rocked her sleeping baby.

What do I do now? Why would he not think about his own children, especially a new three-month-old baby? How could he do this? With my own sister! And what would possess her to leave with him that way?

So many questions flooded her mind and she longed for answers.

Oblivious to how long she had sat or what hour it was, Clinard's cry jolted her to her senses sometime later that night. Aware that he needed caring for, she got out of the rocker, fed him, and put him to bed.

She was still sitting in the rocker as the sun rose the next morning, with swollen eyes, deprived of any sleep throughout the night.

Later in the day, Tura and Lewis brought Clyde home.

"Look, Mama," Clyde said. "Lewis took me to Yates Store and bought me a new pair of shoes."

"Those are nice," Grace quietly responded. "You didn't have to do that, Lewis."

"Now, don't you think nothin' of it," he replied. "Anyway, the boy needed some new shoes."

They were aware of her anguish and were quite concerned for

Grace.

"Let us take Clyde back home with us for a few days, Grace," Tura offered.

As they were about to leave, Bessie stopped in to check on Grace.

"Daddy's gone to take out a warrant on Allen for stealin' mama's money," Bessie said. "They'll fix him for what he's done."

That added even more to her grief. Now alone with Marie and little Clinard, Grace became so despondent that she just sat in the rocker for days, staring into space. All hope and courage seemed to dwindle with each passing hour as she ignored the children. Her family came throughout the day to help feed and care for them. Her depression was overpowering and all consuming. She had virtually given up.

At Dora's beckoning, Walter took Grace to Dr. Hubbard's house in Farmer.

When they returned, Walter and Dora insisted she and the children stay with them a few days while she took the nerve medications the doctor had given her.

Gradually, Grace began to come out of the deepest part of her depression, and knew that Clyde, Marie, and Clinard needed to be home. Even though she felt uncomfortable going back to a house next to the woods where she would be alone with the kids, she was determined to try to make their life as normal as she possibly could.

Dora noticed her hesitation and asked, "Grace, you gonna be alright?"

"Mama, I'm scared back where the house is. But I know I gotta go back."

Walter heard her comment and said, "Grace, we can move that house, it's not that big, and it wouldn't be that much trouble."

"Could it be moved to the road in front of Bud's?" she asked.

"If that's where you want it."

Soon, Walter recruited his boys and a few other men to move the house where Grace felt more comfortable.

She watched as they used logs to roll the house, pulled by

horses, right to the spot she had requested.

She was once again returning to the routine of waking Marie and getting her ready for school, although she was still not always sleeping through the night. But now, it was a problem getting Clyde to go to school. He would go occasionally, but most of the time he stayed home and wandered around the neighborhood. Grace knew an eleven-year-old boy should be in school, but she just did not have the heart or the will to discipline him after the way he had been treated by Allen. Clyde realized this and was glad there was now no one to apply the discipline.

She woke him to see if he wanted to go with her next door to her parents, but he just wanted to sleep.

As soon as Marie was on the bus, she bundled Clinard in a warm blanket and headed out to see if her family had heard anything from Cletie.

She still felt so mentally exhausted and just wanted some rest. Maybe her mama would look after Clinard just long enough for her to close her eyes for a while without worrying about her children being unattended.

Once she was there, Dora instructed everyone to be quiet when Grace finally laid down to nap.

Weary beyond words, she slept much longer than she had intended.

When she awoke, Grace said, "I'm sorry I left you to mind Clinard so long, Mama."

"You never mind now. He was no trouble at all," Dora assured.

"I need to get back and check on Clyde. And besides, Marie will be home in a while," Grace said.

"What does Clyde think about all this?" Dora asked.

"He don't mention it, Mama. He tries to act grown up. I guess it's because of the way he's been treated."

"Well, if y'all need anything, Grace, just come on back."

"Thank you, Mama."

When Grace and Clinard got home, Clyde was nowhere in sight. She wondered where he could be and hoped he was not into anything bad, but she didn't have the energy to fret over it.

She examined the food supply as she began to fix the children something to eat from what was left. There was not enough food to last long and she wondered what they would do if Allen did not come home soon. It was a sobering reality to face. Even though she heard it was now only a recession, it didn't help them much without some kind of income.

She fixed a meager meal, trying to ration what she had, just in case.

Marie arrived home hungry, and apparently Clyde was also, as he came walking up in time to sit down and eat. Grace did not have much of an appetite and only nibbled while she prepared supper so as to allow more for them.

Clyde and Marie finished and then Clyde headed out to the woods again while Marie played dress-up with a few old garments her mother had.

As the next week passed, there was still no word, and Grace was wondering if Allen and Cletie would ever return.

There were days and nights of loneliness and despair as she wondered how she would ever make it and if the whole situation could have been avoided.

She often sat in the rocker with a hundred thoughts running through her mind: How did this happen? And now, how do I find faith during a trial like this, and when did I ever get so far away from it? If only I had left with Allen when he wanted, none of this would have happened.

As she stood at the window reflecting on all these things, she saw the mailman stop. She slipped her coat on and walked down the driveway to her mailbox through the chilly fall wind. She pulled out a single envelope with a car dealership's return address from High Point. She could not imagine what it was as she hurried back to the warmth of her house.

Once inside, she tore open the envelope and began to read:

Dear Mrs. Scarlett,

An automobile that Mr. Allen Scarlett purchased from us
has recently been returned to our lot informing us that
he no longer wishes to continue the scheduled payments.
We are sending this letter as a special offer, allowing you
to continue making the current payments if you so desire
to keep the car or, the payments can be adjusted to fit
a more affordable amount for you. Please contact us or
come by our lot to see if we can help you in this matter.

Sincerely,
Mr. Paul Strickland, Owner

She re-read the letter and then stared at it for a moment with
a surge of anger as she wondered where they could possibly be at
that very moment.

She bundled Clinard and took the letter across the road to
show it to Bud.

"So, he took his car back to where he got it. How on earth are
they gettin' about?" he asked, after reading it.

"Beats me," Grace answered. "They gotta have somebody a
haulin' 'em around."

"What're you gonna do?" asked Bud.

"Not much I can do. I don't have a license, and I sure don't
have money to pay for a car."

As a light rain began to fall, Grace headed back to her house.

When Clyde and Marie got home from school, they had supper and then sat in the room as it continued to rain.

It began to rain hard and Clyde could not go outside as he
normally did, so he and Marie were forced to spend an evening of
ever-swelling tension that Grace patiently tried to endure.

They began to quarrel, and it quickly escalated as they moved
to the kitchen, with Marie grabbing the broom to ward off Clyde's
taunting advances. He grabbed the handle, creating a screaming

tug of war.

Finally, Grace could take no more.

"I wish that dern Allen Scarlett had the both of you," she loudly bellowed.

It was a rare occasion for Grace to become belligerent with them, so the boisterous statement took them both by surprise; so much so, they immediately settled down and became quiet for the rest of the evening.

Once they had gone to bed, Grace sat listening in the silence of the room, with nothing but the sound of rain falling on the tin roof. She sensed a deep, heavy sadness as tears rolled down her cheeks, and she felt more alone than she ever had in her life. With the promise of happier times quickly fading away, she wondered if her heart would ever mend or be at peace again.

Just days later, another letter arrived. The return address was from Stonewall Jackson Training School.

"What on earth?" Grace exclaimed aloud.

As she opened it and began reading, she felt weak and started to tremble.

Mr. Allen Scarlett,

Your recent application request for Clyde Scarlett, age 11, has been reviewed and approved. He has been scheduled for admittance into our training school and will be picked up and transported by our agency truant officer on Tuesday, October 12th, 1937. Listed below are items he will need to have packed for his stay when the officer arrives. You may contact us sooner if issues with your son become urgent.

Headmaster of Stonewall Jackson Training School

She felt flushed as fear gripped her heart. Her mind raced. What would happen to Clyde? What action should she take? For a few seconds she couldn't breathe. How could Allen do such a thing to his own son, and what else had he possibly done that she did not know about?

She picked up Clinard and ran to Bud's house.

Seeing him at the barn in the back, she called and he met her halfway through the back yard.

She was breathless as she presented the letter for him to read.

He stared at the paper for a few minutes and then said, "I think you need to write a letter explainin' what's happened and ask 'em not to go through with it. Surely they'd understand and cancel it, bein' you didn't know anything about this and with Allen bein' gone. You've only got two weeks to do somethin'," Bud explained.

She went straight home, wrote the letter as Bud had suggested, and mailed it the next day.

She anxiously waited throughout the next week for a return letter.

When she thought it would not ever arrive, it finally came. It was not what she wanted to hear. They had declined her request and informed her that Allen had applied and signed the forms and he would be the one required to reverse it. They were still picking him up on the date originally scheduled.

Grace again felt desperate, knowing the situation was urgent. She moved as fast as she could, with baby in arms, back to Bud's.

She was out of breath and tears had begun to stream down her face.

"They're pickin' Clyde up anyway. Here, read this," she panted.

With a concerned expression, he looked over at her and said, "This is not good. I'm not sure if there's anything you can do to stop this, but let's go talk to daddy. Maybe he'll have an idea."

Panic stricken and with a lump in her throat, Bud accompanied Grace out to see their parents.

After Walter studied the paper, he said, "If I ever get a hold of that sorry rascal, by jacks, he'll be sorry he ever knew me. You mark my word."

"Daddy, do you think anything can be done to stop this?" Bud asked. "She's only got about a week before they come to get him."

"You might have to go to the courthouse and ask to speak to a judge. Just explain what that poor excuse of a man did before he left," Walter replied. "And I'd go tomorrow mornin' if I were you."

Grace felt horrified at the thoughts of having to go to a court house and confront a judge, but the fear of losing Clyde was greater than any other fear she had. She had to do it, or he could be taken away for an undetermined period of time. The training school was a place that she had only heard horrible rumors about and certainly didn't want her son to wind up there, whether they were true or not.

"Bud, I hate to ask you with all you got to do, but is there any way you could take me?"

"I'll take you. This needs to be taken care of now," Bud said.

"Any word from Cletie?" Grace asked, as she shivered.

"Not a word," Walter said. "You need to get in out of the chill."

Grace went back home and tried to mentally prepare herself for the next day.

As she left with Bud the next morning, she felt more dread than she could ever remember. But, Bud was there for moral support as she pleaded her case to the judge, actually with more courage than she realized she possessed.

The judge was very compassionate, and being visibly appalled at Allen's actions, he assured her that he would file an injunction with the school, considering her present situation.

She sensed some relief, but she was still concerned that it may not have been addressed in time.

Each day she anxiously rushed to the mailbox looking for the letter. The week was about over and the school's truant officer was to come for Clyde on Tuesday.

By the weekend, the news she desperately sought had not

arrived.

Grace went to church with the family and prayed for intervention. But once she left, her imagination took over as she began to feel sick with worry throughout the evening.

Monday, as the mailman stopped and then pulled off, she thought, I can hardly bear to go look.

Please, God, let the letter be there. If it's not, it might be too late, she prayed.

She hesitated when she got to the mailbox as her doubts returned.

Even if it's in there, it might not be what we want to hear, she thought.

She held her breath as she opened the door and reached in for the two envelopes that lay there. She could hardly see the first one, as a combination of the wind and her anxiety caused her eyes to water, but she could tell it was not the one she was looking for.

As she shuffled it under the other, the next one was addressed to Grace Scarlett from Stonewall Jackson Training School.

She quickly ripped it open and read it, exhaling with a huge sigh of relief.

A smile spread across her entire face as she rejoiced to herself and ran ecstatically to let everyone know that the judge had blocked the order.

Chapter 29
The Confrontation

With such a great relief among Grace and her whole family, the ordeal had temporarily diverted her attention from her own grief while concentrating on Clyde's dilemma.

The hurt and betrayal her husband and sister had inflicted suddenly returned, but she realized if they never came back, she still had to go on.

She wondered how she would ever trust him again, and how could she ever forgive her sister for what she had done.

It had been almost three months since Allen and Cletie had left on September 17th, with still no word from either of them.

But, God had just answered one prayer, and Grace knew He would also answer more if she only asked. Her children were even more important to her now and she would try, with God's help, to raise them the best she could. She had drifted away from Him through the years, but she desperately desired to come back. The road ahead would be difficult, and it would take time to sort out her life.

After the evening meal, Grace wrapped up the children and walked out to Walter and Dora's for a while before dark.

"Grace," Dora began, "your daddy got a letter from your sister Emma today."

"What did she say?"

"She wrote to say that Cletie was at her house. She said Allen's brother, Richard, brought her there along with Allen. They let her out of the car and then they left."

Grace sat silently for a moment. It seemed that just the mention of their names would trigger depression and anger at the same time.

"He just left again. And he didn't even come to check on us. Seems that Emma would have just come up and told you since they just live in Farmer," Grace reasoned. Farmer was only a few miles away.

After a pause, and a lump in her throat, Grace asked, "What's daddy gonna do?"

"He says she can't come back here. He talked to Bud today and Bud's gonna go down to Emma's and maybe we'll have some answers then," Dora said.

"Well, she better have some answers, 'cause I got a-plenty to ask her," declared Grace.

Grace returned home, and the rest of the evening was spent planning what she would say to Cletie once they were face to face. Emma's letter about Cletie renewed the anger and hurt she felt that her own sister would leave with her husband and stay gone for three months. She could not imagine what would ever possess her to do such a thing.

Sleep would not come easily in the dark room with all the thoughts crowding her mind. She was not sure what time she drifted off, but she suddenly awoke early the next morning, trembling.

She had decided how she would handle it, and when Cletie eventually returned home, she would then go take care of matters.

"Clyde, I need you and Marie to watch Clinard for just a few minutes while I run up to Bud's. I'll be right back," Grace said.

As she started out the door, she saw Bud coming across the road toward her house. She met him halfway, noticing the hesitant look in his face.

"Did you talk to Cletie yesterday?" Grace asked.

"I talked to her," Bud said. "Grace, I don't want you to be upset with me, but she came home with me last night. She's up at the house."

Grace stood there somberly without speaking. She had always felt Bud's home was a safe haven whenever she needed someone to confide in. And now, Cletie had taken that away as well.

"Daddy wouldn't let her come home, and she couldn't stay on with Emma, so when she asked to come back with me, I couldn't say no."

"I'm not blamin' you, Bud. I just won't be visitin' as long as she's there. I've decided how I'm gonna handle this, but I'd never cause any trouble at your house," Grace assured him.

Grace went back to her house, but it seemed her attention was constantly drawn across the road day after day, wondering when Cletie would finally come out. But she never did, and stayed hidden away for weeks.

It had been nearly three months when Bud came and told her that their daddy had finally let Cletie come home.

Grace didn't hesitate. With a baby in her arms and Marie trying to keep up, she marched straight to her mama and daddy's house to confront her.

As she walked around the corner of the house to the side door, she found Cletie ambling through the yard, seemingly in deep thought. Cletie had an alarmed look as Grace strode up to her with a raised hand to strike her while holding her baby in the other. Marie was frightened beyond words.

Cletie jumped back, avoiding contact as Grace kept coming after her. Cletie stopped for a moment as if to stand up to Grace, but Grace was relentless. Cletie backed off and started toward the back door of the house as Grace spoke her peace.

"I don't know how you could do such a thing!" Grace exclaimed, out of breath. "I will give you a whuppin' before I leave here."

Cletie disappeared through the door as Grace followed. When she stepped inside, Cletie was nowhere to be found. Walter and Dora came through the dining room as Grace demanded, "Where'd Cletie go?!"

"She just went upstairs," Dora answered.

Grace walked to the foot of the stairs and addressed her.

"Cletie, you might as well come on out, 'cause you gonna get a whuppin.'"

"Now, Grace," Walter interrupted. "You need to just leave her be right now."

"Daddy, she's ruined my marriage and she needs to answer

for what she's done. She needs a good whuppin' and I intend to give her one."

"I said my peace now. You need to go on back home," Walter insisted.

Grace just stood there in disbelief. Perceiving her own family to take Cletie's side, she felt betrayed and abandoned.

Then she turned and walked out the door with her children, following the worn path through the yard and toward home as tears began to flow. And, yet again, she was overwhelmed with a heart that felt empty and crushed. She was not sure when she would ever feel comfortable enough to go back and visit again.

The next day, Grace heard someone at the door.

"Grace, you in there?"

She looked out and saw it was her mother.

"Come on in, Mama."

Grace was folding clothes as her mother entered. She was still hurt by the words her father had spoken the day before, and it was difficult to look her mother in the eyes.

"Sit down, Mama, and I'll be through here in a minute."

"Grace, honey. I'm sorry if what happened yesterday caused you more heartache. We don't agree with what Cletie done. We know it was wrong, but she's still our young'un no matter what she's done. We know you a-hurtin', but there'll be time for reckonin' later. Right now, let's just wait 'til things settle down a bit and we find out what happened."

"I know what happened, Mama. She took off with my husband and ruined my marriage."

"Well, Grace, she'll have to answer for that and ask your forgiveness someday. And you'll have to forgive her, eventually. She's your sister."

Grace knew she was right, but she was not ready to forgive until she could get through the deep-seated hurt and anger that was still burning in her heart.

As Dora sat there, they began to talk about the situation, eventually getting to the subject of the pocketbook.

"I guess he took my pocketbook by mistake," Dora said, hoping to ease some of the pain Grace was feeling. "Cletie said she sent Allen up here to get hers. She said he thought he was taking hers, but he got mine instead."

"That don't matter, Mama. He still took it and never brought it back. And that money is still gone."

Even if her mother's purse was taken by mistake, it did not lessen Grace's resentment toward either one of them, but the talk with her mother helped to soothe her heart if only for a moment.

In the days to follow, Walter, Dora, and all of Grace's sisters except Cletie would come to visit. And eventually, Cletie showed up with them.

Cletie could not look Grace in the eyes at first, and Grace did not offer any gestures of welcome. With such animosity toward her, Grace decided to get out of the house for sanity's sake.

"Do y'all mind if I walk up to Bud's? I need to see him about somethin'. Clinard should sleep 'til I get back."

"Oh, we'll look after him while you're gone," they all said.

When Grace got to Bud's house, she walked in and stated to him and his wife that Cletie had shown up, and she did not feel she could endure her presence at that moment.

After talking awhile, Bud excused himself to go out to the pasture and take care of some matters.

Meanwhile, Bud's wife took Grace to a dresser in the next room and gathered some baby clothes that her own little boy had outgrown.

"I hear a bangin' noise somewhere," Grace said. "Is that Bud?"

"It might be. He's probably puttin' wood on the porch," his wife answered.

When they finally came through the house, they heard Bud step onto the porch and then walk in with a box, handing it to Grace.

"What's this?"

"It was on the porch by the door. The note says it's from Alma Scarlett."

"Oh, my," Grace said, regretfully. "I bet that was her we heard knockin'. We thought it was you. I sure hate I missed her."

When Grace returned home, they all said, "Allen's sister, Alma, came by while you was gone. We told her you was at Bud's house."

"You don't need nobody from that ol' Allen Scarlett's family a-comin' around," one of the girls scoffed.

"She was just tryin' to be nice," Grace responded. "She brought these little white slippers for Clinard. She can't help what nobody else does, no more than we can."

Over the next few months, Grace tried to adapt to the routine of managing her children alone and all the affairs concerning their simple two-room home, although it had become a struggle just to provide food.

Her mama and daddy gave her some flour and a few canned items, but she realized the only way to survive without being totally dependent on them would be to find work.

Grace started taking in laundry for people in the area using her old washboard and earning fifty cents a load, but it still could not meet all their basic needs.

One Monday evening, Bud walked to Grace's house to check on her and the children.

"Bud, it's been several months since anybody's heard even a word from Allen. I thought he would at least check on the children. Do you think somethin' bad happened to him?" Grace asked.

"Well, I don't really think so. I believe he's too scared of daddy to come back."

Since Allen had left, the passage of time was resolving much of her resentment toward him and her heart had begun to soften.

"I've been so hurt and mad at him for the way he's done, but I felt like he would eventually come back someday after everything settled down and maybe things would work out down the road. If only somebody could just find him."

"You could file a missin' person's report on him," Bud suggested. "They might could find him, but you'd have to go to the courthouse to do it."

"The next time you go to town, could I ride along and do

that?" she asked.

"We can go next week after I finish plantin' the garden."

On Tuesday of the next week, they both went to Lexington to fill out the form. Bud realized this might give her peace of mind, nevertheless he surmised Allen would never return.

After Grace explained the circumstances of her family, the clerk asked, "Mrs. Scarlett, did you know you could get help for your children with your husband being gone?"

"What kind of help are you talkin' about?"

"You can get a check for your children," he informed her.

Grace was now listening closely to the information she was hearing.

"This matter of filing a missing person report will take some time, but when it's closed out you could apply. Would you like me to look up the amount that would be allotted for three children?" he asked.

Grace was skeptical about the idea of "free money," but replied, "That would be fine."

As she stood there waiting, she felt hopeful of the help she had just been offered, but could not imagine anyone outside her family, especially a complete stranger, doing so.

"Grace, you better take anything they offer you," Bud urged.

The clerk returned and said, "Ma'am, you're eligible for fifty dollars a month. If you want to go ahead and fill out the necessary forms today, then it can be turned in when this missing person report is resolved."

"I think I will," Grace replied, as her face suddenly brightened.

On their way home, feeling hopeful for the first time in a long while, Grace began to tell Bud about Clyde's latest incident.

Clyde loved the early summer and had been hiking through the woods most of the morning. He hadn't had much to eat for breakfast and was becoming quite hungry.

He came out on a long, dirt drive where Everette Pierce lived in a house barely visible from the main road and decided to visit, thinking he might be offered some food. He walked up to the door and yelled, "Is anybody home?"

No one answered. He looked around and saw that Everette's car was gone and, after hesitating, opened the door and stuck his head inside. He looked outside once more and pondered the thought of going in to see if he might find something to eat.

"Hello?" he called again, then cautiously stepped inside after no one answered. He stepped lightly through the quiet house to the kitchen and was searching to see what he could find, unaware anyone had walked up until he heard the door open.

It was Everette. Clyde froze, clutching a piece of bread, and terrified at the thought of what Everette might do to him for entering his house without permission.

"Hey, Clyde. You fixin' yourself somethin' to eat?" he asked, smiling.

Clyde nodded his head cautiously as Everette encouraged him to carry on, aware of the family's plight at home. After they talked awhile, Clyde thanked him for the food, and Everette invited him to come back sometime and have a meal with them.

"And there's no tellin' where else he's been," Grace added, as they arrived back home. Having someone to talk to gave her a lighter feeling, a pleasant awareness she hadn't felt in a very long time.

"He needs to be careful whose house he goes in," Bud said, as he chuckled. "The next one might not be so kind."

Although there was not a large amount of bills to pay each month, Grace doubted what little she earned would be enough for food and provisions for her family. Food was scarce at home, and pride kept her from asking family for handouts, so she made do with anything she could put together.

Becoming a boy of the woods and somewhat of a hunter and scavenger at the age of twelve, Clyde brought home anything he could catch and Grace would cook it, even down to the legs of captured frogs.

Chapter 30
The Wagon Race

As Grace began feeling more confident about being alone, she decided she now wanted their little two-room house moved away from the road and back closer to the trees. She asked her dad about moving it again, so he arranged for neighbors to come and soon had it situated in its new spot.

Although concerned about leaving her children at home, Grace felt she needed to go back to work. After she found a ride, Grace went to the Dogwood Hosiery Mill in Thomasville and applied for a job. Having previous experience and also a good work record, she was hired that day and given the position of inspector. Marie was only eight, but Grace had to trust her to take on the responsibility of babysitting little two year old Clinard. Clyde was thirteen and old enough to watch after them, if only he would stay close to home and not wander about the entire countryside all day. Her relocated house was still within sight of her parents' home, so Grace's mother and sisters assured her they would help keep a watchful eye on things while she was gone.

Managing her affairs was becoming less difficult now that Grace had a steady paycheck. She was thankful that God had gotten her through the toughest part of her life and made it possible to better provide for her children.

Three years had now passed since Allen left, and although the sadness resurfaced when she dwelled on it too long, she managed to block out much of the sorrow she had endured.

Grace and her three children slept in one room until Clyde got older, and he then wanted to sleep in his own space. He considered himself grown now at age fourteen, so Grace found a small cot and placed it in the kitchen near the stove for him.

As she gradually adapted to supporting her family on her

own, she managed to occasionally buy things for her three children that had not been possible before.

As they all rode along on a trip to Thomasville with Walter, Dora, and Arlene on a crisp, fall Saturday, Grace decided to go to Effird's Department Store. Marie saw a dress that any nine-year-old girl would absolutely feel grand to own. It had caught her eye and captured her heart.

It was a mingled burgundy skirt and top with three-quarter-length sleeves. It had a sewn-in loose scarf in the top that draped down and bunched in front.

"Mama, look at that dress," Marie said, as she gazed at it with a most earnest desire. "That's the prettiest dress I've ever seen!"

"It is pretty," Grace replied. "But I'm afraid we don't have money for that right now. That dress cost fifteen dollars."

Marie was visibly disappointed, but to Grace it seemed foolish to pay that much for a dress when Dora and Bessie could make one at only a fraction more than the cost of fabric.

After they left and walked to another store, Grace kept thinking about the dress and noticed how disappointed Marie looked. She had a little extra money saved and put back for an emergency.

"Marie, let's go back down there and get your dress. I'm gonna go ahead an' buy it for you."

Marie couldn't get there fast enough as she ran through the door ahead of Grace and grabbed it up. She hugged it tightly with a broad smile.

Once they got home, Marie asked, "Can I wear it for a while?"

"You need to put it up and wear it for special occasions," Grace said. "That cost a lot of money. You sure don't want to mess it up."

"Can't I wear it for just a little while?"

"Well, just for a while. Mind you don't get it dirty."

She put it on and wore it all that day, and would have slept in it that night if Grace had let her.

The boys had never had much of anything to play with other than homemade things, so she checked around and found a good used bike for Clyde and a tricycle for Clinard.

They soon began riding up and down the driveway and around and around the house until Grace would call them for dinner.

"Turn them wheels," she hollered out the door. "Dinner's ready!"

As they were finishing their meal one afternoon, there was a knock. Grace stopped what she was doing and opened the front door. It was her Aunt Allie's twin sister, Maggie, for whom Grace's sister had also been named.

"Well, hey, Aunt Maggie. Come on in."

"Hey, Grace. I went over to Allie's for a while and thought I'd stop by for a minute."

Clyde, Marie, and Clinard darted out the door to play in the yard while Grace and Maggie sat down for a talk.

"How is everybody out at Walter's?" Maggie asked.

Grace began to tell her of their visit there on Saturday.

"We all walked across the field to mama and daddy's for a while. When we got there, Clyde and Arlene were out the door."

Maggie listened intently as Grace relayed the story of two kids making their way down to the edge of the woods by the pasture. Marie followed along as they discussed what games they could play. Although Arlene was their aunt, she was only four months older than Clyde.

Walter had let Clyde play on the old wagon time after time, but he always told Arlene to stay off.

"Daddy won't ever let me play on that wagon, but he ain't here, so we can play like we're from the Old West," stated Arlene, excitedly.

The three climbed up on the seat and into character as Clyde pretended to command the imaginary horses, and the lady folk rocked the wagon and laughed. After they tired of that game, Clyde had an idea.

"Hey, why don't we push the wagon up to the well house and ride it back down?"

The three agreed and pushed it up the slight grade with Clyde holding it in place until the girls got on. He had tied a rope to the wagon pole to hold it up off the ground, then he jumped on and they all rode the wagon slowly back to the place it was before.

"That hill's not steep enough," he said. "Let's push it back further and try goin' down through the field."

They all pushed and strained attempting to conquer the steeper hill.

"Push harder, Marie!" Arlene demanded.

"I'm pushin' hard as I can!"

They were exhausted when they finally got it far enough to make a faster descent, then they pointed the front wheels toward the field next to the side of the house.

"Y'all get on quick! I can't hold this thing long!" Clyde yelled.

Arlene and Marie climbed up on the back of the wagon with their legs dangling just as Clyde jumped in the seat and pulled up the wagon pole. They started to ride it down the hill in a slight arc while they all whooped and hollered.

"This is gonna be the best ride y'all ever had!" Clyde exclaimed.

The uncontrolled wagon gained a little more speed this time as the girls kicked their legs over the side of the wagon, laughing hysterically.

All of a sudden, one of the wheels hit a large clump of dirt and pitched them sideways while Arlene's leg slid straight into the wheel's spokes, catapulting her into the dirt so fast that it left her dazed and confused. Marie looked back in awe, watching Arlene appear ever smaller in the distance as Clyde rode his make-believe stage coach until it stopped, unaware of losing a passenger.

"Arlene fell off!" Marie yelled, as they both jumped down and ran back to find her now screaming in agony.

"Get up, Arlene!" Clyde persuaded.

"I can't!" she cried.

"Let me help," he offered, as he tried to pick her up, but she screamed all the more. When he noticed her leg was twisted abnormally, he realized she was injured and panicked, running off into the woods out of sheer habit.

Hearing the commotion, Dora, along with Grace, Ruth, and Ora, came out and rushed to her side to evaluate the injury as Marie looked on.

"Get up and walk, Arlene," Dora demanded.

Arlene just cried as she tried to move.

"You know your daddy told you not to be on that wagon. Now, you need to get up and walk," Dora repeated.

"I can't, Mama!" Arlene cried.

"Mama, I think her leg's broke," Ora said.

After her coaxing failed, Dora came to the conclusion that she might be right.

Clyde finally came out of the woods and sheepishly returned to the scene of the accident, figuring he would be blamed for what happened.

"Clyde, run over to Corbet's and ask him to come over here," Dora said. "Walter's gone over to visit Bob and Janie and I don't know when he'll be back. We gotta get her to the doctor somehow."

While they were waiting, Walter arrived home to find everyone down in the field with Arlene.

"What's goin' on down there?" he hollered.

"Arlene was ridin' on the wagon with Clyde and her leg caught in the wheel. I think it's broke," Dora replied.

As they attempted to pick her up to move her to the house, Walter started whipping her with his hand as she screamed in pain.

"I told you to stay off that wagon, now, didn't I?" he scolded, as he struck her with every word he spoke. Ora and Ruth backed away and just looked at each other in disbelief.

When Corbet arrived, it was difficult to get her in the car but they finally maneuvered her in through crys of agony and drove off to the hospital.

"Well, I'll say!" Maggie exclaimed, when Grace finished telling the story.

"After all that excitement, Clyde and Marie was more than ready to get back home where it was quiet," said Grace, as she chuckled.

Chapter 31
The Rabbit Hunt

While the healing of old wounds inflicted upon the whole family was a gradual process, it also took a lot of soul searching. Grace had now relented to forgive Cletie for the heartache she had caused, even though Cletie had not yet formally asked her forgiveness. Grace was determined to get along for the family's sake.

As Grace searched and strived for peace, at times there still just seemed to be something missing within her. She knew she hadn't relied on her faith as she once had as a young woman living at home with her family, and she prayed for strength to strive harder and reclaim the faith she once knew.

Sometimes, that faith was tested.

Clyde was becoming even more independent as a teen and wanted to do things the older boys did.

Grace was visiting her mother and dad when Clyde walked up the driveway with Fred Klass, each carrying a bundle of clothes across their shoulders. Clyde called through the screen door for Grace when he got to the steps as Fred stood by the cedar tree.

Grace came to the door and stepped outside to see what he wanted.

"What are you doin' with that stuff, Clyde?"

"Me and Fred decided to catch the train when it comes through and go see the sights," Clyde informed.

"What in the world? – Clyde! You could get hurt or even killed tryin' to jump a train!"

"Ah, Mama, I can take care of myself."

"Clyde, please don't run off like that. I'll be worried sick. I won't even know where you are."

"I'll be alright. We already packed up and Fred's waitin'. I'll be careful," he said, as he turned to leave.

As they started down the driveway, Grace shouted in dismay, "Don't you leave here. You tote yourself back up here right now!"

"I'll be alright, Mama," Clyde repeated, without looking back.

Marie had appeared at the door and heard the alarm in Grace's voice as the two boys walked out of sight. Grace then walked around the house and sat down on the ground under the apple tree. She began to cry and sat there for some time as Marie repeated, "Mama, don't cry."

"I'll never see him again," she sobbed. "Somethin'll happen to him and we'll never see him again."

"Well, don't cry, Mama."

Grace awoke throughout the night, fearful of what could happen to Clyde, and prayed if only she could be shown where he was, she would go get him and bring him back home. Finally at daybreak, she got out of bed and got dressed, hoping he would have returned. Several troublesome days went by until Grace received word that Clyde was at Preacher Hopkins' house in China Grove, North Carolina. He had made it that far and then changed his mind. He told Fred he wasn't going any further. They all presumed hunger may have played a part in his decision to cut their adventure short, but Grace felt otherwise. The Hopkins' brought him home to a much-relieved mother, who was hopeful Clyde had learned something – for the present – from his short-lived experience.

Soon Fall arrived. It was a cool October day when Corbet Hill's boys who lived over the road, made plans to go hunting. Clyde had accompanied them on other occasions and wanted to go along this time.

"Mama, I'm goin' huntin' with Jay and Willie today," Clyde stated.

"That's awfully dangerous for a fourteen year old to be goin' out huntin' with a bunch of boys," Grace reminded him, as her words fell on young, invincible, and essentially deaf ears.

His cousin, Jack, had also wanted to go, but his dad made

him stay home to do chores.

When Bud's son, Raymond, now twelve, asked his dad if he could go, he was told he could not, but he slipped away anyway, against his wishes.

They had hunting dogs and guns the boys needed, and there was good hunting way back among the small hills behind Walter's Grove Baptist Chruch. They left Friday morning and entered the woods near the upper end of the church.

The walk to their favorite spot took a while as they trudged through thickets, up hills, and across a creek to a broad meadow next to a patch of trees.

Grace could occasionally hear the echo of gunfire from far across the hills, as many people hunted back in that area this time of year.

But she still felt concerned, wondering if Clyde was over there, and hoping he was safe.

Just after lunch, the door flew open as Clyde bolted into the house.

"Mama!" he said, out of breath. "Willie got shot. I gotta go get Bud."

"How did he get shot?!"

"Jay shot him, but he didn't mean to," he said, gasping.

He bent over and put his hands on his knees, trying to catch his breath before heading out the door.

"Willie's still layin' over in the woods."

Clyde raced out the door with Grace, Marie, and Clinard close behind, while Jay crossed the road toward Bud's house. When they got there they started yelling.

"Bud! Bud! Where are you?"

"I'm out here at the barn. What is it?"

"Willie's been shot. Somebody's gotta go back there and help him."

"How'd he get shot, boys?"

"Jay accidentally shot him," Clyde exclaimed. "I was standin' with Jay, and Raymond was right beside Willie. We jumped a rabbit and Willie stood up just as Jay fired."

"Raymond?!" Bud asked. "He watn't even supposed to be gone. Where's he at now?"

"I don't know. He was runnin' toward home the last time I saw him. He was scared."

Bud called his family out to look for Raymond while he got the truck out.

"We'll help find Raymond while y'all are gone," Grace offered.

They called and called but heard no answer. They soon found him, hiding, terrified, and crouched down in the corn crib.

"Raymond, you get out of there and go on in the house," Bud ordered, as he was leaving.

"Come on, boys. Let's go over and get Jim to go with us. You can take us back there and show us where Willie's at."

They jumped in Bud's truck and took off as fast as they could. Once they picked up Jim, Jack was instructed to go down Hill Road to Albert Gurley's and have him go tell Willie's parents what happened. They headed back, trying to figure out the fastest way into the woods.

They decided the best option would be to hitch up Walter's wagon and try to drive the horse through the woods. It took some maneuvering, but they finally arrived where Willie lay. Jay had taken his coat off earlier and wrapped it around Willie's head. They all jumped off the wagon and rushed over to Willie, but one look told them nothing could be done for him. Willie was gone and Jay just stood there, grief stricken and visibly in shock.

They carried Willie's lifeless body and laid it on the wagon, as Jay and Clyde climbed on and started the dreaded, silent trip out of the woods.

Meanwhile, Jack delivered the message to Albert. After he told Albert and his mother the story, they presumed the worst as they immediately went to tell Corbet and his wife, Vellie. Realizing Corbet was not home, Albert's mother decided to tell Vellie that he had only been shot in the foot to avoid upsetting her until they received definite word.

When the men brought Willie out of the woods, they decided that Pierce's store, just on the other side of the church, would be the best location for the undertakers to find. They took him off the wagon and laid him on the back of the truck to carry him there.

When they arrived, Bud and Jim gently lifted Willie off the truck and placed him against the corner pillar of the store until the family could get there.

Reality had set in for Clyde as well, especially when Willie's mother arrived. Her lamenting and wailing was almost more than he could stand. He just wanted to go somewhere and hide to escape the anguish that engulfed his heart and mind, almost feeling nauseous when he finally headed home.

He went to bed early under Grace's sympathetic and watchful eye, and secretly desired comfort, but his young masculine toughness and pride prevented him from reaching out.

Recurring dreams of all the graphic and disturbing mental images from the day's tragedy constantly replayed in his mind through the night as he drifted in and out of sleep, at times abruptly waking in a cold sweat. And, he couldn't imagine what Jay was going through.

When he thought the night would never end, daylight came, finally easing his dark fears and mental anguish. But there was no easing the secret pain in his heart and the grief of losing a friend.

Clyde felt only dread in the following days, not knowing how to act or what to say when he and his mother rode with Bud and Raymond to visit the home where Willie's body lay in state. Jay stood somberly and undeniably troubled, leaning against the outside wall beside the front door as visitors came and went. Raymond appeared discontent as they got out of the car to go in, and Clyde wished he could just run far away to a peaceful place where the whole incident could be forgotten. But there was no place he could go to erase the recurring thoughts, and in his heart, he never wanted to see or touch a gun ever again. Intently trying to comfort him, Grace realized this would be something he would have to deal with in his own way.

As the years passed, Clyde would eventually, and cautiously, carry his rifle out for short walks alone through the woods.

231

The images of that day gradually became easier to deal with, but Clyde would never completely erase the awful memories that were forever seared in his mind.

Chapter 32
Germany Awaits

All of Walter and Dora's children, except Ora and Ruth, had now gotten married and moved away to start their own families.

Walter seemed to be spending a lot of time back in the woods himself lately, and unfamiliar visitors were beginning to come regularly.

Grace had just walked in to visit her mother when Ora came into the kitchen and asked why so many people had been coming to see her daddy.

"Mama, is daddy runnin' a still back in the woods?" Grace asked.

"I'm afraid so," Dora admitted. "I told him he oughn't to be doin' that. He's gonna get a bad name. But, he said we need the money an' it's an easy way to make it."

"I've been noticin' a lot of people comin' out here lately," Grace noted.

"And they all headin' straight to the woods," Ora added.

"I don't approve," Dora continued. "But maybe it won't last long."

The visitors continued arriving through the next few weeks as Dora and the girls kept a cautious eye toward the busy roadbed down to the spring.

After Ora finished hanging clothes out in the mid-morning sun, she happened to notice someone on the ground down near the persimmon tree by the road. It was a man, partially sitting, but slumped over on one elbow.

She took a closer look. "Oh, no," she gasped, "it's daddy."

She had her suspicions as to why he was there, so she quickly slipped into the house without her mother's knowledge and found Ruth.

"Ruth! You gotta come help me get daddy up to the house. I

think he's been in the spirits he's been a-makin down there."

They both ran to where their daddy was lying on the ground and tried to get him up.

"Daddy, get up!" they said, as they managed to get him on his knees and help him up to steady him on his feet, one on each side as they held him under each arm. His weight was almost more than they could bear as he continued to lean on one, and then the other. After finally getting him as far as the cedar tree in the side yard, Ora said, "Ruth, stay here and I'll go get mama."

Ora ran into the house and called Dora.

"What is it?" Dora asked, as she stepped into the room.

"I believe daddy's been in the liquor, and is layin' out in the yard! We found him under the persimmon tree and got him up here to the house."

"Well, he ain't comin' in the house in that condition," stated Dora.

"But, Mama. He's layin' on the ground."

"I don't care. I warned him about that stuff. He can just lay out there 'til he sobers up."

Ora went back to the cedar tree where Ruth stood guard and said, "Let's get him back there under the oak tree so at least nobody'll see him layin' out here."

After they had gotten him moved and started back to the house, Grace walked around the corner and asked, "What in the world is daddy doin' there under the tree?"

"He been drinkin' that brew he's a-sellin'." Ruth replied.

By late afternoon, Walter had slept off most of the effects while they all checked on him throughout the day. Although he was quite apologetic, it was days before Dora exonerated his actions. He went back to church and made things right, promising her to get rid of the still and never make that mistake again.

Considering all the difficulties up to now, Grace had managed to get one child grown with no major ramifications. Following him was an adolescent daughter and a seven-year-old son.

It was 1944. The world was at war and many young men were being shipped out to Germany. Grace was dreading the possibility of Clyde having to go, aware that many had lost their lives in battle as they listened to the news day after day.

Clyde had recently met a sweet girl named Mozell Byerly, who he thought was the prettiest girl around. And she thought he was the best-looking boy she had ever seen. They immediately became smitten with one another.

Now eighteen, Clyde received his examination letter from the Local Board. Left to wonder if he would be drafted soon afterward, he began visiting his new love as often as he could. Assured of being sent overseas if he passed the examination, he decided to ask Mozell to marry him, with Grace's blessings.

On November thirteenth, Clyde and Mozell went to the justice of the peace in High Point to be married, accompanied by Mozell's mother, Allie. Mozell had only turned sixteen just a month and a half earlier, so the young couple had asked her mother to sign so they could marry. Mozell's family lived in a much larger farmhouse where the newly wedded couple decided to live while Clyde awaited further notice from the government.

They had not heard anything by the first of 1945, and Mozell was hopeful that he would not be called.

Then, the letter arrived. He was to report for basic training in the U.S. Army. When they went to tell Grace, she felt distressed for them, and could tell that Mozell was heartsick and a little frightened, for they had just found out that she and Clyde were to have their first child. Wondering if he would have to be away for this very special occasion, she began to cry while Clyde and Grace attempted to console her.

"Everything will be alright, Mozell," Grace assured her.

"I don't want to leave you, honey, especially now," Clyde said. "But, I'll be fine."

"Mozell, you can stay with me some while he's gone, if you want to," Grace offered. "Between your folks and me, we'll all look after you."

"I don't want you to go," she cried. "I want you here when our baby's born."

But Clyde soon had to leave as he hugged his mother and

siblings, and then kissed his tearful wife goodbye.

He arrived in Little Rock, Arkansas, for his training, and then departed with his combat regiment to Germany by ship the first part of May. Mozell and Grace were both worried sick at the thought of him going into combat, which was, at that point, inevitable.

Then on May 8, 1945, while Clyde was still aboard ship and headed toward their destination, Grace and Mozell heard the good news. Germany had surrendered. It was an immense relief for everyone.

The ship continued on its course until it reached Germany, changing the duties and outcomes for all who arrived there.

Grace soon received an offical letter. She opened it and found a check, written to her. Clyde knew firsthand the difficulty his mother had experienced through the years and had somehow arranged for her to receive money, explaining in another letter that he wanted to help her as well.

Grace was happy to have Mozell there with her and was excited about the upcoming arrival of her very first grandchild. Mozell stayed with her parents some, but she loved spending time with Grace as well, for Grace kept her amused and her mind occupied. And, the arrangement was advantageous for both of them.

Mozell had been there a couple of days when Grace walked in the bedroom and in fun sat down heavily on the bed beside her. The force bounced Mozell up and down as Grace repeated the action a couple more times.

They were both laughing hysterically as Marie walked in and exclaimed, "Mama! Don't you know better than to do that? She's expectin'!" And they laughed all the more.

Mozell welcomed each letter and photograph she received from Clyde and treasured each one, holding them close at night, sometimes crying herself to sleep.

Her sister, Blanche, and husband, Jesse, had been in the stages of building a new house and offered the rental house where they were living to her and Clyde when they moved out. When their new house was completed, they sent word to Mozell that the house was now available, and they had even left their old furniture for her to use.

"We'll just go up there and stay with you 'til the baby's born since the time's gettin' close," Grace offered.

Mozell, Grace, and Marie left for Thomasville to wait for the much-anticipated birth. They had not been there many days before she went into labor.

"We gotta get her to the hospital," Grace insisted, understanding that very few young mothers gave birth at home anymore. Hospitals were safer, she thought, as she began to think about her own dear baby Peggy from years ago.

"I'll go next door and call a cab," Marie said.

The cab arrived and hurried off to the hospital with the expectant mother.

It was a beautiful day on the eighth of June in 1945 when Mozell gave birth to a little girl she named Glenda. Mozell longed for Clyde to be there and could hardly wait for him to get home and see his new daughter.

She began sending photographs of the baby to Clyde with notes she had written on the back. He in turn would send photographs of himself and his Army buddies to Mozell.

Finally, Clyde wrote to inform everyone that he would be coming home soon.

After what seemed like ages, he arrived home to hugs, kisses and tears.

The next day, Clyde and Mozell paid Grace a visit.

As they sat around the kitchen table, Grace asked, "What did you do while you was over there, Clyde?"

Clyde had felt fortunate to have been given the task appointed to him as he replied, "I got to drive a truck transportin' prisoners most of the time I was there. I even got to look inside Hitler's bunker. They didn't let many people do that."

Grace got up out of her chair after they had talked for a while and walked out of the room. She came back with a thick envelope and handed it to Clyde.

"What's this?" he asked, as Grace looked down at him and

smiled as if she had no clue.

He opened it and saw that it was full of money.

"What is this, Mama?" he asked, as he looked up, rather puzzled.

"It's the money you been sendin' me."

"Mama, I sent that money for you to use. I wanted you to have it."

"No, you take it on, now. You gonna need it for a place to live. Go buy you and Mozell a piece of land and build you a little house."

Clyde tried persuading her to keep it, but he finally realized she had no intentions of taking it back.

"Thank you, Mama."

"Yeah, thank you, Grace. That's awfully nice of you," Mozell reiterated, as they both stood up and gave Grace a hug.

Grace was just glad that all the worry and anxiety everyone had felt while he was a soldier was all over. She was assured they would all rest and sleep peacefully now.

Several months later, Marie made an announcement to Grace. She had become an attractive young girl at fourteen, and had begun seeing a young man she had recently met. Grace told her she was too young to be dating, but she was determined to see him. Although Marie had also been concerned about Clyde during his time overseas, her new, handsome beau, Marvin Harrison, had captured most of her attention.

"Mama, me and Marvin wanna get married."

"Marie, you know how hard we've had it. You need to think about it before you make a decision. It's a decision you'll have to live with. You're too young."

"I've already made up my mind and we gonna get married," Marie stated.

"Well, I ain't a-gonna sign for you," Grace said.

Marie then decided to acquire the necessary form for the marriage license. She filled it out, stated she was eighteen years of age, and signed it herself.

Marvin asked his dad to go with them to Chesterfield, South Carolina, and on February fifteenth, 1946, they were married.

Marvin's parents invited the newly married couple to move in with them until they could find a place of their own. Grace had reservations about the idea of marriage all along, but she accepted that Marie would now make her own decisions.

They were still the happy honeymooning couple a year later on February fourth, 1947, with the announcement to Grace of a new grandson. Marvin and Marie named their first child Jerry.

Grace and Clinard were now the only ones left at home. The next two years left Grace often wondering how the time could have slipped by so fast, with Clinard quickly growing up and becoming the man of the house. He wasn't yet a teenager, but he took on a more assertive role, being the only one left for the devoted attention of his mother.

Clinard was at school one afternoon when Grace was at home and heard someone urgently calling her. She rushed to the door to see Ora running across the field.

"Grace! Somethin's happened to mama. I think she's had a stroke."

As Ora neared the house, she could hardly get the words out. "We're gonna have to take her to the hospital. Come on if you wanna go."

"Just let me leave Clinard a note so he'll know where I am when he gets home from school," Grace said.

She hurriedly scribbled on a piece of paper and ran out the door. Ora and Grace arrived at the house in an instant.

"Mama! What's wrong?" Grace asked.

Dora's eyes were open wide, but she didn't speak as she glanced at one person and then another, appearing confused.

"Help me get her in the car," said Ora.

They all lifted and carried her to the car, propping her in the backseat with pillows, as Ora sped out of the driveway toward town.

When they reached the hospital, Ruth got out first and rushed inside to alert the staff of their emergency. They immediately rolled a bed outside and lifted Dora onto it to take her inside. Ora parked the car while Walter and the whole family followed Dora as far as the waiting room.

They sat there in tears, wringing their hands for what seemed an eternity before the doctor came out.

"Grubb family?" he asked.

"That's us," Ora said. "How is she?"

"Is she alright?" they all started asking at once.

"Your mother has had a stroke, and…"

Immediately, they all burst into tears and began to wail before he could finish. They had the whole room in an uproar.

"Please calm down," he pleaded. "It was a bad one, but I think she will survive. She is paralyzed on her right side and can't speak. The next couple of days will be crucial, and then we'll know what damage has been done. If it's not too bad, with therapy, I feel that she should regain her speech."

He wasn't sure if they heard everything he said, and noticing Grace seemed to be the calm one, asked her to step to the side. Ora followed and he explained everything to them.

"Can one of us stay here tonight?" Ora tearfully asked.

"Yes, I think that would be fine," he answered.

"Well, I'm gonna take everbody home and then I'm comin' back," she informed them.

Grace was troubled about her mother's condition and didn't want to leave, but someone had to see about Clinard. They had been at the hospital for several hours, and she was sure he had been home from school for some time. She was relieved to find Clinard at home safe, but hungry.

Grace lay awake in her bed that night, wondering about her mother's condition and if she would recover. When daylight returned, she quickly arose, got breakfast ready, and then saw Clinard off to school. She knew someone else in the family would be going to the hospital early.

Day after day they made the trip to sit with Dora and give their support. She seemed to be stabilizing as she was trying to speak, and had begun eating small amounts of food throughout the day.

After a couple of weeks at the hospital, the doctor walked in with news.

"I believe she's well enough to be moved to a facility where they can give her the therapy she needs. I don't think she will ever be able to walk again and she has no use of her right hand, but she can learn to use what resources she has."

"How long will she have to stay there?" they all asked.

"I'm not sure. We'll just have to see what kind of progress she makes."

Dora was soon moved to the facility and regained her speech more quickly as the family visits continued. After months of therapy, she was finally ready to return home. Dora was smiling from ear to ear, knowing she would soon be sleeping in her own bed and back home with Walter and her family. She had been extremely patient throughout the whole ordeal, and before she left, the staff all commended her on what a pleasure she had been during her stay.

Once back home, Dora was soon resigned to her spot on the end of the sofa near the kitchen doorway. With a tissue in her hand, she sat there day after day, appearing content and receptive as her family brought her meals, water, and other necessities.

Occupied with her mother's illness, Grace had temporarily forgotten her own troublesome feelings. As she felt more confident about her mother's condition, she gradually tried to get back to her normal routine at home.

Mozell was also expecting again, and Grace wanted to do anything she could to help.

During the next couple of years, Grace was blessed with two more grandchildren from Clyde and Mozell. Judy was born in November, shortly after Dora's stroke, and then a little more than a year later in February 1951, their first son, Bobby, was born. Grace now felt she was needed by Mozell more than ever with two little ones in tow, and she was glad to help.

On a fall, October afternoon in 1955, Marie had received

word of a curious newspaper find and mentioned it to Grace while she visited the next day.

"Mama, I saw Arlene yesterday and she was tellin' me about an obituary she saw in the Greensboro paper this week. It was a Scarlett woman, and it had her husband listed as Allen Scarlett."

"Where they from?" Grace asked, curiously.

"She said Reidsville."

"Ah, that ain't him," Grace replied.

"Probably not," Marie agreed. "I don't think he'd ever let anybody know where he's at after what he did. And besides, y'all never got a divorce. I imagine there's more than one Allen Scarlett."

"I imagine so," Grace replied, without carrying the conversation further. It had been eighteen years since her dad had left and Marie thought it to be only a remote chance of being her father, but she found the idea intriguing, nonetheless. Grace kept her thoughts to herself as she resumed trying to forget that part of her past.

Grace had endured years of deeply painful events and emerged triumphant in most people's eyes. But, deep in her heart there was still something that seemed lacking, and she knew what it was. She had privately anguished and struggled with an inward spiritual battle for as long as she could remember.

Finally, one Sunday while visiting a little neighboring country church service with some of her family, the enormous weight of all her past afflictions seemed to lift from her shoulders. For the first time in her life, she finally felt at peace with everything that had plagued her for so many years.

She joined the Pierce's Chapel Primitive Baptist Church and was baptized shortly thereafter.

"I have had a burden for many years," she wrote to the church, upon their requesting her experience. "It seemed to me I was going to die and hell was going to be my home."

In her closing, she told of a vision of her ascending.

"I came to a long hall. I went down the hall until I came to the old cross. I put my arms around it, and it was shown to me that truth and mercy had met together," she wrote. "Since, I have been the happiest I have ever been in my life."

Afterward, things were much different for her. Although she realized there would still be troubles and burdens ahead, she knew that mercy and grace would now get her through.

It wasn't long until Marie and Marvin announced to Grace that she would once again be a grandmother. In March of 1958, they presented Grace with a beautiful baby granddaughter with thick, black hair. They named her Peggy, after Marie's little sister who had died at only three weeks old.

Grace had watched Clinard grow through his teen years with his suave "fifties" hairstyle and looks that made the girls swoon. He was now twenty-one and all the gals would have to step aside for the one special girl he had met, named Mary Newby, who captured his heart. They were soon married, and Grace invited Clinard and his new wife to stay with her until they could find a place of their own. Clyde had previously built two extra rooms onto the original two-room house, which provided a bedroom for her and one for the newlyweds. The couple accepted and she was grateful.

It had been just Grace and Clinard living at home for the past twelve years, although he had been out of the house more since becoming older, so she was happy to have their company.

In time, Clinard and Mary announced that their first child was on the way. Grace was always considerate, giving them full reign of her small, humble home as she tried to allow them ample space.

Before the baby was born, Clinard said, "Mama, if it's a boy, we're gonna name him Allen, after daddy."

It was a boy, born in August of 1959. When Clinard and Mary brought him home, Grace immediately bonded with him. She doted on him so that Mary would hardly have had to do anything at first. If she and Clinard needed to go anywhere, they were assured that Dicky, as they nicknamed him, would be well taken care of.

Over the next year, Clinard and Mary were able to acquire their own apartment in High Point, and informed Grace that they would be moving. Although she would miss them and Dicky terribly, she knew that she couldn't stand in their way and gave them her blessings.

In October the following year, another grandson was born. This was Clyde and Mozell's fourth child, and they named him Don.

As Grace's grandchildren grew, they all occasionally stayed with her overnight, generating unforgettable memories of her sayings and the amusing things she would do.

In 1959 Grace turned fifty-six, and felt her heart was now at the beginning of the final healing as these new babies filled the empty spaces and helped to dispel the ghosts that plagued her past.

Chapter 33
The Discovery

Almost six years had passed since Marie had been told of the obituary, and although it occasionally crossed her mind during that time, she had pushed the idea aside. It was now 1961, and Marie had begun to question the possibility. It seemed she couldn't get it off her mind, and as the days passed, curiosity got the better of her. The mounting suspense created a strong urge to delve further into this idea. She just wanted to know for sure and put it to rest, once and for all.

After Mary found that she was now pregnant with her second child, Marie visited to share in the joyful news. Marie mentioned her interest in the past information and they began discussing the matter. Then, she and Mary joined forces to begin investigating.

"Mary, your handwritin' is prettier than mine," Marie said. "Why don't you write a letter, and we'll send it to the courthouse in Reidsville to see if they have any information on record about this man."

Mary sat down and began to compose a letter. They mailed it later that day.

A week passed and Marie received a letter stating if she would remit three dollars, they would send information on Allen Scarlett.

Marie immediately sent the money and soon received a document with information of this man's marriage and other dates only pertaining to the Reidsville area.

In the meantime, they found a copy of the obituary and Marie had Mary call the funeral home to inquire about the woman in question, but she was given the same limited information other than some names.

"Why don't we just go to the funeral home in Reidsville and see if they'll tell us who this Allen Scarlett is?" Marie suggested. "I just got a funny feelin' about this and I'd like to know."

"When we goin'?" Clinard asked.

"Why don't we ride up there Friday? I'll call Clyde and see if he can go."

Clyde was all for going when she asked.

Marvin laughed when Marie told him of their intentions.

"That'll be a wasted a trip. You'll never find out anything about him," he said.

"Maybe not, but we're goin'."

Marie then went to tell their mother that they were going to see who this man was.

"Well, go on and see," Grace said. "Let me know what you find when you get back."

On the morning of the trip, Marie met with Clyde and Mozell and then went to pick up Clinard and Mary. Their short trip there was lively as they laughed and talked about the "what ifs," and in almost no time at all they had arrived. They all knew it was a long shot after so many years.

They stopped at a local store while Clyde went in for directions to the funeral home. Shortly thereafter, they were pulling into the parking lot.

They all got out and walked in, and were soon being greeted by the director who asked if he could help them.

"There was a woman's obituary in the Greensboro paper several years back and we was wonderin' if you could tell us somethin' about her husband," Clyde explained.

"Well, I'll try my best. What was his name?"

"Allen Scarlett," Clyde said.

"Oh, yes, that was Mrs. Myrtle's husband," the director informed them.

"Our dad left us when we were little and his name was Allen Scarlett," Marie explained. "We're wonderin' if this could possibly be him."

"Oh, I don't think he would be your dad. I've known him for many years and he has only two children."

"Do you know where he lives now?" Clyde asked.

"No, I'm sorry, I don't," he said. "But I know someone who might. Myrtle's brother, Bernard Mayhew, doesn't live far from here. I'll call him and see if he's available to talk to you about it."

"We would really appreciate it," Marie said.

The director got on the phone and contacted Mr. Mayhew.

"He said he'd be here shortly to talk with you."

After a short wait, he arrived and they were all introduced to one another. The director explained that they were inquiring as to whether this Allen Scarlett he knew could possibly be their father, while Mr. Mayhew displayed a puzzled look. Clyde told him that his dad left in 1937 and would have been thirty-one at the time.

"Oh, no, he couldn't possibly be you dad. He's not nearly that old. He was only nineteen when he and my sister met."

"Did he ever mention any of his family at all?" Marie asked.

"He only has one brother. I remember him saying his name is Richard."

"Well, our dad has a brother named Richard from Thomasville," Clyde said.

"Oh, well, he said this brother lived in Florida," Mr. Mayhew replied.

It didn't sound very promising but just the one fact alone of having a brother named Richard sparked enough interest for them to continue.

"Does this Allen Scarlett still live here?" Marie asked.

"No, he remarried three years ago and is living in Danville, Virginia, with his wife and the two young daughters he and my sister had before she died. He works in the meat department at the Market Basket Supermarket there. In fact, I can show you where it's at. I'm heading that way and you could follow me if you'd like," Mr. Mayhew offered.

"Thank you," Clyde said. "We'd really like to just go and find out."

As she exchanged telephone numbers with Mr. Mayhew, Marie said, "I'll call and let you know if by some chance it is him."

Intense excitement filled the car as they prepared to follow this lead to Danville.

"I can't wait, I can't wait, I can't wait!" Clinard exclaimed, sitting on the edge of the seat with a broad smile as they pulled out. Clinard never had the opportunity to know Allen or to even see his face, and they couldn't get there fast enough for him to fnd out.

"Well, don't get you hopes up," Clyde advised. "It's a real slim chance of bein' him."

As they arrived in Danville a short while later, Mr. Mayhew pulled into the store parking lot and they followed him in, then he circled around to pull up beside their car where he could speak to them before leaving.

"This is where he works, if you want to go in. I have my doubts about this being your dad. I really don't think it's him."

"We appreciate you showin' us where he's at," Clyde said.

As Mr. Mayhew drove away, Clyde parked the car and everyone got out. They were even more apprehensive now, but still eager to go in after a twenty-six-year absence and confront this man, if he was their father.

They nervously walked around the corner, opened the front door and walked in, not knowing what to expect.

"Mr. Mayhew said he works in the meat department," Clyde said. "I think that's it at the back of the store there."

As they got closer, they all stopped and studied the man working behind the meat counter, wearing a long, white apron.

"Is it him? Is it him?" Clinard repeated.

"He sure has gained weight, if that's him. But, I believe it's him, don't you, Clyde?" Marie remarked.

After a pause, Clyde said, "I'm not sure. He looks different than what I remember. It does look a little like him in the face, though."

"What're we gonna do?" Clinard asked.

"I'll just go buy a pound of bologna and see if he recognizes me," Marie said.

"You ain't got no way to get meat back home," Clyde said, chuckling.

"I don't care," she insisted, proceeding to the counter.

They all hesitantly walked up to the meat display as if shopping — all five of them — watching his reaction closely.

He was finishing up an order with the only customer there as she took her order and left.

"Can I help you folks?" the meat cutter asked, politely.

"Mm, I'll take a half pound of bologna," Marie said, staring at him, awaiting a response.

He sliced the meat, wrapped it, then handed it to her and smiled.

"Will there be anything else?" he asked.

Marie turned to Clyde for his response.

Finally, after searching every inch of that face and measuring it by a child's memory, Clyde asked, "Do you know who I am?"

"No," the butcher said. "I don't think I do." He absently wiped his hands on his apron as he studied the customer's face.

"I'm Clyde."

The butchers's brow suddenly furrowed with a look of dread, as his face turned red and then pale, and then he looked down.

When he looked back up, Clyde asked, "Do you know who she is?"

"Yeah, that's Marie."

They now knew this was their father and they all stood there awaiting their father's next move.

Allen turned and walked into the back room, leaving them to stand there waiting and wondering if he would come back out.

Mary, being pregnant, had become flushed and excited to the point of almost passing out, and had to be seated to regain her composure.

Allen eventually returned, realizing there was no way to escape this encounter. He had not acknowledged Clinard, and they wondered if he had forgotten him, since Clinard was only three months old when Allen had left, so Clyde pointed to Clinard and asked, "Do you know who he is?"

"I'm not sure," he answered, hesitantly.

"Well, you ought to. He's your baby boy," Clyde replied.

As they stood awkwardly for a few minutes, Allen nervously

made a suggestion.

"I'll be through in about fifteen minutes if you can wait for me under that tree out there," he said, while glancing around to see if anyone was watching.

They all turned and walked outside to wait, realizing their presence in the store was making Allen extremely nervous.

When he finished his work, Allen came out and they talked for a while, with everyone trying to grasp the reality of the discovery.

"I knew you'd find me," Allen said, as they all sat silently for a moment. "I'd been seein' you in the dark."

"I hear you got two daughters and you're married again," Marie replied. "I'd like to meet 'em."

"Oh, no! You can't do that. Please don't let my wife know about this," Allen pleaded. "She'd kill me or I'd have to kill her, one."

Clinard was not sure what to say, so he mostly listened, as he had no memory of him or any events as Clyde and Marie did.

Allen explained that he would visit in three weeks and asked for their telephone numbers, assuring them he would be in touch. Clinard gave him directions to his house in High Point for his first visit.

As they left, Marie scribbled "September fifteenth, 1961" on the paper band wrapped around the meat she had just bought so she would not forget the date. How strange, she thought, as she looked at the date. They had found Allen almost the same date that he left – the seventeenth of September, twenty-four years earlier. Even more odd was the fact that Cletie had eventually gotten married – on the sixteenth of September.

The next day, Marie drove to her mother's house to reveal their find.

"Mama, remember that woman's obituary six years ago that listed her husband as Allen Scarlett?"

"Yeah, the one Arlene was tellin' you about?"

"We all went to Reidsville yesterday to check it out — and it was him!"

Grace just raised her eyebrows and pursed her lips as if studying the news.

We found him workin' at a supermarket in Danville, Virginia."

"Is he livin' there?"

"Yeah, Mama. He's been married twice since he left."

Grace had learned to mask whatever feelings she had toward this matter, although some old memories resurfaced briefly by this news.

Arriving back home later that day, Marie remembered that she had promised to call Mr. Mayhew, so she dialed his number from the small piece of paper she had written it on.

"Mr. Mayhew?"

"Yes ma'am."

"This is Marie Harrison. I told you I'd call and let you know what we found out yesterday. I just wanted to let you know that he is our dad."

"Oh, my!" he said, with a moment passing before he spoke again. "I can hardly believe this. I would have never thought."

"Well, it's a pretty big surprise to all of us."

Each had questions about Allen and the events that led up to this day. Before hanging up, Mr. Mayhew said, "Whatever you do, please don't let my sister in Spencer know about this."

This was somewhat puzzling to Marie, as she replied, "Mr. Mayhew, I don't even know your sister. But could I ask one favor of you?"

"What is that?"

"Would you call me if anything ever happens that we should know about?"

"Yes, I'll certainly do that," he replied.

Three weeks later, Allen arrived at Clinard's house as he had promised. Grace did not go to the meeting, but her three children and all their families were there to greet him as he entered the front door. He was visibly nervous and uncomfortable as he faced his children once again, along with the seven grandchildren he had never met. It was obvious to all that he did not know how to approach the little ones.

Mary served ice tea and snacks to everyone as Allen cautiously watched the door the entire time he sat and talked with them. When he announced that he should leave, Marie decided to seize the moment and asked him if they could take a few photographs. He reluctantly agreed, knowing he could not refuse as the women gathered around him to pose, and then all the men took their turn. He walked out the door and headed toward his car, with a look of relief to a degree, but very much aware that his obligated visits were not, by any means, over.

Allen visited periodically, bringing each of them hams and other peace offerings from the market where he worked.

On one occasion, before he left after visiting at Clyde's home, Marie asked him to sit in the passenger seat of her car for a moment.

"I just wanted to talk to you for a minute before you go," Marie explained.

They sat and talked for a while, then the discussion turned serious. Marie began to ask why, and her emotions began to build. Allen remained silent and without the answers she desperately needed. Finally, after holding back as long as she could, she broke down.

"How could you just leave us like that and not even look back?" she sobbed. "Do you have any idea what you put mama through?"

More than a minute passed before Allen spoke. "Did your mom never tell you why I left? Marie, I could have never gone back down there. Walter Grubb would have seen to that," he said, without elaborating.

Marie knew it was useless to press him any further. At least she had finally let him know how she felt, but it did little to soothe the bitterness she carried for so many years. There was nothing left to talk about, so they said their goodbyes until Allen's next visit.

Clinard and Mary were still living in High Point in October 1961, when their second son, Timothy, was born. Shortly afterward, they decided to move to Darlington, South Carolina, where they started their own upholstery and antique business. Although they regretted moving so far away from Grace, they felt they should not dismiss the opportunity to build a successful enterprise together.

Clinard and Mary worked hard dividing their time between taking care of two boys and managing a business for the next five years.

Clinard was out on an errand when Allen arrived for a visit.

Mary welcomed him in and said, "Clinard should be back shortly."

Mary's boys, Dicky and Tim, played with their toys on the floor nearby as she and Allen chatted, until someone knocked on the door. Allen jumped up, seemingly wanting to hide. It was only a customer needing something from their shop.

When the customer left, Mary asked, "Allen, why are you so nervous? Nobody even knows you're here."

He attempted to give the impression that he was calm, but never answered her.

Clinard soon returned and visited with Allen as he constantly watched the door and appeared edgy every time he heard a car pull up.

Chapter 34
Sharing Grandma's Grace

Grace didn't seem to mind her children's discovery of their father, nor their acceptance of his visits. If she did, she never let it be known. Grace was just satisfied to be at home, focusing on family and indulging her grandchildren. She loved all of her grandchildren, having them visit and sometime stay the night, as each one would leave with a memorable experience.

Grace's grandson, Bobby, had occasionally stayed with her during the day while Mozell worked. Bobby was still small enough for Grace to rock him on the front porch.

Clyde and Mozell's oldest daughter, Glenda, was five, and Judy was just over a year old when Bobby was born, prompting family and neighbors to offer support since they had two babies to care for.

Grace felt nervous and uneasy being alone at night, and since Bobby appeared to be comfortable and satisfied at her house, she mentioned to Clyde and Mozell about letting him stay with her overnight. They discussed it and decided that although they preferred him to be at home, they knew he would be fine with Grace. Bobby was always the most secure when close to his mother, so they decided to try him at Grace's for a night. If he was okay, then they would consider letting him stay with her more often.

Bobby was almost four when he first spent the night there. After he awoke from his evening nap, a thunderstorm could be heard in the distance and he began to cry. Grace supposed it was just the thunder that unsettled him, since he had been with her through the day with no problem. She took him to the rocking chair on the front porch and began singing, "Bye-o ba-by, o bye--o," to the tune of Amazing Grace. That seemed to have a calming effect on him and Grace never remembered him crying again, even at night.

Bobby stayed more frequently as he grew older, and by the age of ten, he was content to be with his Grandma Grace in her little wood-framed house as she offered snacks of molasses with butter and homemade biscuits.

With the help of Marie and her daughter, Peggy, Grace planted a small vegetable garden beside her house. All three kept the weeds hoed out through the summer, and when it came time to harvest, they always had packs of field peas and corn for freezing. Grace mixed the two together when cooking, and persuaded Bobby to try some. Mozell had served them at times but couldn't get him to eat any. Once he did, he was hooked.

"These are good, Grandma!" exclaimed Bobby.

Even though he didn't ask her to cook them every day, she now knew it was a favorite of his, and she served peas and corn at every evening meal.

Winter was getting close and Grace began to make preparations.

"It's gonna get cold tonight, Bobby, so we're gonna have to fill up these jugs and buckets with water just in case the line freezes up," Grace said.

"Why does that water line always freeze up ever winter, Grandma?"

"The pipe's not buried deep enough somewhere through that field there from mama and daddy's house. When it gets way down cold, it just freezes up," she explained.

Grace had no bathroom, but next to each bed was a chamber pot with a lid. There was still evidence of an outhouse near the edge of the woods, but it had long since fallen down.

Before they went to bed on a cold night, Grace put a bucket-load of coal into the cast-iron heater and closed the draft. The coal embers smoldered throughout the night as the rooms gradually cooled down, but when Grace reopened the draft the next morning, the stove heated the rooms fast and the pipe into the chimney would sometimes begin to glow red.

As presumed, no water came out of the faucet the next morning, and Grace was glad she and Bobby were prepared. She peered through frosted window panes in the front den window and exclaimed, "Ooo, Jackie Frost, Jackie Frost!" as Bobby appeared in his pajamas, yawning and rubbing his eyes while entering the room.

Grace had purchased an electric cook stove in recent years that made it easier to heat water. She poured some into an agate wash basin for Bobby's bath, then sat on the edge of her favorite rocking chair near the heater. She soaped up the cloth and commenced to lather him up. Bobby knew, at his age, that he was capable of doing this for himself, but he sensed the gratification Grace seemed to get, and didn't protest.

"Now, you wash down there," Grace said, modestly, as she left the room to give him privacy.

"What you want for breakfast?" called Grace, from the kitchen.

"Pancakes!" answered Bobby, as he finished his bath.

He found it impossible to rinse the cloth in such a small amount of water, which left his body with a thin film of soap.

Bobby finished getting dressed and headed to the kitchen to eat as Grace served up the pancakes. Bobby retrieved the large tin of King Syrup from the cabinet and popped the top out with a butter knife. He spread butter on the pancakes and then poured the syrup on thick. He ate them with his favorite fork that Grace made sure he had at every meal.

He was buttoning his heavy coat for his walk to the bus when Grace handed him some change.

"Here's some money to buy you a snack at recess."

He usually spent the money as soon as he got to his bus stop, which was at Pierce's store. The morning walk was frigid, and the store was on the other side of the church, so he was eager to get there quickly and make his candy purchase.

When Bobby got home from school on Monday evening, Grace had another favorite dish ready for him. She set a pot of chicken stew with cornbread on the table, along with peas and corn.

During supper, Grace said, "Ora and Ruth bought'em one of

those televisions over the weekend. After we finish supper and I clean up, we'll go and see it."

Grace had never owned one, and even though Bobby watched television when at home with Clyde and Mozell, he didn't seem to miss it that much when he was at Grace's. There was always something interesting to do there or at the Grubb farm. He had cousins nearby to play with, and he had acres of forest to explore.

Grace still had the old upright radio that Clyde bought when he lived at home. He left it with Grace when he moved out and now Bobby enjoyed searching its dial, finding stations from other countries that spoke foreign languages he could not understand.

When Grace was finished in the kitchen, Bobby walked with her to Walter and Dora's house. Ruth and Ora never married and were still living at home to help Walter care for Dora, who was paralyzed on her right side, and still sitting on the end of the sofa as she had done for the past twelve years. Maggie had eventually married the Reverend Albert Gourley, but after his death, she moved back home to care for her parents so Ruth and Ora could go work at the Dogwood Hosiery Mill in Thomasville.

Everyone was captivated with this box that showed real, moving, black and white images. Although the technology had been around for a while, it was a new experience for them.

Soon, a "western" program came on and all the sisters were riveted to the screen as two back-to-back cowboys began to walk ten paces apart on a dusty street in an old-west town, and then they turned and shot at one another. One fell dead, as all the sisters except Grace jumped up from their chairs and rushed to the television, leaning in toward the screen to get a better look as they hysterically exclaimed, "Oh, God! He killed that man!"

Grace looked Bobby's way to observe his reaction.

"It ain't real, y'all. It ain't real." Bobby explained. But they couldn't hear him over their own commotion.

"Oh, God, he killed him!" they continued.

"Y'all, it ain't real," Bobby repeated.

After their dramatic reaction subsided, they finally settled back into their seats still unnerved. Grace was hopeful there wouldn't be another shootout, and when the show ended, she said, "Well, I guess we might better go."

On the way back home, Bobby said, "Grandma, they thought that was real. I knew it watn't real."

Grace chuckled and said, "I did, too, Bobby."

Bobby had to go home and stay with Clyde and Mozell over the next few weeks after finding he had a hernia that required surgery. During that time, Grace's other grandchildren came to stay. Glenda, Judy, Jerry and Peggy lived nearby and were happy to take turns keeping Grace company until Bobby was well.

He soon returned, and was happy to be back in the quiet and comfortable haven of Grace's home.

"Bobby, you feel up to helpin' me wash clothes today?"

"Sure, grandma, I'll get the tub."

"No," Grace said. "You're not supposed to lift anything yet. You just help me with the rinse."

Grace got an old chair that she kept on the back porch and set it next to the ringer washer, then placed the rinse tub on the chair under the rollers. She filled the washer drum with water, detergent, and then the clothes. After running an electric drop cord out the door to the machine, she plugged it in. Once the lever was pulled, it started to wash. Bobby watched her as she filled the rinse tub with fresh water. When Grace thought the clothes had washed enough, she stopped the machine.

"You guide the clothes when they come through the rollers and make sure they fall in the rinse water," Grace instructed.

After a few garments came through, Bobby asked, "Grandma, can I feed the clothes through the rollers?"

"That's too dangerous," Grace cautioned.

"I'll be careful."

"I don't know. If you get hurt down here, your mama'll get me."

"Let me try just one time."

"Okay, but be careful not to get your fingers caught in the rollers."

Grace smiled as those words brought back memories of her days with Nellie and Anna many years earlier.

After the clothes were hung out on the line, Grace said, "I need to go next door for a while and help 'em do some quiltin'. You want to stay here, or go with me?"

"I'll go with you," said Bobby.

While Grace helped with the quilting, Bobby explored the barn. He climbed the ladder to the barn loft and picked up and examined the door knobs in the chicken nest. Wonder what those are for, he pondered. He lay back in the loose straw and daydreamed, and then rolled around and threw handfuls of it up in the air, pretending it was snow as it came down. After a while he climbed down and went to the grain building and peeped in the door, but was wary of the darkness, and decided against going inside.

Bobby eventually went back inside the house and walked to the stairway door. He reached for the wooden thread spool that had been nailed to the door as a handle to see if Grace was still upstairs quilting.

"Don't go up there," said Maggie. "There's grave robbers up there."

"Grave robbers?" he asked, with a skeptical look. "Where's grandma?"

"She's in the kitchen. Come on with me," she said. "There's somethin' you can help us do in there."

Bobby followed Maggie, but turned and looked at the stairway door once again as he walked out.

"Here. Take this jar and shake it," she said. "You can't stop. You have to keep shakin' it 'til butter appears."

"What's in here?" he asked.

"It's cream, and it'll turn to butter after a while."

He had his doubts about butter appearing, but he kept shaking the jar of cream as he had been instructed. And soon, to his amazement, there were clumps of butter forming in the jar.

It was almost time for the evening news as they finished, and all the sisters gathered in the family room to watch.

"A rock 'n' roll star has been arrested after dropping his pants and exposing himself on stage in front of hundreds of fans!" the newscaster began.

All eyes in the room grew wide with shock as Maggie exclaimed, "God help this world. That's a scandal and disgrace."

"What's this world comin' to?" echoed Ora.

Ruth sat seemingly unfazed, and then looked at Bobby matter-of- factly and stated, "Well, you know, if a man wanted to pull his pants down in front of me, I'd take a nice long look."

"Well, Ruth!" Ora scolded.

Grace frowned and looked at Bobby, shaking her head in embarrassment as Ruth just smiled.

As they were still attentive to the news, Bobby slipped out of the room and back to the stairway door. He turned the wooden latch and slowly opened the door slightly as he peered up the stairs and surveyed the landing at the top. Hmm, he thought, as he stood there contemplating. I will go up there one day… but, not right now, and he closed the door.

"Grandma, Maggie said there were grave robbers upstairs," Bobby commented, as they walked back home that evening.

"They ain't really no grave robbers up there. They just tell kids that to keep 'em from goin' up there and plunderin'." she explained.

"How 'bout we go out there in the field and pick some blackberries for a pie?"

"I like blackberries," replied Bobby.

Grace got two wire-handled buckets and they trampled into the thicket next to the house.

"Let's play a game and see who can pick the most blackberries," she suggested.

But, because of his fondness for blackberries, Bobby ate nearly as many as he picked.

They soon had a reasonable amount of berries in the buckets and returned to the house. The afternoon hours found them sitting at the little chrome edged kitchen table sampling her freshly baked and perfectly flaky blackberry pie.

Summer was about half over and school would soon start. This year, the bus was scheduled to stop at Grace's driveway to pick Bobby up. He would have to get up a little earlier if he wanted to go to Pierce's store first.

As he stepped off the bus that first evening after school, he detected the aroma of food drifting all the way down the driveway. Grace had supper ready the minute he walked in the door to satisfy his voracious appetite after a long school day. He was happy to be back. Even if there were times when Grace had to be gone, she would always leave him a note telling him his supper was on the stove and that she would be back soon.

At the end of 1964, Walter became ill. After learning that his illness was terminal, the family had a hospital bed brought in so they could care for him at home. He passed away on February twenty eight, 1965, at the age of eighty nine.

After a very emotional funeral at Walter's Grove Baptist Church, Ora, Ruth, and Maggie, along with the rest of the family, now would have to concentrate on caring for Dora.

"Would you and Bobby stay with us a few nights?" Ora asked, as her voice broke. "If not, I just don't think we can bear to stay here with him gone."

Grace and Bobby agreed. They slept on the two couches in the den for almost three weeks until everyone was better adjusted to their loss.

At night, before bedtime, Ruth would set the radio alarm to music for the next morning. She would start clogging in an untimely fashion as the music played, giggling like a little girl. Dora would have a big smile as she sat on the sofa, tapping the foot that wasn't paralyzed.

Less than a year had passed when Dora suddenly fell ill. Grace and her sisters began taking turns sitting with her at the hospital, night after night, before she passed away on January fourth, 1966, at the age of eighty seven. The emotional response to her funeral was even greater than at Walter's. Afterward, Dora was laid to rest beside Walter in the church cemetery just down the hill from Grace's little Gladys and Peggy.

Grace and Bobby decided to stay with Ora, Ruth, and Maggie again, knowing how difficult it would now be with both parents gone.

The other family members continued to visit, and as their grief eventually lessened, Grace and Bobby returned to her house just across the field.

"Grandma, can I get some chickens?" Bobby asked, as they walked home. "I know a man who's got some for sale."

"I guess so. You'll have to keep 'em fed though, and build 'em a coop so foxes and 'possums won't get 'em. We'd have good ol' fresh eggs every mornin' then."

Bobby smiled with excitement at the thought of having chickens lay eggs, and maybe even hatching a brood. He got straight to work gathering scrap wood, nails, and some rusty chicken wire to build them a refuge. Before long, he had erected a makeshift coop. He stood back and admired it as he smiled. It wasn't perfect, but it would do. Now he would wait for his mother and dad to pick him up for the weekend, when they would take him to get the chickens.

"Bye, Grandma, see ya soon!" Bobby exclaimed, as he climbed into Clyde's car. Grace waved and smiled as they drove off.

When they arrived at the farm, the man took them to a large, fenced yard and told Bobby to pick out the ones he wanted. He chose three big, fat, red hens.

"You'll need a rooster if you want 'em to set," he informed.

Bobby then picked a rooster of the same color.

"Those are Rhode Island Reds," he informed.

"What's that pretty yellow one in the other fence there, with feathers on it's feet?" Bobby asked.

"That's called an Araucana," the man answered. "She'll lay a blue egg when spring gets here. It's still too cold for 'em to lay right now."

Noticing the sparkle in Bobby's eye, the man asked, "Do you want one of those?"

"Yeah, I'd like to have one."

After returning with the chickens and introducing them to their new home, Bobby and Grace kept them fed and watered during the next few weeks as they eagerly watched and waited for the blue egg to appear. Bobby started turning them out during the day, assuming they would go back to the nest boxes to lay, but would often hear the red hens cackle in the wood's edge.

He could never find the nest, so Grace sat on the back porch one day until they heard another hen let out a cackle. Bobby ran to the brush and searched thoroughly, finding nothing.

"Can't find it, Grandma!" Bobby yelled.

"Go over to the left a little, under that tree layin' down there."

Bobby leaned down to look closer, and there it was, a whole nest of brown eggs.

He now learned to watch closely where the hens entered, in order to know where they were laying. Now, if only the yellow hen would lay that blue egg the man had told him about. He was beginning to doubt that it would even happen. It was days before he heard a different cackling sound, and it was coming from the coop. He rushed to the coop just as the yellow hen was coming out and looked in the nest box. There it was! He gazed in amazement as he picked up the beautiful, still warm, sky blue egg, running to the house to present it to Grace.

It had been five years since Grace's last grandchild was born, and she supposed there wouldn't be any more. Her children seemed to be content with the number of children they now had, but then, Clinard and Mary surprised her with news.

"I'm gonna be grandma again," Grace happily stated.

After long anticipation, Clinard and Mary called to proudly announce the birth of their third son, Samuel, in late July 1966.

Grace was ready for the trip to Darlington to see the new family member when Marie mentioned she was planning to go. Grace was captivated as she saw him for the first time.

The next year, Bobby turned sixteen and acquired his driver's license. He was proud that he could now take Grace wherever she needed to go. Even though it wasn't a burden to her children or her sister, Grace was happy that she didn't have to trouble them as much.

Before getting his license, Clyde and Mozell would always pick Bobby up on the way to a little Baptist church just over in Randolph County where his family had always attended. Now that he had a car, he could drive himself there.

"We're havin' a dinner at Pierce's Chapel Sunday. You wanna come?" asked Grace.

"Yeah, I'll come. I'll go to my church and then come up there," said Bobby.

Grace was busy cooking for most of the afternoon on Saturday. On Sunday morning, Grace packed all her dishes into the car when Ora, Ruth, and Maggie arrived to pick her up.

When Bobby arrived at Grace's church, the service had just ended and all the ladies were spreading out the tablecloths and setting the pots and dishes of food on the tables.

Grace smiled proudly as he walked up.

"This is my grandson, Bobby, that lives with me."

"I've heard her talk about you several times," said Grace's friends to Bobby.

Grace beamed throughout the dinner as she introduced him to the other fellow members.

As everyone got their plate to start the meal, Grace smiled as she leaned close to Bobby and said, "I brought those peas and corn in that dish there just for you."

As hunting season arrived, Marie's son, Jerry, stopped in and asked Grace if he could go hunting back in the woods.

"Just be careful," she reminded. Thoughts of the tragedy when Clyde went hunting with Willie came to mind, but Grace supposed he would be safer hunting by himself.

Jerry always came back with something, and a few hours later he walked out of the woods with his rifle on his shoulder and his catch.

"Grandma, you want this rabbit?" he asked.

"Well, it would sure make a good stew."

Grace turned to Bobby, "You know how to skin a rabbit?"

"I'm afraid not, Grandma. I've never done that before."

"I can skin it for you, Grandma," Jerry offered.

Once that was done and it was washed, Grace cut it up and put it in the pressure cooker.

"Now, you stay and eat with us when I get this stew done, Jerry," Grace said.

"I gotta to get back, Grandma. I would if I didn't have things to do at home. But I'll come back again."

The rabbit stew was done and they sat down to eat.

"This is the best stew I've ever had, Grandma. Nobody can make it like you and mama."

Grace smiled in approval as they both took pleasure in one another's company.

"And these peas and corn are really good, too," he added.

As Christmas approached, Bobby went to the field near where her former two-room house once set, cut down a cedar Christmas tree and nailed a wooden stand to the bottom.

Grace went to her bedroom closet and pulled out the single strand of lights she had stored overhead.

Bobby plugged in the cord to test the lamps.

"They ain't burnin', grandma," Bobby remarked.

"They a-getting' old, but one of the bulbs is probably burnt out. There's some extras in the box."

He knew from previous years that he would have to change each bulb until he found the bad one. When he finally changed the right bulb, they lit up with a colorful glow that warmed and illuminated the room. The small bubblers soon warmed up and began to bubble, and the Santa and snowman bulbs glowed with an excitement of their own. He pulled two, thin, frazzled strands of silver and red tinsel garland from a bag and draped them on the tree, and then strategically placed her small, worn, colored glass ornaments and stood back to observe his work.

"What do you think, Grandma?" Bobby asked, awaiting her response.

"I believe that's the prettiest tree we've ever had," she exclaimed, as she smiled and her eyes sparkled with an almost childlike delight.

"Now," Grace began, "let's eat oranges by the tree light before we go to bed."

Bobby opened the record player and placed a Christmas album on the turntable. As they listened to the joyous and festive sounds, they peeled their oranges, reveling in the warmth of home, one another's company, and the sentiments of the season.

Chapter 35
There is a Balm in Gilead

After learning of Allen's next planned visit, Clyde stopped by Grace's house and said, "Mom, dad's comin' down next week. Why don't you have Bobby bring you up and greet him when he gets there?"

"I don't care nothin' about seein' him," she declared.

"You got every right to be there. You don't have to talk to him if you don't want to."

"Well, I'll think about it," she replied.

On the day Allen was to visit, Bobby asked, "Grandma, have you decided to go today?

"I don't know. There's really no reason to wanna see him again," she said.

"It's whatever you wanna do, Grandma. It's up to you."

"Well, let me get my stuff," she said, without hesitation. "I'll go with you, but I don't know if I'll be in there when he shows up."

"Now Grandma, you go in the back and fix up real pretty," Bobby teased, once they were there.

"Pffft. I sure wouldn't fix up for him," She scoffed.

After sitting on the sofa for a few minutes, Grace excused herself, carrying her brown paper "poke," as she called it, to the bathroom. She was aware that her appearance had changed during the years and she was not the same attractive young lady she was when Allen left. The enduring memory of him was the youthful and handsome man she knew from decades ago.

Grace stayed in the bathroom for quite a while before coming out, donning a nice dress, a freshened-up hair do, and makeup. There were stifled snickers emitted from the family, but no one let on in front of her. She returned to the sofa and there awaited Allen's arrival. Soon there was a knock on the side door from the porch and Clyde welcomed him in.

As soon as he stepped in the door, he looked straight over to the den where Grace was sitting. She immediately threw her hand up with a big smile and said, "Hey, there!"

Allen's face turned red at the unexpected greeting. He turned and put his elbows on the kitchen stove and covered his face in apparent embarrassment.

The incident now seemed to create an awkward atmosphere. Everyone was wondering if Grace would feel hurt over what again might have appeared to her as rejection. But Grace was stronger than that. She had already overcome years of paramount grief and pain.

Allen left shortly afterward without speaking to her that day, but Grace and her children later discussed meeting with him. They all wanted her to finally get a divorce, so Marie offered to call Allen where he worked and tell him.

"Daddy, mama wanted me to call and tell you she wants to get a divorce."

"Okay."

"And, she wants you to pay for it."

"All right. I will."

"We'll have everything drawn up and you can just come down and sign," Marie informed.

They decided on the day and time, and then she said goodbye.

Grace's children accompanied her for their meeting with him. When he arrived at the attorney's office, he signed the divorce papers, and before he left, he handed Grace the money to pay for the divorce and then offered her money for a new dress.

"Oh, you needn't give me money for a dress," Grace said, politely.

Marie glanced over at her mother and shook her head, gesturing for her not to refuse his offer, so Grace accepted the money.

The divorce was soon finalized. Even though a flood of memories — good and bad — had returned, Allen was now a closed chapter in her life.

Grace was sixty-four now and had lived alone for thirty years since Allen disappeared, but she had still been legally married to him up until now.

That was the last time Grace ever saw the man she once fell in love with in her youth and later caused such a grievous life for her. Allen continued to visit their children over the next ten years, but merely out of obligation.

On a warm June morning in 1976, just a few days before Marie's birthday, she was about her daily routine, thinking about the upcoming plans her family had made for her, when the phone rang.

"Is this Marie?" the caller asked.

"Yes, it is."

"This is Bernard Mayhew's daughter, Judy. You asked to be called if anything ever happened to your dad. I'm sorry to tell you, but he passed away this morning."

"Oh, my," Marie said, as she hesitated at the sudden news. "What happened?"

"He had a heart attack last week and had been in the hospital since. I sure am sorry."

"Thank you for callin' to let us know," she replied.

After hanging up, Marie called Clyde and Clinard with the news.

"How in the world are we gonna break this to his family up there?" Marie asked them. "This is gonna be a real shock."

"Maybe the undertakers could have the girls meet with us before anybody gets there," Clyde suggested.

And so, they started making plans for the trip back to Virginia.

On Monday, June 21, the day of the family visitation, Clyde, Marie, and Clinard gathered their own families and followed one another as they drove to the funeral home in Danville.

They arrived early, before anyone else, and the families lingered together in the parking lot until all were out of their cars, and then they all entered together.

"Are you here to see Mr. Scarlett?" the doorman asked.

"We're actually here to meet his daughters," Clyde explained. "You see, he was our dad, too, and we've never met these girls. They don't know anything about us and we was wonderin' if you could call 'em and have 'em come over."

The doorman's eyes were getting wider with each word.

"Oh, my goodness," he said. "Oh, dear. Let me go get the director."

He returned, seemingly in a panic, followed by the director, and Clyde again explained why they were there.

The director seemed slightly perplexed, but calmly said, "Let me call them and discuss this with them," as he excused himself and exited the foyer.

The anxious family members discussed the situation quietly until the director returned.

"I spoke with one of his daughters," he said. "And they have already been told of you soon after he died. They said to tell you they would be here shortly."

When they arrived, the families were introduced to the two sisters.

"This is Lois," the director said. "And this is Aileen. They are Allen's daughters."

As they stood in the foyer talking to Clyde, they appeared to be in awe at the striking resemblance he had to their dad.

"Our cousin, Judy, called and told us about you all right after dad died," Aileen said. "We're just at a loss for words. We had no idea he had another family."

"What about your stepmother? Does she know about us?" Marie asked.

"We haven't told mom yet. We're going to wait until after the funeral is over," Lois said.

After the anticipated meeting, the newly acquainted families left as Grace's three children drove back home that night to prepare for the next day's funeral.

When Clyde, Marie, Clinard, and their families arrived for the funeral, the staff seemed rather nervous when deciding where to put a family that the deceased man's wife knew nothing about.

"We're his children, too, and we'd like to sit up front," Marie said.

"I don't want this to cause any trouble, now," the director replied. "I really don't want any trouble."

"We don't have any plans of causin' trouble," they all said.

They seated Clyde, Marie, Clinard, and their families on the right front pew before the service started. Allen's two daughters, Lois and Aileen, were then escorted in, along with their step-mother, Marion. They were led into the choir area at the front, near the minister and where the coffin was placed. There were wooden louvers postioned that separated them from the sanctuary, obscuring Marion's view of where Grace's children and their families were seated.

Officiating the service were elders from the Primitive Baptist church Allen had started attending in recent years.

Once the funeral was over, Allen's wife, daughters, and all their families were escorted out first and led to the family car.

As Grace's children walked out and past the car, Allen's wife, Marion, turned and watched intently as Clyde, who resembled his father immensely, went by. Clyde, Marie and Clinard followed the line of cars to the cemetery, parked back a short distance and stood secluded a couple of hundred feet away from the gravesite out of respect to Allen's unknowing wife. They were all standing together as the service began. Suddenly, Clyde stepped forward, holding his hands behind his back, with his family wondering what might be going through his mind as he somberly stood there alone until the rites were finished.

Allen Scarlett was only sixty-nine years of age. He was laid to rest along with many unanswered questions of how and why he chose to deceive his family for so many years. Perhaps the stress of attempting to conceal the secrets of his past might have caused his early demise. No one would ever know.

Two sets of families departed from the cemetery that day without the chance of speaking, both wondering if they would have that opportunity again and what kind of future this unusual, new relationship held.

Marie went to see Grace when she arrived home.

"I would have gone with y'all, if y'all had only asked," Grace said.

The statement took Marie by surprise, and she was now feeling guilty. None of them thought she would have wanted to go, considering the unpleasant life she had had with Allen.

"Mama, I'm sorry. I had no idea you wanted to go."

Even though she did not attend, Allen's death was the ultimate closure for Grace as she paused to think of all the family she had been blessed with. She also couldn't help thinking about all the family and events that Allen had missed.

Allen's first family members has stayed in contact with the two sisters afterward, and even their stepmother, Marion, who was Allen's last wife, visited on special occasions.

"I don't know why he wouldn't tell us about you," Marion told them. "We could have been family all along."

Even after all she had been through, Grace now realized that there was a plan and purpose in place long before the trials and heartaches she had endured. And again, to be blessed with devoted children and her precious grandchildren, was now, she felt, worth all the years of pain and grief she could have ever experienced.

Epilogue

Grace Grubb Scarlett was an example of strength and faith to her family and everyone who knew her.

After suffering a stroke, her family remained at the hospital by her side throughout the day and night.

Her family held her hands, kissed her forehead and said their goodbyes with whispers of "I love you" when it was apparent that her death was near.

Outside, the marigolds were beginning to bloom and there was a sweet fragrance in the air the day she passed from this world and into the one she had often dreamed about, where two precious little girls waited for their mother and greeted her with outstretched arms.

Grace died on Sunday morning, May twenty ninth, 1983, at the age of eighty.

Her love for God and family was abundant, with a determination to survive, and now her three children, nine grandchildren, and eight great grandchildren, gathered together, laughing and crying as they took turns telling stories about Grandma Grace, and their hearts swelled with thankful praise.

Amazing grace! (how sweet the sound)
That sav'd a wretch like me!
I once was lost, but now am found,
Was blind, but now I see.

'Twas grace that taught my heart to fear,
And grace my fears reliev'd;
How precious did that grace appear
The hour I first believ'd!

Thro' many dangers, toils, and snares,
I have already come;
'Tis grace hath brought me safe thus far,
And grace will lead me home.

The Lord has promis'd good to me,
His word my hope secures;
He will my shield and portion be
As long as life endures.

Yes, when this flesh and heart shall fail,
And mortal life shall cease;
I shall possess, within the veil,
A life of joy and peace.

When we've been there ten thousand years,
Bright shining as the sun,
We've no less days to sing God's praise,
Than when we first begun.

There appeared a golden thread.

A connection from one heart to another

— A golden connection.

About the Author

Born and raised in the small close-knit country community of Silver Valley, near Denton, North Carolina, Bobby C. Scarlett developed a genuine appreciation of his roots and heritage at a very young age. His large, extended families abound with longevity: he witnessed his great-great aunts become the World's Oldest Living Twins, as well as others in his lineage reaching the century mark.

In his earlier years, he traveled, performed, and recorded with various gospel music groups.

In 1980, Scarlett became one of the first in North Carolina to adopt a child as a single parent, and now, the title of Grandfather is one he affectionately reveres.

He began photographing his son and family as a hobby, which soon advanced to a professional career spanning twenty five years.

Scarlett discovered his passion for writing during recent years and is currently a business owner in the historical tourist town of West Jefferson, North Carolina.

CPSIA information can be obtained
at www.ICGtesting.com
Printed in the USA
BVHW081542201121
622107BV00002B/112